SCARRED QUEEN

NIKITA SLATER

FUCKING OBSESSED WITH YOU

Don't see no colours like you, but you ask me to,
Ask me to see the things you do,
Think the way you do.
Fuck the way I feel, the way I feel for you

Loyal is everything to you, but you want me too,
You take me too, I ain't gonna be for you,
Not loyal no more, not if I go.
Fuck the way you do, obsessed with you too.

Why you gotta take, take everything for you,
Push the way you do, take the things for you,
Make me love you too,
Make me do the things you do, feel for you.

Why you gotta make, make me feel things for you,
Can't hold on to you, make me go,
Make me hate you too,
Push me to go, make me hate you too.

Not strong enough to go, but you gotta push me to,
Make me fuck off, fuck away from you,
Loyal is everything to you, fuck the way I feel,
Make me go, fucking obsessed with you.

PART ONE

Broken Head, Broken Heart, Broken Parts

CHAPTER ONE

I gnacio Hernandez had never before brought a woman to a meet. Then, they'd never met at a club before. The entire scene was unprecedented. Reyes didn't do unprecedented, but he was willing to make an exception because he was curious. He could sever the Miami connection if he had to. It would cause some shockwaves, but it wasn't out of the question. Ignacio was beginning to annoy him anyway. His poor decisions were beginning to affect the Bolivian. Such as bringing a woman like *her* to a meet with a man like *him*. Something that was meant to show off Ignacio's power and wealth would become a big mistake.

His gaze flickered over the woman, calmly drinking her champagne and orange juice as though she weren't sitting at a table with four of the most dangerous men on the continental East coast. Two kingpins and their right hands. Only Reyes didn't think she was as calm as she appeared. Her wrist trembled slightly, giving her away. She had enough presence to make sure that tiny shake ceased by the time it got to her slim fingers where they clenched the crystal of her glass. It wasn't the fingers or her ability to remain coolly poised while the men around her talked business that captured his curiosity. It was the mark on the back of her delicate hand, permanent slash lines, viciously marring her porcelain skin.

Anger burned deep in his gut, surprising him. Reyes rarely felt anything. Ever. Certainly not for a woman. This was how he made effective decisions. How he moved trade across borders with ease and cool logic. Emotion had been removed from him. First by a ruthless father, then by a vicious military stint in his home country and finally by an unrelenting, merciless prison sentence that had systematically broken him before he had, in turn, broken down the prison itself and owned it from the inside out. By the time he was released it was into a world of his own making; a world shaped by him on the inside and ruled by him on the outside.

Yet the sight of this cool, blond beauty, so broken yet utterly resilient was doing something to him, forcing him to *feel*. He shifted in his seat, sliding his arm across the back of the leather, his eyes never leaving her while he listened to the other men speak. Negotiate terms. He didn't need to add his voice. Alejandro, his right hand, knew the terms. Knew not to fuck up while in pursuit of new deals for the boss.

Reyes wanted her. The electrifying anger he felt when his eyes caressed that mark assured him he would take the woman and make her his. Not because it infuriated him that she had been abused. No, he was not a good enough man to care about that. He was under no illusions he would treat her any better than Ignacio. Hell, he'd probably treat her much worse. Because Ignacio undoubtedly set her up like a trophy in his great mausoleum of a house and then ignored the unapproachable beauty.

Reyes had no intention of ignoring her. He was going to take her and fuck every inch of her, just the way he wanted. Hard, brutal, mean. Exactly how he was. Exactly how this world had shaped him. Because he could. She was about to become spoils of war.

No, he wasn't angry about the mark on her hand at all. He was pissed that the mark was twisted into the shape of an "H" and not an "R." He wanted her to belong to him, to the King. When he got his hands on the woman, that would be the first thing he changed.

Finally, after nearly an hour of sitting in the booth together, his eyes rarely leaving her face, she lifted hers to meet his uncompromising gaze. And for the first time in his life, he felt his heart stop in his chest. He was unprepared for the impact. Her eyes — one startling green and the other amber brown — were vivid, stunning and unrelenting. Though her expression didn't flicker once from the blank mask of icy beauty, he saw the burning disdain, the heated fury buried deep within those fiery orbs for the men that surrounded her. She despised all of them.

His lip lifted in an answering sneer. She refused to drop her eyes from his challenge, despite her husband sitting at the same table. He wanted nothing more, in that moment, than to take this scarred Queen from her throne and tame her. He vowed, then and there, that he would eventually have her.

CHAPTER TWO

C asey Hernandez, the beautiful and untouchable wife of Ignacio Hernandez, did not leave his mind for the next several months as Reyes negotiated trade with her stupid fuck of a husband. He'd left most of the footwork with Alejandro, while he retreated to his compound, deep in the mountainous Altiplano region of Bolivia. Alejandro and several of his most trusted men had been back and forth between the two countries, discussing terms and moving product. Building business in the safest, smartest way possible.

Reyes continued to do what he did best. Manage his kingdom with an iron fist. Though it burned him to leave the woman alone, he'd learned patience over the years through the most brutal of methods. Learned to understand his prey before making a move. Reyes moved to his desk and sat. He reached for a Cohiba, lit it, took a long draw and leaned back in his sturdy leather chair. He rarely smoked or imbibed alcohol, preferring clarity, but indulged once in a while, particularly when agitated. When his rigid control was tested or felt somehow... overly restrictive. His glance flicked to the newest set of prints scattered across his desk. They'd been taken three days ago.

After a moment, he picked one up and allowed his forefinger to brush across her delicate features. In the picture, she was shopping, her long, perfectly manicured fingers skimming carelessly over an exquisite cashmere dress while her empty gaze remained unfocused. Somewhere else entirely, somewhere not in the room she was standing in. Except for her eyes, she looked perfect. Not a hair out of place, her long, tall form packed into a cream-coloured pencil skirt and a pink flowery blouse. Her pale blond hair flowed down her back like a silk waterfall. Reyes grunted and crushed the picture in his fist, tossing it over the top of his immaculate desk.

He was ready to admit that, despite his best efforts, he knew very little about the woman he'd been obsessing over since the moment he set eyes on her six months earlier. He'd had her investigated by no less than three private investigators. He'd had her photographed every time she stepped foot from Hernandez's garish mansion, which frustratingly, was not often. She appeared to have the markings of exactly what she was; a kept woman. Yet, she was more, an enigma.

She shopped, but she didn't take enjoyment in her purchases. She picked things out, colours that didn't even match, handed them to her bodyguard without trying them on, then moved on to the next shop without a backwards glance. She moved like a robot, shopping, not because she wanted to, but because it was expected. She went out for lunch with "friends" once a week on Tuesdays, but she rarely said a word and she never smiled. Her so-called friends were the wives and daughters of local politicians and businessmen. She showed up because she had to, not because she liked the people that she ate with. Anyone could tell from the pictures that she hated those lunches. Other than to shop and eat lunch on Tuesdays, Casey never left the mansion. Reyes wasn't able to dig anything else up about her, she had no past that he could discover. It was like she'd been buried when she'd taken the Hernandez name.

Reyes didn't like mysteries and he didn't like women that eluded him. He was straightforward in business and straightforward when it came to fucking. He wanted both to be quick and efficient with as little mess to his personal life as possible. He knew, without a doubt, if he continued to pursue the growing obsession he felt with the Hernandez woman, that he was in danger of doing something he'd vowed never to do. Creating a mess. A weakness for exploitation.

His mother and siblings had been caught in the crossfire of such a weakness. He'd ended his own father in bloody retaliation, finally taking out a broken man before dismantling his empire and rebuilding from the ground up, better, more brutal and unbreakable. Now he had to decide if he was going to allow this woman to crawl further inside him, burrow her way deeper under his skin. Because something told him if he didn't do what he knew was right, and put a bullet in her head now, take care of this weakness, he was going to bleed for her. And he didn't bleed for anyone.

He had less than a week to decide. He was going back to the United States to see the woman and to take care of the Miami connection. It was time to make the power move and set up his own organization with men he trusted at the top. He glanced down at the array of pictures scattered across his desk, his dark eyes moving to one in particular. A close up of her face as she glanced over her shoulder toward the hidden camera. Every time he looked at her, he saw that tiny scar next to her eyebrow. Something about it bothered him. How had she gotten it and why hadn't his investigators found out a damn thing about her? Why was she such a mystery? And would she survive the coming war long enough to answer his questions?

CHAPTER THREE

"Boss wants to see you."

Casey jumped and dropped her concealer stick. It clattered against the top of her makeup table, rolled from the smooth glass surface and onto the carpeted floor. She took a calming breath before turning slightly in her seat and bending over to pick it up. Her long, pale blond waves swished around her shoulders as she reached for the tube, snatching it up. She set it back on top of her vanity and then glanced over her shoulder at the rugged, stocky bodyguard standing in her doorway. He hadn't knocked to announce his presence. She would have heard and been able to prepare herself for the intrusion of her private sanctuary.

They never knocked. It was like they took deliberate pleasure in walking in on her any time they wanted, interrupting her private moments. So, she made damn sure those moments were few and far between. She locked the washroom door when she was in there and *always* changed in the closet. When Ignacio's respect for her had nosedived it was like he'd given his men free reign with their disregard of his wife as well. Perhaps it had bothered her at one time, but she didn't really remember what that felt like anymore. Now her feelings were more geared toward survival. She didn't like the way his men watched her. Like a pack of hungry dogs, awaiting the release order from their master. So far, the command hadn't come; they weren't allowed to so much as touch a single hair on her head. He still seemed to value her trophy status.

The bodyguard standing in her door wasn't her usual full-time man. This was one of the relief guys that took over from time to time. She nodded a little and said quietly, "I'll be out in five minutes."

He continued to stand, tense and looking at her as though he had no intention of leaving. She turned her head, gave the best impression of haughty she could come up with and repeated, more steel in her voice, "Five minutes. You may go now."

His eyes narrowed and his shoulders stiffened, but he left, closing the door with some force. Casey sighed in relief and slumped against her vanity for a moment. She now had five minutes to prepare for a meeting with the devil. And she'd pissed off another bodyguard.

She ran a quick brush through her hair and added a little mascara to her pale lashes, then pushed away from her makeup table. She didn't take too long in her closet choosing an outfit because she knew the bodyguard would be back right on time to collect her for the meeting with Ignacio. She was lucky she was even getting the five minutes she'd insisted on. She snatched a pair of distressed skinny jeans from the shelf and pulled them on underneath her robe. She chose a black bra with little embroidered roses on it, her favourite, and then pulled a soft black knit sweater off a hanger. She added a pair of three inch heeled black boots to complete the outfit. Ignacio hated it when she was taller than him. Not too hard, considering she was already the same height as him at 5'8."

She hurried out of the closet just as her bedroom door banged open. She lifted her chin in cool defiance and moved toward the door. The bodyguard, whose name she didn't know, took her arm in a painful hold that told her he wasn't pleased with her current attitude, and led her out the door.

"A little slower, *help*," she muttered as she stumbled to keep up with him, her heels sliding on the marble tiles. His hand tightened on her arm until she flinched. He was going to leave bruises. The man must have a death wish. One word to Ignacio and he'd be toast. She sighed and tried to shrug him off. Too bad she was a better person than that.

He practically flung her down a flight of stairs toward her regular bodyguard, Alonzo, who took a quick step back before he accidentally touched her. He took one look at the hold her temporary bodyguard had on her and stepped threateningly toward the pair. Casey dropped her eyes and turned her head away, not wanting to watch the display of masculine posturing in her own foyer.

Alonzo sent the man a sinister glare and snarled, "Hands off the woman!" He poked a finger in the guy's chest, then swiftly grabbed a finger from the hand that held Casey's arm in a brutal hold. Alonzo snapped it so hard that she went stumbling into the wall as soon as she was released. She heard a sharp crack and a pained gasp. She suppressed the sound that threatened to escape her throat and sent her mind to a better place. This wasn't the first time she'd seen or heard something awful happen in front of her and it wouldn't be the last. "Never fucking touch the woman. Understand?"

"Yeah, man!" the guy panted, doing everything he could not to drop to his knees in front of the bigger, angrier bodyguard.

"Alonzo," she mumbled.

"What?" he grunted not bothering to look at her.

"I... I fell on the stairs and he helped me. That's the only reason he touched me. Please d-don't tell Ignacio," she whispered, keeping her eyes averted from the brutal tableau. She edged along the wall toward Ignacio's study. Though he was the master of these horrible men, he usually kept some semblance of calm around her. Kept the savages at bay. Sometimes, like now, they got out of hand when they were allowed off their leashes. Though if he found out one of them touched her... the consequences would be so much worse. She shuddered in memory of the last time one of them touched her.

"This true?" Alonzo demanded of the man whose hand he was ruthlessly crushing.

She could feel the guy's gaze on her, but she refused to look at him. She'd done what she could. She didn't like him, didn't really want to help him. But she also didn't think a few bruises was worth the brutality Alonzo was delivering now, or the punishment she knew he might deliver later if she didn't diffuse the situation. Her bodyguard was extremely efficient at following through on the boss' orders.

"Yeah man," the guy wheezed. "I was just helping 'er. Never touch 'er again. Promise, man."

She straightened against the wall, shook her hair back and forced herself to meet the scene head on. She met Alonzo's gaze with an icy look meant to convey her boredom and disdain. She knew her regular bodyguard understood her better than anyone in the mansion, including her own husband, but acting was all she had to fall back on. She knew it. He knew it. And there were cameras everywhere.

"Can we deal with this later, Alonzo?" she demanded, sending an annoyed glare toward Ignacio's office. "I have things to do today."

Alonzo stared back at her for a moment, their eyes

clashing in a shared moment of understanding. Alonzo let the man that had dared touch the mistress of the household sweat for a further thirty seconds before releasing him with a shove that sent him sprawling across the marble foyer. Casey held her ground, continuing to watch the scene with cool indifference, though she wanted to turn away in disgust.

"If Mrs. Hernandez says you were only helping her," Alonzo drawled, "then you were only helping her." He tilted his head to the side, his dark eyes taking on the dead look she'd unfortunately seen so many times before. Casey dropped her eyes, hoping she wouldn't have to witness an execution. Fuck, she already had enough trouble sleeping at night. Alonzo pointed a thick finger at the guy, his gold ring, a gift from Ignacio for his years of service, glinting in the light. "Touch her again though, and you die."

Casey shuddered and turned away, satisfied that they were finished. She strode toward the study door and waited for Alonzo to open it for her. He joined her and reached past her, his hand brushing the bruises of her arms ever-so-slightly. She stepped quickly to the side and glanced swiftly under her lashes at the man that had stood next to her side for the better part of a decade. She didn't understand him. Sometimes she thought he hated her guts and sometimes... she didn't think he hated her at all.

Alonzo knocked and waited for Ignacio's summons before ushering her inside. Casey entered the large, opulent room and took a seat across from the husband she hadn't seen in a week, not even in passing. Partially because she avoided him like he had herpes, rabies and bird flu all rolled into one. Plus, their schedules differed significantly and Casey lived reclusively, choosing to take most of her meals in her room. Unfortunately, Ignacio would insist on these meetings where she would have no choice but to see him. He was currently on the phone so she waited patiently for him to finish, crossing her legs and folding her hands over her knees.

She allowed her gaze to trail over the expensive, masculine furnishings that outfitted his office, declaring him mafia royalty among those men lucky enough to enter into his exalted presence. She knew better than to let him see the hatred in her eyes as her gaze flowed over the items in loathing. She'd had no hand in the furnishings as a wife might. She cared little for the things he chose to surround himself with. He cared even less for the things she might enjoy.

Ignacio ended his call and Casey felt the physical shift of his focus on her body like an actual touch, though she was the untouchable princess in his elite tower. Her gaze was locked on a statue that he kept on a pedestal a few feet from his desk. It was the horrific depiction of a cherub with a bow and arrow. Casey knew it must have been insanely expensive, but she didn't understand what else it could possibly have going for it.

Ignacio brought his open palm down heavily on the desk, startling her attention back to him. It had taken years of practice, but her heart no longer sped up in trepidation at his cold, twisted visage. That face. The one that drifted along the edge of her nightmares without ever stopping to feature too closely. Mostly because she didn't have enough respect left to be truly scared of him. Unlike that clown from IT. Now *he* was worthy of featuring in a nightmare or two.

Ignacio was twenty-three years older than Casey and she thought he looked every one of those years right now. Not from stress or worry, but from self-satisfied overindulgence. His dark, silver-threaded hair was filled in with surgical plugs and slicked back from his scalp in a sharp widow's peak. His light grey suit was not well complimented by the awful wide-collared flower-patterned shirt he wore underneath. The entire ensemble would have cost as much as the gaudy desk she was forced to sit across from. She rather thought he should've at least looked in a mirror before leaving his bedroom. He tried so hard to look old-school mafia. She didn't know how all of his associates didn't just laugh in his face before turning a gun on him. God, how she hated the man with every fibre of her being.

His lips curved in a cool smile of welcome. As though he were happy to see her. Of course, the smile didn't reach his eyes. It had never reached his eyes, not even in the early days of their marriage. "Casey, my dear. Thank you for coming on such short notice."

She nodded her head, not returning the smile. "Of course," she said quietly, her hand twitching involuntarily. She clasped her hands together, to stop the tremor before his eyes fell to her lap. As if she had a choice. If Ignacio demanded his wife meet with him then she made time for him, no matter what she was currently doing.

"What are your plans for the week?" he demanded.

His cold eyes roved over her. His look was possessive, but not in a passionate, caring sense. No, he was picking her apart piece by piece. Checking her for faults or flaws. Making sure the merchandise wouldn't embarrass him. She resisted the urge to shift in her seat, like a child under inspection. She knew exactly what he would see anyway; her appearance was flawless. She wouldn't have it any other way. If he had no complaints then he wouldn't have a reason to interview her.

She also knew he didn't actually care what her plans were for the week. He received a schedule of her calendar every Sunday and it never deviated. Lunch on Tuesdays, shopping on Fridays. She clung to the mansion with stubborn tenacity the rest of the time, like it was some kind of replacement family. She wouldn't even bother with lunch or shopping except that it was expected.

She forced herself to meet his dark, empty gaze once more and said in a level voice, "I have lunch with Maya Steel, Elvira Montana and the rest on Tuesday and then shopping plans on Friday."

"Huh," he grunted, his eyes narrowing.

What exactly did he want from her? Those were her exact plans. She never deviated from them. The only time her schedule changed was when Ignacio changed it up himself. Yet he looked at her as though he thought she might be lying to him. She tried to force her frozen brain to move, to think about what his motivations might be for this meeting. It wasn't an easy task. She'd learned from her years with him that it was easiest... or best... to just turn her thoughts off and flow in and around his life with robotic ease. He paid less attention to her that way.

Plus, the medications his doctor prescribed for her headaches helped her maintain this sense of fuzziness. They didn't seem to help much with the pain though, and she'd tried to stop taking them when she was younger and feistier, which hadn't gone over well with Ignacio. Now the meds were like an ally in her quest for invisibility.

He placed his elbows on his black marble -topped desk and drew his chair in. Folding his fingers in a way that made the light glint off his rings and throw reminders of his position of privilege and power in all directions. Ignacio stared at her with a mixture of undisguised longing and hatred that could easily have equalled her own. That look almost rocked her back in her chair. He usually took pains to mask his every expression, which was probably how he'd managed to avoid a grisly death from his many enemies despite his rampant greed. Ignacio wasn't completely stupid, much as she wished to imagine otherwise.

Casey was convinced that the only reason she wasn't dead yet by her husband's order was because he still wanted her, despite several years of growing impotence on his part. That, and she still held value to him as a figure of beauty. Something to lord over his friends and bodyguards. She didn't like feeling like a trophy on his arm, a pretty doll that other men could watch, but never touch. She wasn't allowed to speak when they were out in public together because she didn't have sufficient control over her words. Perhaps a by-product of her accident, or maybe it was just who she was; Casey didn't have enough memories left to know for sure, but she rarely controlled the words before they popped out of her mouth and thus often chose silence. Or silence was chosen for her by Ignacio. Thus, she was a kind of broken doll, mute and frozen at his side.

"There's a man," he began, his voice drawling the words, while his eyes took in every micro-expression on her face.

Panic threatened to well up and ruin her carefully controlled exterior. If there is one thing she knew to the core of her being, it was that Ignacio expected fidelity. She shook her head and quickly denied, "You know my every move, Ignacio. There's no man."

He shook his head and waved his hand impatiently over his desk, indicating she should shut up immediately. She closed her mouth, pressing her lips together and dropping her chin. He'd not had to follow his words with a physical correction in years. She'd learned from a young age what was expected of her.

After a few seconds of silence, he continued. "This man is important... very important, Casey. He's coming here, to our country to inspect my operations and make sure our association is running smooth. My business here depends on his continued benevolence." She struggled not to frown down at her lap, to keep her expression smooth. It was very unlike Ignacio to admit that his business might hinge on another person. And since when did he discuss business with her? In front of, yes, because she was invisible to him, but never with. "He seems to have taken a liking to you, my love. My sources tell me he has even discreetly looked into you, tried to find out about your past. Of course, he has found nothing, but I'm of a mind to use this information to my advantage."

Casey bit her lip to stop the dangerous rush of breath that might give away an emotion. She slowly, steadily stiffened her shoulders and lifted her head to look at her husband. She forced herself to ask the question that she knew could get her killed, either by Ignacio himself or by this mysterious man that would be her husband's equal, or worse. "And what do you want me to do about this man, Ignacio?"

He smiled coldly across the desk at her. "You will be nice to this man, Casey, and make him happy while he's in Miami."

CHAPTER FOUR

She'd had a bad night. Emotionally. Physically.
In every possible way.

She knew what was waiting for her when she opened her eyes. She wanted to be grateful, but fuck them all, she wasn't. It was their fault she was a pitiful wretch of a human being to begin with; a frail ghost who was too useless to function without an army of prescription pills and vitamins. Speaking of which... she managed to crack an eye open to survey the dim lighting of her bedroom. Oh, thank goodness, the maid had left the blinds closed. Alonzo must have warned her about Casey's terrible night.

She shifted carefully under the blankets, as much as she dared, and snaked an arm out, reaching for the plastic cup on the table next to her bed. Just as her fingers closed around the smooth surface, slippery with condensation, Alonzo's voice rumbled from the doorway, interrupting her peace, "Take the meds as well, Mrs. Hernandez."

Casey flinched and nearly lost her hold on the precious drink. She slapped her other hand over the cup and hauled it into her chest, just barely managing to save her cherry Cola flavoured Slurpee from ultimate doom. She sighed and pulled the blankets further over top of her head, covering both herself and the cup.

"Please, just leave me alone," she mumbled, propping herself up on an elbow and sipping from the straw. The cool rush of frozen drink soothed the raw pain in her throat from vomiting and crying the night before. She held the cup against her aching head and closed her eyes in pleasure.

"Take the pills, Casey." Alonzo's insistent voice came from directly beside the bed. She heard him pick the tablets up off the side table where either he or the maid had left them at Ignacio's orders. "If you don't, then I'll be forced to report to Mr. Hernandez."

And she would be punished.

Casey stuck her hand out and felt two small pills fall into her palm. She pulled them under the covers with her, but he yanked the blanket abruptly back from her face. Her already tousled hair went flying. She didn't bother flipping out at him. There wasn't much point since this was their usual Casey-had-a-bad-night morning after game. She glared at him through red-rimmed eyes, stuck her tongue out and flung the pills in her mouth so he could see her swallow them. Then she took a long pull on her drink.

"Happy?" she asked fake-sweetly.

He grunted in response, turned away from her and began tidying the room. It was a weird chore for him to do considering it definitely wasn't his job, but occasionally he seemed to enjoy going above and beyond his usual duties. She tilted her head to the side and listened for a moment. Then she shoved the covers to the side and struggled off her big bed with one hand still clutching her Slurpee cup. She ignored the way Alonzo straightened quickly from where he was collecting stray clothes littered across her floor, his eyes averted from the mistress of the mansion.

"I think I'll go for a swim," she announced, heading for her closet. "It'll help wake me up. Please call the kitchen and order a mimosa, Alonzo."

"But it's raining outside, Mrs. Hernandez," he muttered.

"Even better," Casey replied, slamming the door of her closet behind her.

———

She appeared like some kind of apparition. One minute he was gazing absently out the patio doors of Ignacio's office toward the pool, wondering if it ever stopped raining in Miami at this time of year, and the next she appeared. She was by herself, arms down at her sides, shoulders slightly slumped and head bent. She wore a white silk robe that clung wetly to her tall, willowy form as though embracing her like a lover. Something inside him, an invisible pull, desperately wanted to see her face, wanted to know if the same magnetism he felt before was still there.

As though hearing his silent summons her shoulders suddenly jerked back and she lifted her head, those strange eyes turning slowly toward the window. He knew she couldn't see him through the darkly tinted window panes and she would soon be completely obscured from his sight by the rapidly increasing rainfall. The thought was both unsettling and untenable. Under normal circumstances, if she were his woman, he would have one of his men bring her inside and warmed up.

But there was something wrong with her, this perplexing woman that captured his attention in a way she shouldn't. Her eyes held a glazed, faraway look in them and she wasn't shivering as she reached up to gather her hair loosely in one hand, wrap it around her wrist and drag it over her shoulder. She took a few steps forward, but stumbled, nearly falling on her too-high heels. Her bodyguard lunged forward, seeming to come out of nowhere. The hulking giant snapped at her, but didn't so much as lay a finger on his delicate mistress to aid her.

Reyes frowned, anger and confusion growing as he watched her crouch and place a palm on the stone pool tiles while, what he suspected was, a severe bout of dizziness passed with absolutely no help from the man that was supposed to be her protection. Reyes had to squint now to see what she was doing, his muscles locked against the urge to stalk out the door, sweep her up and cradle her against him. Eventually she picked herself up and made her way slowly to a patio set where she collapsed into a seat with a hand against her head.

"Beautiful, isn't she?"

Reyes' lips began to pull back in a snarl and his hand twitched toward his gun, a primal reaction to Ignacio Hernandez coveting what was *his*. It didn't matter that she'd belonged to the other man first, that she had, in fact, exchanged vows with the fucker. Reyes saw her and he wanted her, end of story. She would become his. The thought of Ignacio's hands anywhere near such a perfect creature enraged him to the point of instant, blind homicide. Reduced him to the feral beast he so often unleashed when faced with an enemy.

But he could not attack Hernandez. Not yet. He must remember that he, Reyes, was in control. Not this half Cuban, half American fuck. He needed to remember that he ruled entire regions through calm, cool logic. By maneuvering his enemies into the perfect position for a fall. And then he unleashed his fury. Never before.

Reyes turned to Ignacio with a raised brow and a smirk. "She's stunning, *amigo*," he admitted and nodded toward the pool, now completely obscured by the pouring rain. "You did well for yourself with that one."

Ignacio's chest puffed and he reached for a cigar box. Reyes waved the proffered cigar away and forced himself to keep his back to the window. He couldn't see the object of his fascination now anyway.

"She was promised to me long ago by her family. She was a beautiful child too," Ignacio told him, his eyes glinting in a disturbing way that made Reyes want to remove his teeth. Slowly, one at a time. "She almost slipped through my fingers... an accident. But it worked out for us, we married just after her eighteenth birthday."

"You are a lucky man," Reyes acknowledged with a grunt, remaining deliberately behind Ignacio's desk next to the big leather chair; the power position. It left the other man standing opposite him, where his minions would usually place themselves. Ignacio shifted uncomfortably, but seemed to shrug it off.

"She could be yours, Señor Reyes," Ignacio said slyly. "For a time."

Reyes could feel the vicious pull of his lip sliding back along his incisor in a snarl. He could not contain his disgust this time. He was forced to dip his head as though in thought. His voice was tight when he drawled, "That is very generous of you, Ignacio. Perhaps I will take you up on your offer. After all I am in Miami for a short time only and such a beautiful companion would make me the envy of my men."

His lips tightened further while disgust flooded his chest. The need to tear out Ignacio's eyes and slam them down his throat before setting into an earnest bout of torture rode him strong. The other man had just boldly offered Reyes the use of his wife. Hernandez clearly had no instincts for self-preservation or he would have stepped much more carefully around the Bolivian boss.

"I am a generous man," Ignacio said proudly, puffing away on his cigar, pride blinding him just as much as the smoke curling around his mustached face.

"How generous?" Reyes asked, trying not to growl at the other man. "I don't want a woman that has been passed around half of Miami, you understand?" Fuck his plan, he was going to murder Ignacio Hernandez with his bare hands in the next five seconds if he didn't like this answer.

Ignacio looked alarmed for a moment, as though his own plans weren't quite going the way he wanted. He was quick to reassure. "No, never. She is practically untouched, except for myself, of course."

"Of course," Reyes growled, turning from Ignacio. It went against his instincts to turn his back on an enemy, but he couldn't look at the man without seeing red.

"So, you'll consider Casey as part of the negotiations?" Ignacio pushed.

Reyes gripped the top of the chair, crushing the leather beneath strong fingers, imagining it was the other man's trachea. *Impudent fuck*, he thought to himself. *How dare he presume to dictate the terms of our agreement and then use my woman as a bargaining chip.* The death of Ignacio Hernandez would be something to be savoured.

"Yes, I believe she will be part of the negotiations," Reyes murmured, gazing into the pouring rain toward where he knew she sat. Alone and vulnerable.

"But only to use in Miami?" Ignacio was quick to clarify. "Not to take back with you to Bolivia. She is my prize, after all."

"Of course," Reyes lied.

CHAPTER FIVE

Casey hadn't thought about the man in over six months. It took her a second to realize who he was when he suddenly appeared next to her in the pouring rain, on the pool deck, water dripping down his tanned face and running into his collar. She was damp herself, but sitting comfortably underneath her patio umbrella lounge set. Her fearful gaze flickered toward Alonzo, who was standing underneath the overhang of the towel cabana. He didn't move or indicate in any way that she might be in danger of the man standing arrogantly next to her, as though he had every right to invade her space, so she figured she was safe enough.

She looked back up and forced herself to try to remember him. Her memory was not always the best, not since the car accident that had cracked her skull open ten years ago. Sometimes she had difficulty remembering things, which seemed to annoy people. Her bad memory coupled with her sometimes impulsive words and other little quirks tended to get her in trouble.

"You're an associate of Ignacio's." She finally managed to come up with. "We met at that club several months ago."

He jerked his head in a short nod and moved to sit across from her at the small table, his eyes never leaving her face. She thought it was a little rude of him to sit without an invitation, but in their world, guys like him were used to doing whatever they wanted. Which Included invading the spaces of women. Sadly, she was used to it by now. The man continued to stare at her as though she were available or something, though he should know by now that she was married.

Now she definitely remembered him, remembered the way his eyes roved over her as the men conducted business in the club. How she'd hated every moment of that meeting. Ignacio had forced her to go as punishment because she'd mouthed off to him earlier in the day, told him she wouldn't leave the house. He knew she hated leaving the safety of her bedroom.

Casey picked up her mimosa and took a long sip, forcing the tremble in her hand to steady out before placing the glass back on the table. She saw his dark gaze flicker to her drink for a moment and then back to her face with a raised eyebrow, saw the judgment there. He was probably calculating the time, 9:30am. Her own eyes narrowed and she dared him to say something. He didn't live with Ignacio Hernandez, couldn't possibly understand what her life was like. What the fuck was he doing in their house for a meeting at that time of morning anyway?

"A little early, eh *nena*?" he asked, his deep accented voice caressing each syllable.

She stared at him, determined not to give in to the urge to unleash on the man. Strange, she rarely allowed herself to feel anything other than cold dispassion. Especially toward Ignacio's business associates. Yet, something about this man assuming she was a morning drunk rubbed her the wrong way. Woke something up inside her. And calling her *nena*? She knew her Spanish well enough to know he was calling her a combination of baby and party girl all rolled into one. An endearment if they'd known each other, but an insult otherwise. She eyed him, completely taking him in for the first time.

He wore his thick, black hair short and spiked up, shaved to the scalp at the sides around his ears and collar. Almost militaristic, except it was a bit too long on top. His features were broad with deep, pitted scars marring enough of his face to make her heart lurch. How had she not noticed that before? The scar next to her eyebrow twitched in sympathy and she resisted the urge to reach up and brush it with a fingertip. She'd erased that particular tell years ago. She forced her eyes to linger on his face, the way his relentless gaze lingered on hers. His high cheekbones, prominent forehead and sculpted lips would have made him quite handsome except the scars and his demeanor gave him an almost feral look. She knew without a doubt that the assumption she'd made about this man six months ago was wrong. He was not an underling or a bodyguard, he was the boss. And he was not to be lightly dismissed.

Finally, she dropped her eyes and went for her drink again. His hand reached across the table, landing on her wrist, stopping her. She jerked in surprise nearly spilling the drink. His skin was warm against hers. Her heart pounded against her chest as she took in the feel of another man's touch against her flesh. She hadn't been touched by a person in over a year except the woman that did her hair and nails. And the hapless bodyguard with the now broken fingers. She glanced unsteadily toward the windows of the house, but the downfall of rain obscured anything past a few feet. Even her bodyguard couldn't see exactly what was taking place on the tabletop from the way they were sitting. His hold wasn't tight and she knew she could slip her hand away if she wanted. Instead she lifted an eyebrow in question looking at him fully again. Instead of judgement she now saw pity. Her second least favourite emotion.

"Why?" he demanded.

She took a quick breath in, savouring the fleeting touch and then pulled her hand away. Deliberately she picked up her champagne flute, tipped it against her lips and emptied it. The man across from her made an annoyed grunting sound. Her heart responded with an erratic thump. She set the glass back down and pressed her hand against her chest, rubbing a little. She was surprised at how her body reacted so quickly, so readily to the presence of this man.

Then, maybe it wasn't so surprising. She spent so much time alone, that maybe she was like a sponge, ready to soak up any kind of attention. She turned to him and tilted her head, studying his broad shoulders under the dark shirt he wore, unbuttoned at the top, and the way he sprawled his legs out as though relaxed in her presence. Only she suspected he wasn't truly relaxed. He seemed to be absorbing everything about her. And he was hyper-aware of her bodyguard. She could tell by the tension in his body, the placement of his hand next to his hip, near his back and the way he relaxed in positon so he could see both her and the man over his shoulder.

"I use it to wake up," she finally told him, her soft voice carrying to his ears alone. She was ashamed of her substance use, though her bodyguard knew everything about her, right down to her underwear size. It wasn't like she had any secrets from Alonzo. He was the one that kept secrets from her.

"What do you mean?" he asked, dark eyes cutting to her face, demanding more of an explanation.

Casey blushed. "I... sometimes get bad headaches. I was in a car accident when I was eighteen and there was head trauma. I had surgeries, but there was only so much doctors could do... there was some brain damage... not much! Don't look at me like that. But now I get migraines and I take prescriptions for my head, only they don't always work and the pain just gets to be too much, more than I can bear. I can't sleep because of the pain, but I just want to sleep the pain away." She knew she was talking too much... she did that sometimes when she was nervous. Started babbling and couldn't seem to stop. It was why she often chose not to talk, so people wouldn't get to know this side of her. But he'd asked the question. "Well... sometimes I also take stuff to help me sleep too, pills and... and alcohol together. It helps my head. But when I get up in the morning I feel fuzzy. I guess I just need to de-fuzzify."

"Fuck..." he murmured, his gaze darkening. He was quiet for a moment before he said, "That's dangerous shit, Casey. You do this often?"

She wanted to deny it. It was on the tip of her tongue to tell him she hardly ever did as she'd just described. In fact, she'd never admitted out loud that she took that dangerous combination before. Of course, Alonzo knew, which meant Ignacio also knew. And neither man had put a stop to her drug use, so she assumed they were okay with it. She didn't know what else to do. She had terrible headaches almost every day that medication barely controlled and Ignacio would only let her see his personal physician. A man who wasn't a neurologist and not even remotely specialized in migraine therapies. She was forced to manage the pain as best she could. And then there were the prescriptions Ignacio and his doctor forced her to take, for her health.

She bit her lip and nodded.

"How often?" he demanded in a growl.

"I don't know," she whispered, shifting in her chair, sitting up straighter. "Why do you care?" she asked suddenly, piercing him with her eyes.

He turned fully toward her, placing his arms on the table and closing the distance between them until the small table felt like no barrier at all. She knew it was significant that his back was to her bodyguard, opening him up to possible attack. In the dark world of mafia, men of his standing just didn't do that sort of thing. She glanced nervously around them, but they sat in a private cocoon of rain and patio furniture. His thick brows lowered in a frown as he studied her features, taking in her vulnerability, the side of her she tried so hard to hide from the world.

"Fuck if I know," he told her. "But I want your promise never to do it again. Even if you're fucking head feels like it's going to explode right out of your damn skull. You call for help instead. Got me, *nena?*"

Tears filled her eyes suddenly and she looked away from him so he couldn't see. It had been so many years since someone had cared enough about her to make such a demand. Anyone that had cared enough had died in a fiery crash on the side of a highway. Just distant, fuzzy memories. People she knew she loved, but couldn't quite remember.

He reached out and snatched her hand, pressing it hard between his long, brown fingers. She flinched at the intensity of his touch and saw her bodyguard shift uncomfortably out of her periphery. She flicked her wrist, waving Alonzo back, hoping he would stay. He was her husband's man, after all. She didn't know what his actual orders were. He subsided though and continued to stare at nothing.

"My name is Reyes. Vow to me you will not harm yourself again, *nena*. No more sleeping pills, no more mixing pills and drinks."

A shiver ran through her from head to foot. She forced herself to meet his dark eyes, knowing it was what he was demanding of her. She frowned a little. Though he was highly compelling, she didn't want to make a promise to a man she barely knew and definitely didn't trust. "I'll try... Reyes," she whispered, his name feeling foreign but good on her tongue.

He let her go, releasing her hand from his warm grip, apparently satisfied with her answer. Wanting to put distance between them, she stood and walked out from under the umbrella and into the rain. Without looking back, she slipped off her heels and robe and dove into the pool. The water enveloped her body in a cool embrace, reminding her once more what it felt like to be alive. This is why she loved swimming so much. She needed the reminders so she wouldn't slip too far into the shadows. She didn't watch as he walked away from her, but she felt as though he were taking a piece of her with him. She didn't know how it was possible. It was like waking up after a lifetime of slumber.

CHAPTER SIX

"When do we make our move?" Alejandro asked, leaning against the doorframe of Reyes' Plaza condominium. He'd rented an entire suite for himself and two more for his right hand and the rest of the guys.

"Soon," Reyes grunted, flicking him a look, daring him to keep talking.

Alejandro was as good as a brother, but some lines were not to be crossed. This one question was the only one that would be allowed. Reyes would set the date and time when he was ready. He knew the guys were talking about his hesitation. So far, the talk had not crossed any lines into dangerous territory or Reyes would have had to deal with his own men. But he knew he would have to act soon, before his hesitation to act swiftly and brutally on the Miami front was perceived as weakness.

He just wasn't certain yet what to do about the woman. He needed more information and so far, getting that information was harder than getting into a bank vault. His private meeting with her had not gone down as he'd hoped. He thought maybe he would look into her beautiful, vapid face and feel nothing. Expose that feeling of six months ago for the fleeting fraud that it was. Instead, the woman... Casey, had shaken him to the core of his very being with her bald admittances.

"Go," he said without looking up.

Moments later he heard the door open and close, indicating Alejandro's exit. He ran a hand over the thick spikes of his hair and then stood to pour himself a drink. His hand hovered over the bourbon as he remembered her pathetic story and he glanced at the clock, 3:00pm. Then he closed his fist over the bottle and strode to the window overlooking the city. A city that would soon belong to him.

He needed to make a decision about the woman. Did he go with his original plan and clean house or did he take the scarred woman for himself? With a growl, he twisted the lid off the bottle and drank deeply, allowing the smooth alcohol to slide down his throat, soothing the questions that burned him with unfamiliar doubt. Unfortunately, it was the uncertainty that burned so heavily in his gut that made her fate become more and more likely.

He was Reyes. He was a king. He couldn't take a scarred queen from a despotic man and set her up at his side. She was weak and pathetic, a drunken shell of a woman. She wasn't strong enough. She would fail and she would collapse. He would eventually be forced to put her down if she didn't find a way to do it herself. He'd found the iron will to clean out his own house. He'd harden his heart and do another man's house.

Yet, despite this resolve, he found himself tipping the bottle once more, then turning to put on a shirt so he could intercept the woman he had every intention of letting go of with brutal finality. It was Friday.

Shopping day.

"What colour, Alonzo?" she asked absently, handing her silently suffering bodyguard another dress.

Perhaps if she cared enough to examine her motivations she'd question why she tortured Alonzo this way. He never actually hurt her or touched her in any way, unless called upon by the boss to touch. Which was extremely rare. Alonzo didn't allow so much as a flicker of malevolence to cross his expression when he looked toward her. He was nothing but coldly solicitous of her every want and need unless it conflicted with something Ignacio wanted. Then, Ignacio's desires came first.

And then it struck her; this was why she needled Alonzo. Because he looked through her instead of at her. Because he'd stood at her side for nearly a decade. Stood at her side during her surgeries after her accident, watched over her during horrific migraines and tried to wake her in the mornings when she'd taken too many pills or too much alcohol. He'd made the panicked call for an ambulance when she'd tried to kill herself three years ago and he'd stood next to her hospital bed, pity finally lighting his expression as Ignacio had ranted at her for daring to try to leave him while she was strapped to a bed, forced to listen to every word.

And still she knew deep in her gut that her "loyal" bodyguard would put a bullet in her if the boss ordered it. Because he was the one that had held her down while Ignacio had burned her hand after her single escape attempt, though she'd screamed and pleaded for mercy, finally passing out in his arms. This was why she played with him, but never crossed the line toward true friendliness. That and she couldn't bear to get closer to another human, feel that affection and then watch as Ignacio took away something else she cared about.

"Blue, Mrs. Hernandez," he grunted, doing an excellent

job of disguising the annoyance he must be feeling at their weekly sojourn, which included some variation of the same conversation every time.

"Now, would you say it was more of a royal blue or a sky blue?" she asked softly as though she actually cared. She really, really didn't.

He shifted next to her, barely glancing down at the fabric she was holding before sweeping their surroundings with a thorough check. "Royal."

"Excellent," she said brightly, tossing the dress into his arms without looking at the tag.

They both knew she didn't care about the size, fit or price. That it was hit or miss whether she would ever wear it or whether it would end up in a bag headed for a charity clothing drive. She shopped because it was expected and because it forced her to leave the house. And because if she didn't dress well, then she was even less useful to Ignacio. They all knew there was only one way out of the life she was in and it wasn't through a divorce lawyer.

She held another item up and looked it over. "What colour, Alonzo?" she asked.

Before he could answer, a deep voice startled her from behind. "It's red, *nena*."

Casey whirled around, the blouse she was holding up slipping from her grip. Long, dark fingers reached out and snatched it before it could hit the floor. His quick movement brought him a step closer to her. Casey instinctively tried to move back, used to having an entire large bubble of personal space, but the clothing rack to her back stopped her.

Reyes' eyes never left her as he spoke. "I do not think red is your colour, *cariña*."

Another endearment from a man that was almost a stranger.

"I wouldn't know," she whispered, unable to tear her eyes

from his rough, scarred face, but knowing she should. They were in public and Alonzo was a few feet from her watching her every move, listening to every word. Ready and waiting to report back to Ignacio.

"Why wouldn't you know?" Reyes asked, replacing the blouse on the rack.

Casey forced her brain to follow the conversation and catch up to his meaning, then shrugged. "I'm colour-blind. Red, blue, green... they mean nothing to me," she told him.

He looked startled for a moment, his face changing from his usual hard, difficult-to-read expression to a sudden softening. She was used to the men in her world never giving anything away in their looks. She'd adopted the same look, emulated it for self-preservation. She knew it saved lives. But she... liked the way he looked at her now when she revealed her latest little quirk. His eyes squinted a little, narrowing in laughter, his lips lifting a little as he huffed out a small chuckle.

"What?" she asked, a small, breathless laugh escaping her throat as well. She couldn't help herself. He looked different when he laughed and she wanted to join.

He studied her face, the way her bowed lips curved upward in amusement and her pale, pink cheeks flushed as he watched her. "So damn defective, woman."

Her amusement fled with his words as a slice of pain streaked through her. She touched her chest, pressing her fingertips against her breastbone for a second. She ignored the way he watched her, like a hawk or something. She didn't need his razor-sharp eyes or his razor-sharp wit taking her down every time she saw him. How had she let this man, a stranger, get close enough to cause pain? Where had her frozen, sleepy life gone? Why was she even telling him these things? Making herself vulnerable to men like him, men used to exploiting weaknesses in others. She dropped her eyes and turned away from him.

"If you'll excuse me," she murmured. "Alonzo and I are just finishing up here."

Reyes stepped around her, blocking her path. She felt Alonzo's tension thrumming from several feet away, but the bodyguard didn't step in. She was positive he'd had the same conversation with Ignacio that she'd had. Don't piss off the Bolivian boss.

"I came to see you, Casey," Reyes said.

She rolled her eyes. "Of course you did. I didn't think it was a coincidence that you just ran into me in a city this size."

She felt him stiffen next to her, saw his fingers twitch and realized he had to stop himself from grabbing her. She backed a step away from him. He followed her, his eyes capturing hers and hardening. "Do not roll your eyes at me again, *nena*. You understand?"

Her heart stopped in her chest and she couldn't breathe for a second. How could she forget how dangerous these men were? She hadn't made a mistake like that in many years. She would never have dared to roll her eyes anywhere near Ignacio. She brought a hand up to her mouth and nodded quickly. Fuck, she was going to have to be more careful.

He watched her every reaction, his hard, dark eyes narrowing with understanding. Of course, he knew. She'd been married to the mafia for nearly a decade. She knew what was expected of her. Mob wives didn't make stupid mistakes that could cause pain, or worse, cost them their lives.

"Come, I'm taking you somewhere else," he told her.

Casey glanced at Alonzo who jerked his head in a quick nod, giving his permission. Of course. Keep Bolivia happy. Before she could utter a response, Reyes took her arm, touching her for the second time. She closed her eyes for a moment, trying to steel herself from feeling the warmth of his hand seeping into her skin, the tingle of another body against hers, the rush of blood through her veins clambering to wake up. Her lashes lifted and she met his dark, satisfied gaze. His fingers wrapped more firmly around her and he pulled her tighter against the side of his heavily muscled body as he led her from the shop.

CHAPTER SEVEN

C asey laughed out loud, amusement animating her features when Reyes pulled up outside the club. She waited for him to come around to her side of the car and open the door for her. She raised a pale eyebrow at him as he took her arm. "Why are you bringing me here again?" she asked with another laugh. "You didn't get enough of this tacky place last time we were here?"

"I wanted to have you here again, just you and me. Now we can talk like we should've done the first time we met. You'll class the place up, *nena*."

His low chuckle sent a thrill through her body and she turned toward him, helplessly drawn to his power. She was slightly taller than him in her four inch Luis Vuitton heels. Though he wasn't a massive man in comparison to her body-guard, he exuded raw Latin masculinity, the type that Ignacio had always tried so hard to express but failed at on every level. She suspected from the lean flexing of his hands and throat that a tough musculature roped his body beneath the tastefully expensive suit that fit him to perfection. Though his clothing and bearing spoke money, he didn't throw it out in gaudy waves the way her husband did. His clothing, car and jewelry were all tasteful. He wore only one ring on his right middle finger. A thick gold band with an insignia on it.

"I'm not dressed for the club," Casey said, feeling self-conscious.

He looked her over, taking in her soft black leggings, black heels and the low-cut pink sleeveless silk top she wore with an old comfortable wrap. "You look beautiful," he told her, taking her arm in a gentle hold and turning her toward the club.

He handed his keys and a generous tip to the valet, took the ticket and led her inside, completely ignoring Alonzo who followed a few feet behind them. She didn't see Reyes' men, but suspected they were around somewhere. Heavy hitters like him didn't wander around an unknown city like Miami without protection though she was certain he could take care of himself. The aura of violence surrounding him was real. Not studied or postured. She knew this man was capable of backing up the threat that his body betrayed with every bunch and tense of his lithe muscles.

With a hand at her back he led her into the club. Casey forced herself to lift her chin and meet the bouncer's knowing gaze at it slid over her body with familiar ease. She met his look with icy disdain and strode forward at his nod, but stumbled when Reyes caught her arm and pulled her back against his chest. She gasped and rocked on her heels, reaching for the bouncer's table. Heat seeped through his shirt warming her from behind. He slid a hand around her waist and anchored her back into the cradle of his hips. The back of her shoulder grazed his.

"Why're you looking at her like that?" he asked the bouncer, his low voice a chilling demand.

Her mouth fell open and she moved her head to the side to look at his face as he spoke. The glare he was giving the giant man blocking the door was enough to convince her she was currently in the hands of a very dangerous man. His dark eyes were flat and merciless, promising pain beyond anything the man who'd insulted her with a single look had ever known. And though Casey knew that deadly look well, having seen it in the eyes of the men that inhabited her world, seeing it on Reyes' face was unlike anything she'd ever seen before. The fact that it was meant for her, that is was *about* her, made her both want to run away as fast as she could... and also curl up like a cat and bask in the warm glow of his protection.

The bouncer shifted uncomfortably on his huge feet and slid his gaze away from the pair of them. Casey felt sorry for him. She turned her head further until her lips were only a few inches from Reyes' face. Her breath rushed across his skin as she spoke. "Ignacio owns this club, Reyes. This man... he recognizes me, that's all."

Reyes stiffened against her, his shoulder knocking hers and his fingers flexing into her hip, biting into the flesh over her thin leggings. She shook in his hold and could barely manage to keep her gaze steady as he flicked his eyes from the bouncer to her, sweeping her face with a heated look. The savage possession in that one look was enough to set her dormant body on fire in a way she'd never felt before, but always wondered about. It took her breath away. It frightened her on an instinctual level.

"You don't need to talk right now, *nena*," he told her before turning his attention back to the man at the door. "Now you, friend, will keep your eyes and your thoughts off this woman. I don't care who she belongs to. I even hear of you disrespecting her again, I will take you apart piece by piece and have my people mail the bloody pieces to your mother. Understand?"

The bouncer jerked his head in a quick nod and stepped out of their path. Hurt rushed through Casey as Reyes ushered her into the darkened interior of the club with Alonzo at their backs. She hated the way Reyes spoke to her, with such careless chauvinism. Yet, she understood it. She had been part of the mob for so long she understood the disrespect that women endured. Or at least she suspected she wasn't alone. It wasn't like she got out enough to meet many mob wives.

Casey despised that Reyes treated her the same way her husband would. It sickened her that he could wake something up within her, make her respond to him, then treat her as though her opinion didn't matter. She stopped walking, digging her heels in and turned on the spot. She brought her hand up to press against his chest so she wouldn't crash into him. The incredible heat from his body penetrated through the fine fabric of his shirt and warmed her palm.

"I've changed my mind," she mumbled, glancing at the people moving all around them, dancing, eating and drinking. Having a good time in one of Miami's favourite hotspots. "Please just take me home."

He took her hand and jerked it away from his chest, pulling her closer to his body. She silently cursed her heels as she once more stumbled against him, her legs giving way against the pull of his unbreakable hold. The breath whooshed out of her lungs and she held her face stiffly back from his so she wouldn't accidentally brush her lips against him. He looked at her with a mixture of dead eyes and triumph. It made her shiver in his arms.

She could feel Alonzo at her back, seething angrily, unwilling to intervene and mess with Ignacio's most recent edict, but also taking major issue with his years-long standing order that no man should touch Casey Hernandez. Casey felt a little bad for the man. She was swamped with all kinds of emotions herself. Her body felt like it was coming to life after a decade of sleep. The hard hands that held her were lighting a sort of delicious fire inside of her. Yet, she was horrified that a man like him could do this to her. A man from a world she despised with every frozen fibre of her being.

"I'm not ready to let you go," he said, his voice a softly accented growl. He turned his head, deliberately brushing his lips against her cheek before wrapping an arm around her waist, holding her tight against his side and leading her to a booth.

Casey shook her head and resisted the urge to roll her eyes. It was the same booth they'd sat at the first time they met. Clearly, he had a sense of humour. A sick, dark sense of humour. She sighed and slid into the booth, resigned to the idea that she wasn't leaving until he was ready to let her go. He immediately got the attention of a server and ordered drinks for them. Casey didn't bother protesting. What was the point?

"Why am I here?" she asked, turning to him as he slid closer to her. "Are you trying to piss my husband off?"

His dark eyes studied her intently as she spoke. Then he ignored her question and reached to touch her face. She jerked in her seat, but he just leaned forward, persisting. He brushed the hair off her forehead and tapped two fingers against the edge of her eyebrow. "How'd you get this?" he asked with a slight frown.

He dropped his hand to her shoulder, cupping her as though he had every right to touch her so casually. Her heart thumped in both anticipation and trepidation at his touch and she had to take several calming breaths. She wasn't used to being touched so much. If he kept this up she was likely to pass out at his feet from all the gasping and heart stuttering. She had to force her brain to keep up with his words. He wanted to know about her face? Ah... right, the scar.

"A car accident," she told him. "I have other scars."

He reached for her lap, picked up her hand and curved it

so they could both clearly see the shiny scarred "H" on the back. She shuddered and shook her head. "Not that one, of course."

He nodded and let her hand drop. "How bad was the accident? When was it?" he demanded. He leaned back in his seat as their drinks were served. She immediately reached for hers, grateful for the respite.

Then she rolled her eyes, careful to conceal the movement under her lashes when she realized her companion had ordered her a straight up orange juice. Twenty-eight years old and she was being treated like a child. She wanted to storm at him and tell him with all of the haughty sophistication of her Tuesday "friends" that she wasn't an alcoholic as he'd no doubt assumed from their encounter by the pool. She rarely drank unless she was forced to go out to clubs with Ignacio or when she had a bad headache.

"You answer when I talk to you, *nena*," he prompted when she took too long.

She turned to look at him, staring at him, showing him some of the loathing she felt for men like him. She felt safer with Alonzo nearby. Surely, despite Ignacio's orders to keep this man happy, Alonzo wouldn't allow the Bolivian to harm her in public. Especially in this particular club surrounded by men loyal to her husband. "I don't like the way you talk to me, *nino*," she hissed back at him, insulting him in his own language.

A short bark of laughter burst from between his lips. Then he abruptly cut the laugh off as though he hadn't meant the sound to escape. He raised an eyebrow and stared at her as though she were insane. Well, she was. The faster he learned it, the faster he might leave her alone. He reached out, too quickly, and brushed the pale blond hair back from her face again. She flinched a little, but held steady when his touch barely registered against her skin. His dark eyes caressed her, warmth searing right through her, piercing the sleepy fog within her body.

She knew he wanted her to see things in his eyes. Knew it, because men like Reyes only let a person see what they wanted a person to see. They might let a man register the lick of anger right before death. Or a woman feel that warm rush of passion before they made love to her body. The rest of the time, their eyes were dead. Reyes wanted her to know the sizzling heat of lust as his eyes touched every part of her that he could see and every part he couldn't.

"There is the fire I saw that first time you turned those strange eyes on me, *cariña*," he murmured, lightly running his fingers across her cheek, over her shoulder and down her arm. "I thought I had imagined the burst of hatred that had so intrigued me." His hand landed on her thigh and his fingers tightened. Not painful, but almost threatening. "But you will have to learn to answer immediately when I speak to you."

She looked down at his hand, eyes wide, mouth open in bewilderment. Then she lifted her face to search out her protection. Alonzo stood about ten or so feet back from the table, his own gaze burning holes in the booth and the couple. He was still as a statue, his bulging arms crossed in front of him, his chin down and his eyes narrowed in rage. He was definitely angry enough to tear Casey from the booth and walk her forcibly out of the club, but he didn't so much as twitch in their direction. He wasn't going to help her. Once more she was at the mercy of a powerful man, surrounded by people that wouldn't lift a finger to help.

Reyes tightened his grip on her thigh, forcing her attention back to him. Her eyes jumped to his. He didn't look angry as she thought he might. As Ignacio would be if he had to teach her how to behave. Instead, Reyes looked as though he truly wanted her to understand. "If I ask you a question, you answer me. When I tell you to do something, you do it.

This will keep you safe in my world, understand? Repeat the words, Casey."

She frowned at him, her brow wrinkling, but she nodded slowly. "You tell me to do something, I do it... for safety. T-to keep me safe," she whispered her eyes widening and meeting his as the full impact hit her. She felt herself slip past the usual bullshit as she spoke, as he absorbed her words and slowly nodded as if to praise her. What did he mean by that exactly? Was he trying to keep her safe from him or safe in their terrifying mafia world of false friends and sinister business associates.

He moved his hand from her thigh up to her arm, wrapped it around her and then pulled her toward him. She brought her hand up to brace herself against his chest, but she was practically sitting in his lap now, his face almost touching hers when he spoke. She hardly dared to breath, though a tiny whimper escaped her throat when she felt the impossible steel of muscle threading his body. The promise of a human cage if she was ever unlucky enough to be captured by this man so intent on treating her as his prey. He brought his other hand up between them and took hold of her chin, tilting her face until her eyes met his once more.

"And Casey?" he said huskily against her lips.

"Yes?" she whispered.

"Never call me 'boy' again. In any language. I don't care when or where we are, I will bare that beautiful bottom and beat it until you can't sit down. Understand?" His deep, accented voice vibrated through her entire body, taking her breath away. The dark promise of erotic violence did something to her it shouldn't have, something she never would have expected.

"I understand," she whispered. Then she sighed, her breath rushing across his lips in an unconscious invitation. His hands tightened on her arm and chin until she flinched in his hold and he was forced to set her back along the seat in the booth.

He nodded slightly and kept his arm around the top, near her head, as though ready to reach for her if she tried to bolt. Which wasn't far from the truth. She was exhausted and ready to go home. The anxiety and intensity of her emotions were becoming overwhelming. She didn't know how much more she could take. She really didn't understand why Ignacio was allowing this to happen to her. He'd never allowed other men this close before. She understood the need to keep Bolivia happy, but when had keeping a business contact happy meant allowing them to take his wife out to a club?

"Now tell me about the accident," he demanded.

She shrugged and reached for her orange juice, desperately wishing it was something stronger. She wondered what he would do if she lunged for his drink and downed it before he could stop her. He probably wouldn't be too impressed and chances were pretty good, he could stop her before she got very far into that course of action.

"I was eighteen," she told him, tracing the edge of her glass with one light-pink tinted nail. "I don't remember anything about it at all actually. I was told it happened on the highway when we were driving back from out of state. My entire family died in the accident; two sisters, a brother, my mom and my dad."

He lifted his hand and touched the tiny scar on her face again before running his hand over the top of her head in a soothing motion. He dropped his arm back behind her. Oddly, she felt relaxed with his arm behind her. As though nothing could happen with him in the booth next to her. She turned her body so she could face him a little better as she spoke about one of the most painful things in her life.

"I... I had to miss the funerals," she told him quietly. "I was in a medically induced coma for nearly five weeks while I recovered. Th-there was a lot of swelling in my brain so I had to have time to heal. But... waking up to find out that my entire family was gone and that I'd missed the funerals... it was devastating."

He nodded, not saying anything. Just watching her as she spoke. She so rarely talked to anyone, let alone discussed her family and the car accident, and yet it felt strangely okay to do it here, with Reyes. Like he was safe somehow. Which was utterly ridiculous. He was as far from safe as she could get. She didn't know what kind of business he had with her husband and she didn't want to know, but it wouldn't be anything good. Nothing she wanted to be involved in.

"They shaved a bunch of my hair off and I had staples in my head from here to here," she pointed at the side of her head, indicating a line across the left side. "There were also a couple of holes in my skull... I guess to relieve the pressure. It was terrifying and very painful whenever the medication started to wear off."

He nodded again, his jaw tightening a little as he listened to her. "What other injuries did you have?" he asked.

"Except for the cut on my face, none really," she murmured. "I was very lucky actually."

He growled incredulously, "You call having your skull cracked open luck?"

"I just mean that my entire family died in that accident and I got away with a few scratches except for the crack on my head. I guess it could have been so much worse for me." She was startled to find tears stabbing her eyes and she blinked them rapidly away. "I'm grateful for my life. Ignacio was there for me too. He was one of my father's close friends and he took care of me as soon as I was released from the hospital. He made sure I didn't have to worry about anything."

He leaned back and watched her with a brooding expression. She got the feeling he didn't really know what to do with her. That there was something about her that bothered him and that he was bothered by his reaction to her. It was almost exhilarating for her to sit here with him and to have a real conversation.

"What about the headaches?" he asked, his voice issuing another demand. "They part of the accident?"

She shivered under the dark scrutiny of his penetrating gaze. The way he pinned her to the seat and forced her to talk to him about some of the most personal things in her life. She played with the edge of her wrap, stretching it and running her nail along the fabric before answering him. He wasn't going to like the answer anyway.

She lifted her shoulder a little in a careless shrug. "I guess."

"What does that mean?" he asked, his voice taking on an annoyed edge. He picked up his glass and finally took a drink of the amber liquid.

"Well the headaches started right after the car accident so, of course, they must be linked," she answered quickly. "But I guess it's impossible to prove. Doctors don't know enough about migraines to be able to find out if mine are caused by the accident. And there's no way to stop them anyway."

His frown turned even darker until she was truly squirming against the seat. "What do you mean 'doctors don't know enough'?" he repeated her words in a tight voice. "You see a bunch of head doctors for this problem? They send you to specialists, right? Get it taken care of."

She didn't know what to say to him. How much should she tell him? She couldn't say anything that would make her sound disloyal toward Ignacio, but the truth was, she'd never been allowed to see more than his personal physician since the accident. She had done a lot of reading on the internet about her condition though. "Uh... it's fine, really," she said quickly. "There's not much anyone can do. I take medication to control the symptoms and that seems to help most of the time. Sometimes I still get really bad ones... and I just deal with those as best I can."

He made an angry sound and slashed his hand through the air. "Yeah, I saw how you dealt with that yourself."

She looked away from him and said softly, "I told you I'd try not to do that again."

"And you never lie?" he asked, skepticism clear in his voice.

She looked him in the eye and said, "Never."

He held her gaze for a long, uncomfortable moment. She refused to break eye contact. She knew it didn't really mean anything. Anyone could profess to tell the truth and look a person in the eye. It was a stupid myth that people thought they could get away with a lie if they looked a person in the eye. But somehow, when his dark scrutiny swept over her and finally captured her eyes with his, she knew he could discern truth from lie.

"Tell me, *nena*... for I find I am curious. Why would you bother to match words to actions with me? I am nothing to you. You could tell me one thing and then go home and do quite another. I would never know." She felt his fingers drop from the back of the booth and ever so lightly touch the soft strands of her hair.

She shivered at the slight contact. She closed her eyes for a moment and resisted the urge to press into the touch. She was a little breathless when she spoke, her voice serious, "I don't have much, Reyes, but I do have integrity. It's something I had to teach myself over the years. Every time my husband and his men looked at me and lied, I promised myself that I wouldn't allow a lie to pass my lips."

His hand suddenly clenched into a fist behind her head

making her flinch and he swiftly glanced around. His voice was a sharp growl when he spoke. "That is a stupid and reckless thing for a woman in your position to say. I hope you are smarter than to speak things like that around Ignacio Hernandez. He doesn't strike me as a patient man."

Casey shrugged carelessly and continued to play with the hem of her wrap avoiding his eyes, knowing he was getting a better glimpse inside her head now that he was forcing her to speak to him at length. "Ignacio knows how I feel about him. There's a reason we don't spend time with each other and haven't shared a bedroom in years. Well... we've never actually shared a bedroom. He doesn't like my shoes and girl things invading his space. What I mean is, he knows how much I despise him, so he hasn't summoned me to share his bed in well over a year."

Oh shit, she was babbling again, way oversharing. The strained look on his face convinced her to slam her lips shut and seal them.

"Fuck," Reyes snarled.

He dropped his hand to the back of her neck, wrapping his fingers around the slim column of her throat through her hair. She cried out and brought her hands up to protect herself as he jerked her across the booth toward him. She sprawled in his lap, gasping as her hip grazed the hardness of what could only be his erection. She scrambled against him, trying to push herself back from his chest, but his fingers bit into her arms denying her the space she desperately sought.

Finally, when he refused to allow her an inch and the fight ebbed from her, she allowed herself to lay stiffly across his chest and swallowed the sob that threatened to build up in her throat. A painful throbbing was beginning to pull from behind her eye socket. She wanted to shout at him, ask him why he was doing this to her. Was he truly interested in her? Or was he playing some sick game with Ignacio?

He pulled her steadily closer until she was fully in his lap, her long legs dangling awkwardly, half on the booth and half across his muscular thighs. She wasn't able to brace herself and was forced to trust him to hold her up against his shoulder and chest. He leaned her in, angling her toward him until his scarred cheek brushed the pale smoothness of her own. She shuddered as the slight stubble of his shaven face scraped against her and the heat from his body warmed her. A whimper escaped her lips and it was on the tip of her tongue to break down and beg him to release her. But before she could speak, his deep voice interrupted her.

"When you come to my bed, *cariña*, I can promise you..." his warm breath touched her cheek and nose as he spoke and the pleasant smell of him combined with whiskey swamped her already overwhelmed senses, "I will never let you leave."

The way he said it felt like a promise, not a hope. Like he somehow knew that she would end up in his bed. Vivid images of herself entwined with this man, embracing him in the throes of sexual ecstasy flooded through her. She made a distressed sound and tried to push against him again, but his hold was unbreakable. She bowed her shoulders and dropped her head, letting her forehead rest against his shoulder.

"I'm sorry, Reyes," she whispered.

His shoulder jerked a little against her as though he were surprised. He brought a hand up and smoothed the hair back so he could see her face. "Why're you sorry, *nena*?" he asked with a frown.

"You can't have me," she whispered, her eyes boring into his. "Even if you truly want me."

His dark eyes widened for a moment, trapped in the innocent beauty of her multi-coloured gaze. Before he could reply, argue with her, she brought a hand up between their bodies and pressed it against her chest and said, "I don't have many things, Reyes. Oh, I have clothes and I have jewels. Things I don't want and never really cared about. Things I would give away in a heartbeat for five more minutes with my family. But the things that are real in life? I don't have many of those. But the things that I do have are mine. I taught them to myself over painful years of Ignacio's lessons. The things I taught myself are honesty, integrity and loyalty. You understand what I'm saying, Reyes?"

He swore savagely, baring his teeth at her. Then he jerked his head in a nod. He took her hair in his fist and crushed the soft strands for a moment. "Yeah, I understand, Casey."

"Loyalty," she whispered.

He growled and jerked her head back, baring her throat while pulling her closer against him, into the incredible heat of his body. She moaned, knowing her body was reacting to him in a way she'd never before experienced, flooding her with wet heat. "You feel that, woman?" he growled, leaning in to run his lips whisper soft across her throat, barely caressing her.

"Yes!" she gasped, her voice barely a whimper of sound. "It doesn't matter, Reyes. I belong to him."

Rage vibrated in his voice as he spoke against her soft skin. "He doesn't fucking deserve you." He stood with her still in his arms, handed her off to Alonzo and said, "Get her home safely."

CHAPTER EIGHT

"Fuck that woman," Reyes growled, downing a generous drink straight from the bottle before slamming it on the table.

Casey Hernandez was dangerous. She was testing his calm. She was driving him to drink.

He strode to the window and glared into the night. His meeting with her had not gone as he'd planned. Instead of clarifying things, he'd found himself more confused, more entangled. She was an infuriating mixture of world-weary siren and stunted half-child that never grew up. When she'd flat out told him that her husband hadn't touched her in over a year, he'd damn near torn her clothes off and fucked her right there in the booth, despite the few hundred witnesses swarming around them and her bodyguard a few feet away.

Then she'd given him the one gift he couldn't refuse, the one thing that was guaranteed to save her life in all this. She'd promised him loyalty. Well, not him. But as good as. She'd given her loyalty to Ignacio Hernandez, a disgusting pig of a man. One of the poorest excuses for a business partner that Reyes had ever had to work with – a situation that had only been allowed to go on this long because of the female. If she'd given her loyalty to such a man, because of a vow, most likely forcibly given when she was barely more than a child, then what would she give to Reyes when he finally had her wholly within his power? The thought took his breath away.

He would settle for nothing less than Casey Hernandez's utter and complete surrender; her loyalty. He would heal the damaged beauty and she would stand tall at his side as his scarred queen.

He reached for the bottle again, swearing viciously when he knocked it sideways, spilling the contents across the table. He snatched it up, took another long drink and then threw it away from him in an uncharacteristic moment of rage. The satisfying shatter of glass barely calmed him.

He wanted nothing more than to drag the woman out of that fucking mansion and away from the husband that should never have had her. Every time he saw her she managed to claw her way under his skin a little more and he feared for her safety in that damn gilded cage she lived in. If her husband didn't do something to her, she might manage to fucking hurt herself. Either with the pills or her own reckless disregard for her safety. She'd say something stupid to Ignacio or one of his men. Roll her pretty eyes at the wrong guy at the wrong time. She seemed incapable of perfect obedience, no matter how hard she tried.

He'd just have to go with his original plan. The one that would make her safe and ensure her freedom all in one stroke; Mrs. Hernandez would become a widow.

Casey woke to the beautiful aroma of subtle, flowery perfume. A smile curved her lips and she sighed, stretching under her blankets, enjoying the smoothness of her sheets against bare legs and arms. She usually wore light cotton sleep shorts and a tank top to bed. Not very sexy, but it didn't matter since she slept alone. She enjoyed the comfort and she liked the feel of her fluffy quilt wrapped around her body.

Today was one of those mornings where she preferred to wake up slowly and allow the day to creep in with soothing sluggishness. She wiggled her face against the blanket, enjoying the softness against her cheek. The lovely sweet smell wafted around her, tantalizing her and drifting softly next to her face. Her lashes fluttered open and she forced herself to focus on the thing that had touched her.

It was a petal. Like from a flower. She untangled her arms from the blanket and pushed herself up on an elbow, reaching for it. She picked up the silky rose petal and rubbed it between her fingers. It was an honest to goodness rose petal. Looking around she realized she was surrounded by them. Hundreds of rose petals drifted over her prone, blanket covered body and all across the tall Queen Anne bed. She frowned, trying to register where they had come from.

It wasn't unusual for the maid to come in while she was sleeping to drop off breakfast or laundry. Casey was a terrible sleeper, so when she did finally get to sleep she tended to sleep hard, oblivious to the world around her. But the quiet woman, who rarely said two words to Casey was unlikely to randomly shower her mistress in rose petals unless ordered to. Sitting up with a frown, Casey felt several petals fall from her hair and float to the warm bed. She plucked one that had tangled in the ends of her long, disheveled hair. She wondered what colour they were. Red?

As she started to climb from the bed a vase filled with what had to be at least three dozen roses caught her attention. It was perched on her vanity table. Her mouth fell open in surprise. Somehow the gorgeous arrangement was even more of a shock than waking up in a pile of rose petals. In the

ten years that she'd been married to Ignacio, he'd never once
bought flowers for her. He'd never even bought her a birthday
present. She doubted he knew her birthday had just passed a
few weeks ago.

So, the odds that this beautiful gift came from her
husband were extremely small. And there was only one other
man who was pursuing her with any kind of dedication. Her
heart tripped in anticipation as she approached her makeup
table and reached for the small, white envelope nestled carefully within the perfect, delicate blooms. She let her fingertips linger against the velvety tips, enjoying the feel of them
against her skin; absorbing the quiet loveliness of such a gift.
Pretending for just a moment that she was free to accept such
extravagance without all the baggage that came between
them.

She pulled her hand away and opened the envelope,
tugging the plain white card out. It said:

Pink is your colour.
  8:00pm tonight,
  Room 1228, Plaza condos.
  Reyes

She looked toward the bed and then back at the vase. The
flowers were pink. He remembered that she couldn't see
colours and he wanted her to know what colour he chose,
that he didn't choose red for her. She let a tiny smile linger on
her lips for a moment, allowed the rush of emotion in as she
felt what it was like to have a man pay real attention to her.
Lavish a gift upon her even though he wouldn't be there to
see her reaction or receive a thank you.

Then reality intruded. She couldn't allow this to continue;

whatever *this* was. She'd had enough. Ignacio could just work this deal alone. She wasn't going to allow her emotions to get involved any more than they already were and then get crushed when the big boys were done playing with her. For once she wanted to call the shots, and she was calling this one.

She didn't bother changing. She walked swiftly into her washroom and pulled her robe over her sleep outfit, washed her face and brushed her teeth. Then she strode into the hall where Alonzo stood waiting for her to show her face and tell him her plan for her day. She crossed her arms over her chest and lifted her chin.

"I want to see him, now," she informed him, using the best impression of "snotty voice" she could come up with, a useful by-product of her hated Tuesday lunches.

Alonzo flexed his shoulders until they cracked. "You don't have an appointment."

Casey huffed out a breath and snarled, "I don't give a shit. He's going to see me on my time for once." She walked past him down the hall, her bare feet slapping against the marble. His eyes widened as he finally looked at her and took in her lack of proper attire. Casey rarely left her bedroom unless she was fully clothed or going to the pool. She glared over her shoulder when Alonzo fell into step behind her. "Unless you plan on touching me, you won't be stopping me, Alonzo."

Alonzo didn't touch her, but he dogged her every step through the mansion toward the foyer. She stormed toward Ignacio's office, never losing momentum, despite the terrified beating of her heart begging her to reconsider, to remember his temper and the years of hard lessons on obedience and her place within his household. She was too angry to listen to her own common sense. She wanted answers.

The doorknob to Ignacio's office opened easily under her hand, but she had to shove hard to get the heavy panel to open under her thin frame. It swung wide and she stumbled a little in the doorway, her robe gaping to reveal her long, bare legs. Ignacio looked up from behind his desk. Both he and his second-in-command, Diego, reached for their guns, but seeing a disheveled Casey, they subsided.

After a brief moment of observation, taking in her stubborn stance, Ignacio waved Diego from the room with an annoyed, "Give me ten minutes."

Casey stepped quickly out of Diego's way as he approached the door, his cold, malevolent eyes crawling over her body. She quickly twitched the robe back into place and tugged the belt tighter. She despised Ignacio's second-in-command even more than she hated her own husband. He was the one who delivered her husband's punishments over the years when Ignacio was too weak-stomached or too busy to follow through. She knew if she was ever truly left in Diego's care she wouldn't last long. There was something about the man that took sadistic to a new level. And the way he looked at her made it clear he would love to get his hands on her.

"What do you want, Casey?" Ignacio demanded the moment the door closed behind Diego. "You know better than to burst in here. I don't have time for you this morning."

She shivered at the menacing tone of voice Ignacio was treating her to. He was usually cold and distant, but this spelled danger. She forced herself to remember her reason for seeking him out. She needed to remember her outrage. "I'm done playing nice with the Bolivian," she announced bravely, approaching his desk. "Allowing him to take me to your club was one thing; tacky, but okay, fine. The flowers, though, they're too much. You allowed another man to send me flowers in our home. The place where we live together. Have you no shame, Ignacio?"

His eyes suddenly took on a gleam that she didn't like. It

was greed combined with something else. Something awful and disgusting... something she couldn't quite place. "You don't like his attentions, my dear?" he drawled, watching her carefully.

She felt her face flush and she avoided his eyes. "I don't understand why you're allowing him to do this to me. In a decade of marriage, you haven't allowed another man to lay a hand on me except for punishment, but now, suddenly this man is allowed to do whatever he wants?" She wrapped her arms protectively around her middle and forced herself to meet his eyes. "Why are you doing this, Ignacio? What do you hope to gain by handing me to this man on a silver platter?"

He snorted and slapped his hands on his desk, pushing himself back. He stood and slowly circled the desk, his eyes sweeping her tall, lithe form. "You're a beautiful woman, figure it out. You belong to me, Casey. You always have and for as long as you live, you always will. You float around this house like a useless piece of nothing. I ask you for one little thing? Just to be nice to this guy, my business partner... and that's a problem for you?"

She turned to look at him and lifted her chin, the tangle of her pale hair swaying with the movement. "Yes, it is a problem for me," she said defiantly. "I don't want to see him again."

The strike came so quickly she didn't have time to so much as flinch. He slapped her on the side of the face, then before she could collapse, grabbed a fistful of hair and slammed her forward into his desk. She cried out as her hip smacked hard into the wood and then she was forced to sprawl face down across his paperwork. She bit her lip to stop further shrieks from erupting, knowing the punishment would be worse if she made a fuss. She tasted blood where she bit down too hard.

He leaned across her back, crushing her further against the side of his unyielding desk, bruising her hip even more. His hot, horrible breath slid over her bare shoulder where her robe had slipped. Involuntary tears of pain glittered in eyes that stared straight ahead, frozen on his big, fancy leather chair.

Unlike years past when he'd struck her in anger, his voice was surprisingly calm as he spoke. Now he seemed intent on hurting her with dispassionate malevolence, simply to get his point across. "You will do as I say tell you, Casey. Or I have no more use for you. Got me?"

Casey nodded and blinked rapidly, tears spilling over her cheeks and dripping onto the papers on his desk. Absently she hoped they were ruining something important. Maybe whatever business deal he was trying to seal with the Bolivian. Ignacio pulled her abruptly to her feet and steadied her when her legs would have given way. She was the exact same height as him in bare feet, taller in heels, which of course annoyed him. Fleetingly it occurred to her that Reyes wouldn't care about something stupid like that. He was enough of a man to feel pride in the presence of a striking woman, whether she was taller than him or not.

Ignacio smoothed his hands down her arms, wrapped his thick fingers around the thin columns and drew her closer, his thumbs rubbing absently against her chilled skin. She stood stiffly, holding herself as far back as she could, making sure any expression of loathing was wiped clean from her face. Her ear was still ringing and her cheek was on fire from the vicious blow she'd taken.

"You will dress up, you will look beautiful and you will go to his room at the Plaza at 8:00 tonight. You'll do whatever he wants to do with you and you won't disappoint me, will you Casey, my girl?" he asked, his voice cajoling. They both knew he wasn't asking her a real question, but stating a fact.

He'd only given her a small taste of what he was really capable of. Why had she so stupidly forgotten how little power she had under Ignacio's regime?

"Of course, Ignacio," she murmured through stiff lips.

He led her to the door and opening it, handed her off to Alonzo, who was silently ignoring whatever Diego was saying to him. The two men had never gotten along.

"Make sure she's presentable for tonight," Ignacio said before turning his back on Casey and her bodyguard, dismissing them.

CHAPTER NINE

C asey stared at her reflection with a mixture of resigned despair and anger. No amount of makeup could disguise the mark high on her cheek or the swollen bite mark on her lip that were clearly visible through her careful efforts. Absently she wondered if it was part of Ignacio's plan. To present his wife, damaged goods, to another man who clearly wanted her. Only she wasn't sure what the other man ultimately wanted with her. A quick fuck? A way to mess with his business rival?

Ignacio had sent an entire outfit for her to wear, including a dress, heels and jewelry. As the day had progressed and she'd prepared for her meeting with Reyes she began to feel more and more like a pawn in some deadly game. She wore a beautiful white dress that clung lovingly to every curve. It was curved along her legs to give the illusion of length along one thigh, but if she moved wrong it would also give a tantalizing glimpse high on her other thigh. It was sleeveless with a neckline that plunged halfway to her stomach. She didn't bother with a bra. She'd been blessed with decent cleavage, but hadn't been eating well lately, which had shrunk some of her curves.

The dress fit her perfectly though and looked stunning when paired with the four-inch silver stilettos and diamonds Ignacio had sent from the safe room, a bracelet, teardrop pendant earrings and her wedding rings. She almost never wore her wedding set. Ignacio said they were too expensive to wear in public and, honestly, she was relieved. They were so big and gaudy, she hated the sight of them. But tonight, clearly, he intended to send the message that she was taken... even though she had orders to give Reyes anything he wanted. Which presumably included her body.

Casey sat on the edge of her bed, a hairbrush clutched tight in her hand. The thought made her feel sick to her stomach. Not the thought of Reyes touching her. God, his touch melted everything inside her. Like nothing she'd ever experienced. No, it was the thought that her husband could so easily sell her to another man. And that she had no idea what the true intentions of that other man were. She was beginning to think she was in danger of really caring about Reyes, but he was mafia, just like her husband. No... he was worse than her husband. She could sense the lurking predator in him, getting ready to strike. She just wished she knew whose throat he intended to tear out. She lifted the brush and absently ran in through her hair, trying to hold the tears back so she wouldn't ruin her make-up and piss Ignacio off. She would have pretended she had a headache if she thought it would get her out of seeing Reyes again, but she knew that wasn't an option.

Less than an hour later she was standing in front of his hotel room door with Alonzo and another man, one of Reyes people at her back. She could feel the tension sizzling between the two men, but kept her head tilted down, her hair covering her cheeks when Reyes opened the door.

"Casey," he greeted her, his deep voice caressing her name with warmth.

She wanted to look up, but kept her eyes on his waist. He wore dress pants with a leather belt and a nice shirt, tucked in. She wasn't sure what colours he wore, but she thought maybe dark, either black or grey. His shoes were very nice and shined dully in the light of the hallway. She wanted to laugh bitterly. If Ignacio hadn't marked up her face she would never have noticed the man's shoes.

"Reyes," she greeted him, infusing ice into her voice and quickly moving past him before he could question why she wasn't looking at him.

He closed the door behind her and offered to take her wrap. She nodded and let it fall from her shoulders as he tugged, gently moving her hair aside so he wouldn't catch the strands. She shivered from his soft touch at the back of her neck and rapidly stepped away from him toward the darkest part of the room, a table next to the window. She could stand in the shadows there.

"Thank you for coming," he said, approaching her from behind.

She wanted to laugh out loud and point out that she didn't have a choice, but she kept her mouth closed. It was always smarter to stay silent. When she opened her mouth she said too much, got herself in trouble. Instead she focused on the view outside the window, the incredible swath of lights that swept Miami's coast before plunging toward the ocean.

"A drink?" he asked.

He was standing so close she felt his heat touch her bare shoulder. "Yes, please. Maybe something a little stronger than orange juice this time," she murmured a hint of wryness in her voice, her eyes locked on the darkness of the water far below.

He chuckled and moved away from her for a moment,

returning with a glass of white wine. She reached to take it, without turning to look at him. The coolness of the glass against her fingers told her he'd chilled the wine before she arrived. "Thank you."

"You like the view, *nena*?" he asked when she still didn't move to look at him.

She nodded and took a hasty sip of the wine. It was delicious. Smooth and sweet with a hint of tartness. "I love this part of Miami," she told him. "Especially these high up condos, they're so beautiful. Do you own this one?" She hazarded a quick glance around the penthouse suite before moving her eyes back to the window.

"No," he said shortly, not bothering to continue that line of conversation. She wasn't surprised. Reyes didn't seem like a man that tolerated idle chat. He said what he wanted to say and moved on.

He reached past her, deliberately brushing her arm with his sleeve. She swore he inflicted those light touches on her as a form of torture. They seemed to do just as much to her senses as when he outright grabbed her. He opened the door leading to the expansive deck and flicked his wrist, indicating she should accompany him outside. She stepped over the threshold, her heels clicking softly against the tiles as she stepped toward the balcony railing, taking in the breathtaking view of the Miami coastline. She made sure to keep her back to him while they stood together.

He allowed the silence to reign for several long minutes as she sipped her drink and tried valiantly to steady her nerves. It didn't help when he caged her against the railing, gripping the metal on either side of her body and bracing his arms so she was trapped between him and a long, long drop. She glanced down, the liquid in the glass shaking a little as she let that dark voice in the back of her mind run free for just a second. The one that whispered to her, every once in a while, that it would be easier to just let go. That if she succeeded this time Ignacio couldn't punish her the way he promised after her last botched attempt.

She tore her eyes away from the beckoning darkness and focused on the strong fingers flexed against the railing. It didn't matter. Reyes would grab her before she even completed the thought, let alone the action. Besides, she didn't want him acquainted with that sad, dark part of her. He already had a pretty good idea of how messed up she was and he still seemed to want her. His next words proved it.

"Stay the night with me," he said huskily, his accent caressing each syllable as he leaned into her back to speak into her ear from behind.

She nearly moaned out loud from the feel of him against her, his groin grazing her ass. Her thin dress made it so she felt every small touch from the fabric of his trousers and the graze of his belt buckle against her curve of her cheek. His broad shoulders brushed hers as he leaned in. The cool evening breeze gently lifted her hair and flipped it back across his bicep where it was braced next to her, caging her body in. From the corner of her eye she could see the barbaric beauty of her pale hair laying across the darkness of his shirtsleeve.

"No," she sighed.

He made an impatient sound from behind her and eased closer, surrounding her with heat. Her long hair snaked back around them, enveloping them in a cocoon. His knuckles tightened against the railing. In anger or frustrated lust? Both, maybe. She was certain this man wasn't used to denial.

"I want you to stay with me, *cariña*," he growled in her ear, his voice throbbing with authoritative energy. "Leave Ignacio and come to me. Not just tonight, but permanently. I can do things for you, give you things you can't even imagine. I can protect you. Set you up with more luxuries than you can even hope to experience here in this narrow world."

Casey gasped and whirled in his arms, her hair whipping around them. She was careful to tilt her head away though, keeping half her face in the shadows still. He straightened and moved back a little to give her room. She stood to her full height, which, in her heels, brought her eye to eye with Reyes. It didn't matter that he was much broader than her and outweighed her by at least eighty pounds, she glared at him, showing him exactly what she thought of his offer.

"Never," she hissed pressing her hands back against the cold, unyielding glass of the balcony. "Fuck you and fuck your offer, Reyes. I already have all the material shit that I need in my life and I'd give it all up for a taste of freedom. If you had any idea what I've done to leave..." Abruptly she brought a hand up to cut off the flow of words and pressed shaking fingers against her lips, reminding herself not to let her tongue get away from itself.

"What?" Reyes demanded, his too sharp brain catching on to her words. "What would you do to leave him? Apparently, you won't accept offers from other, more powerful men. Tell me, *nena*, what exactly will you do to escape a lifetime with Ignacio Hernandez?"

She tried to turn away from him, dismiss his words in the hope that he would drop it, but he grabbed her arm and swung her around. She moved quickly on her heels, reaching out to catch herself so she wouldn't fall. He steadied her and she looked up at him, full in the face, the light falling across her. His eyes roved over her, lingering on her swollen lip and bruised cheek.

"Shit," she gasped turning her head, but it was too late. She could feel the instant stillness in his body as he absorbed the meaning behind her battered face. She felt the incoming storm as emotion swelled and seethed within him.

"Who hit you?" Reyes demanded, his voice lashing her.

Casey shivered but lifted her chin defiantly. "Who do you think?"

"Don't give me that shit, Casey," he snarled, rage vibrating thickly in his voice. He took hold of her chin and impatiently brushed the hair back from her face so he could see the marks better. "Did Ignacio do this to you?"

"Of course it was my husband. Do you really think he would allow anyone else to do this without permission?" she confirmed jerking her chin, but he refused to release his hold on her face. He smoothed a finger across the graze on her cheek, his touch gentle despite his seething anger.

"Why the fuck would he hit you, especially knowing I would see you tonight?" Reyes asked incredulously. "Does he have a death wish?"

She stared at him, at the threat of violence glittering fiercely in his eyes. All for her, all over the momentary pain Ignacio had caused her. She sighed and brought her hand up, closing it over his and forcing his hand away from her chin. Her bracelet slid along her arm as she moved, a reminder of the ownership another man had over her.

"Why do you think he hit me? I told him I didn't want to see you again," she admitted.

She could feel the heat of his fury rise further and flinched back, pressing against the railing of the balcony. She expected him to have the same reaction as Ignacio. To attack her for not wanting to see him. Instead he slowly reached out so she could see what he was doing and pulled her away from the railing. She shivered as the cool evening air washed over her bare arms and shoulders.

He gently brushed her hair back from her face once more

and touched the bruise with the back of his fingers. "He hit you because you were reluctant to see me again."

She nodded miserably and stood stiffly in his hold. He cupped the back of her head, holding her still and leaned forward to touch his lips against hers. Her lips parted in surprise at the feathery light touch of his mouth to hers. He took advantage by licking the cut on her bottom lip where she'd bitten herself. She jerked back, but he held her immobile with one hand at the back of her head and another around her waist. He brushed his lips back and forth across hers, with gentle purpose.

Heat sizzled through her veins with the force of a lightening strike. She tried to concentrate on not passing out as every nerve ending in her body lit up with pleasure from the soothing touch of his lips against hers and the firm hand wrapped around her, forcing her to hold still while he overwhelmed her senses. Her legs wobbled on her heels and she probably would have collapsed if he hadn't been holding her up.

Finally, he pulled back from the most perfect kiss she'd ever had, his mouth only a few inches from hers when he spoke. "I was already planning to kill your husband, *cariña*. Now that I know he's put hands on you, I will make it so much fucking worse. He'll beg me for death long before I let that miserable fuck go to hell."

Casey's eyes widened in shock and she opened her mouth to protest, but before she could, he interrupted her, his hands falling to her waist in a tight hold. "I know what you will say and I want you to think, Casey. Think hard about who your husband is, what he's done to you and what you want."

She shook her head, her hair swinging. She pushed against his chest, but he wouldn't let her go. She dug her nails into his chest over his shirt, trying to hurt him, to force him to release her. His hold was unbreakable. "Stop it, Casey. Hold still and listen to me."

She whimpered and shook her head.

He shook her until her head snapped up and they were staring at each other, her eyes wide and fearful, his snapping with fierce energy and anger. "He's fucking handed you over to me to use however I want. He gave you to me bruised and..." he grabbed her hand and lifted it, her wedding rings glinting in the faint evening light, "wearing his fucking rings. Why? So I could fuck his wife, knowing I was taking a woman I want but can't keep? He's a disgusting, degenerate fuck and you know it. He deserves worse than the death I'm going to deal him."

A sob tore from her throat and she covered her mouth with one shaking hand. She moaned and tried to turn away from him, to deny his words. She didn't want to hear this. It was too much, more than she could handle. She'd been sleep-walking through life for a decade. In the space of barely a week she was forced to deal with a whole barrage of emotions and now the man that woke her up was confessing plans of murder on his penthouse balcony.

A laugh escaped her and she looked around wildly for escape. It was either a twelve-story fall or back through the penthouse into the cold presence of her bodyguard. Her life was a cage no matter where she turned. His grip on her waist tightened painfully as he forced her attention back to him.

"Don't you dare drift away from me, Casey. I know how you work, woman, and when we're together I won't let you have your little escapism tricks. When we're together we'll be together," he growled.

"Stop it," she cried out, the words wrenched from her. She shoved harder against him, struggling in earnest now. "Just stop, Reyes. We'll never be together!"

"You think not?" he snarled, turning to the balcony door and dragging her through.

She squirmed against him, dragging her heels against the floor as he hauled her against the table, shoving her until she was almost sitting on the marble top. Her skirt had twisted until it was nearly hiked up to her waist. He glanced down and groaned as he reached for her. She tried to dive away from him but his hands gripped the outside of her bare thighs and his chest pressed against hers. Capturing her, stilling her. He slid his hands up her thighs, his thumbs caressing the edge of her panties. Casey sucked air into her starved lungs and resisted the urge to tilt her hips to give him better access as scorching heat flooded through her belly and ran like a river through her pussy.

"Ah god, *cariña*," Reyes growled against her throat rocking his hips into the cradle of her thighs and forcing her to feel the thick hardness of his erection. He licked her exposed throat, running his tongue down the side and then gently nipping the place where her neck met her shoulder. His teeth turned more savage with each word until he bit down hard enough to leave a mark. "Let me have you... let me fucking have you and I promise I will make it so fucking good."

She slapped her hands down on the table behind her and dropped her head back, unwittingly giving him better access to the front of her body. He immediately moved his mouth across her collarbone, taking stinging bites until he reached the hollow between her breasts. He sucked and licked, touching and seducing her body. He flicked the top of her dress to the side, exposing her breast to the cool air before covering it with his hot, skillful mouth.

Casey's breath whooshed out of her and her arms gave out. He caught her before she could hit the table without ever taking his attention from her breast. She whimpered and cried out underneath him, squirming against the hardness of the table. She clenched her hands into fists to keep from grabbing hold of him and demanding he devour her the way she desperately wanted, the way she needed. She couldn't, she just couldn't participate, no matter how bad she wanted it.

He reached for her skirt, shoving it up her thighs and then slid his fingers into her panties, touching her. She felt the rumble in his chest before he spoke. "So fucking wet. Fuck, it was like you were made for me, Casey."

She felt pressure as he slid his fingers further into her, felt the explosive pleasure of him sliding across her clit and into her pussy. Her eyes flew open and she gasped, "Stop!"

He froze, his body going from warmly fluid to completely rigid over top of hers. He pulled his hand from her panties and reached for her. She cried out in fear as he dragged her into his chest, her legs still spread and dangling on either side of his hips. She could still feel the insistent press of his cock straining between them and moaned, half in need and half in distress. She fucking hated this situation!

"Your husband told you to fuck me?" he demanded, his dark eyes fierce on hers.

Tears flooded her eyes and she nodded. "Y-yes, that's pretty much what he said."

"And you're saying no to me?" he asked, his voice a quiet snarl.

The breath shuddered in and out of her and real fear of his retaliation began to replace her arousal. But she held her ground. She nodded and said in a shaking voice, "I'm saying n-no."

"Because you're loyal to that sick fuck?" he demanded, his fingers tightening on her arms.

"Because I made a vow to be loyal to that sick fuck," she cried out, hardening her voice and forcing the tears in her eyes back. Yes, this situation was fucked, but she was a mafia wife and she had her principles.

He smiled, his face hard and strained, but his eyes gleaming triumph. "Good girl, Casey," he said, his voice thick with passion. "You are my good fucking girl."

"I... I don't understand," she whispered, frowning, trying to figure out what was happening. Was she about to be raped? Coerced into sex? Or kicked out of the penthouse for being a good girl?

He chuckled and pulled her further into his chest, embracing her lightly, running his hands down her back soothingly. She lay stiffly against his chest and listened to the beat of his heart against her ear and the rumble of his voice as he talked. "Your loyalty is stunning, *cariña*. You give it to a man that doesn't deserve it because you must. Because you promised and you know no other way. Now I am going to crush that man and turn your loyalty to me. You will become my queen. *Mi Reina*."

Her heart sped up, pounding with each word. He was going to take her away from Ignacio, give her another cage, turn her into another version of her current self. Mafia wife. And she would hate him for it. She pushed back, shoving away from his chest to look him in the eyes.

"No," she told him. "I won't be your queen."

His face hardened into granite lines and he pulled her off the table, standing her in front of him. He straightened her clothes with quick efficiency. "You won't have a choice," he said, his voice holding a cold ruthlessness she was familiar with from Ignacio and his men but hadn't heard from Reyes yet.

"I'll tell Ignacio what you're planning, he'll stop you," she said, edging back in case he got angry at her threat.

He merely took her by the arm and led her to the door of the condo, retrieved her wrap and folded it around her shoulders, careful to cover every inch of her exposed cleavage. He leaned closer, murmuring in her ear, "I'm counting on it, Mrs. Hernandez."

Casey's mouth fell open and she looked over her shoulder at the man who was proposing insanity. At the man who was planning on murdering her husband, taking over his business and stealing his wife... all while his enemy knew his plan. He was either incredibly confident, insane or he knew something she didn't. He dropped a stinging kiss on her lips and opened the door to usher her out.

CHAPTER TEN

"I want to speak with Ignacio right now!" Casey argued with Diego as she'd been arguing with him for the past few days without results.

Ignacio refused to see her.

Diego's dark, sadistic eyes swept over her body, taking in every inch with a look that suggested she shouldn't have bothered with the terry cloth robe over top of her bikini because he was picturing her without it. Probably without the bathing suit too. She crossed her arms over her breasts and gave him the coldest glare she could come up with.

"You need a reminder what happens when you get demanding of the boss's time, little girl," Diego sneered, his eyes lingering on the top swell of her breasts. "You probably like being smacked around like that though, don't you? Bitches like you'll take whatever attention you can get."

Casey flared her nostrils as she tried to bring her temper under control while Diego postured in front of her and did his best to make her feel small and insignificant. He came within a hairsbreadth of touching her, lifting his hand toward her bruised cheek and running his knuckles down her face without actually making physical contact. She whipped her head away from him and backed up a few steps, her sandaled feet slapping against the floor.

Alonzo shifted at her back and snarled, "No touching."

Diego laughed, the slimy sound drawing a shudder from her. He shrugged and nodded absently. "Yeah," he drawled, his dead eyes piercing her, marking her. "For now."

Casey tightened her arms around her middle and took a steadying breath. Diego made her sick. He'd done things to her over the years, hurt her, at Ignacio's behest. Usually small things, like hit her with a belt or locked her in a closet. But the look in his eyes when he'd punished her told her just how much he enjoyed every moment of her pain, wished he could inflict worse. He'd been one of the three men in the room with her when Ignacio had burned her hand. Watching her face as Alonzo had pinned her down. She'd known that he'd been desperately turned on by her excruciating pain, seen the terrible lust in his eyes as she'd screamed while her flesh had burned.

That day had convinced her that she was better off going dead inside, sleeping through life, rather than attempting to resist the marriage that had been forced on her. So, she had essentially tucked Casey safely away from these ruthless men until such a time came that she could emerge. The look in Diego's eyes as she begged to see Ignacio frightened her. Not only was he refusing her, controlling her ability to see her husband, but he was silently telling her something with those terrible dark eyes. Telling her that their time would come and that it was coming soon.

"Fine," she snapped, looking away from him. "Since you refuse to allow me to see him, or he refuses to see me, whichever it is, then I'll tell you what I need to tell him."

Diego waved his hand in front of her. "By all means, *chica*. Speak to me."

She gritted her teeth, but forced herself to voice the warning that she'd been trying to get to Ignacio since her meeting with Reyes. She turned icy eyes up to Diego and said as coldly as she could, "The Bolivian's are planning some kind of takeover. Reyes intends to kill Ignacio."

The mockery fell from Diego's face for a moment and shock replaced his expression. "Reyes told you this himself?" he asked incredulously, his voice sceptical.

"Yes," Casey replied.

Why wasn't Diego freaking out and dragging her in to see Ignacio? Shouldn't he be more concerned? Unless they already knew of Reyes plans. Suddenly the look on Diego's face became speculative as he looked her over. "Now, why the fuck would the Bolivian tell *you* of his plans?" He stalked closer to her. Casey moved swiftly backwards until she bumped into Alonzo who jumped quickly out of the way so he wouldn't accidentally touch her again. "You got a pussy made of gold?" Diego demanded crudely, lunging toward her.

Casey cried out and fell backwards as her sandal slid on the marble floor. Unable to catch herself she hit the side table and fell, crashing hard on the unyielding marble. She heard Alonzo swear viciously, but there wasn't much he could do. Diego hadn't actually done anything except frighten her. She was the idiot for letting a thug get to her. She shoved herself up onto her knees and shook her hair back, glaring at Diego for all she was worth. She might be down, but she was still going to let the guy know exactly how much she fucking hated him.

She felt his eyes crawl all over her exposed flesh where her robe had come open during her fall. Her hands moved automatically to pull the two halves closed while she kept her eyes on him as he crouched down in front of her. He flexed his biceps, making sure she saw how massive they were next to her insignificant strength. She breathed hard through her nose, forcing herself to hold his gaze.

"Stupid woman," he drawled. "You think we don't know what the Bolivians are planning? You are just a distraction for that lowlife savage while we move our people into place and call in some favours."

She frowned in surprise. She'd been used to distract Reyes? Somehow, she thought he was too smart to fall for that. But he had definitely been interested in her. Had pursued her. Was still pursuing her, sending gifts to the mansion for her. "I don't understand any of this," she whispered.

"Poor, baby," Diego mocked her, his cold eyes raking over her breasts while he talked. "You don't need to understand, you had your chance to be useful. And it seems you were more useful than we thought. I'll tell Ignacio that Reyes revealed his plans to you. Only a man in love does something stupid like that."

Her eyes widened in horror as the impact of his words hit her. Had she been utterly wrong in telling Diego of Reyes' plan? Had she taken her loyalty to Ignacio too far? She'd lived by her own personal code for so long that maybe she didn't see the right path any more when it was directly in front of her. But... no. Reyes seemed to understand her, seemed to understand how she worked. He knew she was unfailingly loyal to Ignacio. He knew she would rat him out to her husband, had been counting on it. She had to believe that the man who made her body sing and was starting to look toward her scarred heart knew what he was doing. Because she sure as fuck didn't.

She jumped when the door to Ignacio's office slammed

open and he stood glowering in the doorway. He stared with open hostility at the tableau in front of him for a moment. Then, completely ignoring the fact that his wife was sprawled on the floor next to his second-in-command, snapped, "Diego, I need you."

CHAPTER ELEVEN

"He has a sense of humour," Casey murmured with amusement, eyeing the array of gifts Reyes had sent her.

Each one had significance and, if she were being honest, chipped away a little more at the armour around her heart. She hadn't seen him again since their erotic and stormy encounter in his penthouse suite almost a week ago. But each time a new gift arrived, it was a reminder that he hadn't forgotten her. Nor had he forgotten the things that she'd said to him in each of their conversations.

None of the gifts were overly expensive, which told her that he'd listened when she told him that the luxuries surrounding her meant little to her. Her fingers drifted over a framed picture of herself. She had no idea when it was taken because it was a close up of her face. In the photo she was leaning forward, her hair covering most of her face, except for a carefree smile curving her lips as she stared off at nothing in particular. The expression on her face surprised her since she so rarely smiled. Casey lifted her fingers and touched her lips, wondering when she'd smiled like that and what she'd been thinking at the time. How had he gotten such an intimate picture of her? The mansion was locked down tight and she so rarely went out.

She put the picture down and picked up the next item, a book. This one made her laugh out loud and roll her eyes. It was a tourist's guidebook to Bolivia. She'd actually read the entire thing cover to cover in one evening, eager for knowledge of Reyes' home country. She wondered which region his home was in since there were several. She tried not to think too hard about the significance of his giving her the book.

"Kantuta," she whispered, picking up the gorgeous blooms, yet another gift. They looked so exotic she wondered if he'd had to go to great lengths to find them. They were strange looking, but hauntingly beautiful with a long tube-like bell instead of petals. On a suspicion, she'd looked up the national flower of Bolivia to discover that there were two. This one was native to the cooler, western side of the region that contained the Andes. She wondered if he was telling her, indirectly, where he lived.

She flipped the guidebook open and pressed the flowers inside, wanting to preserve them for as long as she could. This was the second time in her life she'd received flowers. Both times from the same man in the space of a week. She was beginning to think he liked her.

The other gifts included a lovely silk wrap that she discovered was a light pink colour by asking her maid. He also gave her several books on the science of migraines written by reputable neurologists from around the world. This particular bundle had filled her eyes with tears and made her think he was doing more than playing terrible games with her. It also broke her heart a little. Because it didn't matter how thoughtful he was, how much he treated her as though he actually cared. She still belonged to another man.

And Reyes had made it clear to her that he valued her

loyalty, even if it belonged to someone else. That was the tragedy of her blossoming feelings for the Bolivian mafia boss. Though she suspected he could be as much of a monster as her own husband, she also thought maybe he was capable of loving her back. His thoughtful gifts proved that he felt something. But she couldn't go to him, no matter how much she wanted to.

Ignacio owned her.

"We move as planned," Reyes growled to Alejandro.

His second nodded sharply, but hesitated. Reyes stiffened and waited. He knew the other man had something to say, but was so used to heeding the boss's orders without question that he didn't know if he should verbalize the thought. Smart decision. However, Reyes had appointed Alejandro his second for a reason. The man was uncommonly intelligent and had survived twelve years in Venezuelan intelligence before moving on to the head of a mercenary organization and then to Reyes who had lured him away with the promise of unparalleled riches and a medical treatment for his mother that would have been out of his reach without Reyes' intervention.

"Just say it," Reyes snarled, already knowing where Alejandro's thoughts were, but knowing they had to have the conversation anyway.

Alejandro stood a little straighter, his eyes on the window behind Reyes. "What about the woman?"

"What about her?" Reyes spat.

Alejandro sighed a little, clearly unable to say exactly what he wanted. They were both ex-military men and thus used to plain speaking, but the big, beat-up head of Reyes security had no idea how to handle this unique situation. Women didn't usually fall under their jurisdiction. At least not the kind they kept. "We have no extraction plan for her. If we move in as planned, she'll be at the house when we hit it."

Reyes stared coldly at the other man. He could feel fury rising up within, but forced it back and responded in the only way he knew how. "She's his wife, she chose her loyalties. I asked her to come to me and she refused. Just make fucking sure nothing happens to her when we move in. I have a contact on the inside who'll help keep her safe."

Alejandro looked as though he were chewing on nails. Reyes understood the dilemma. They would be walking into a bloodbath, no matter what happened. And Casey Hernandez would be sitting right in the middle of it. It chilled him to the bone that there was nothing he could do to spare her from the coming war. Except extract her and keep her for himself. Take her from the keeping of one monster and move her into the keeping of another, infinitely worse. He only hoped she was smart enough to keep out of the path of the flying bullets.

Alejandro grunted. "We'll do our best, boss."

"You better," Reyes told him, turning his cold gaze on the man he'd trusted with his life for the past several years. "If something happens to my future *reina*, I can assure you, I will come after you and whoever else was careless enough to allow her harm. I don't care who puts the bullet in her, everyone will suffer my wrath."

Alejandro met his eyes and nodded his understanding. The idea that Casey Hernandez *would* become the Queen of the Reyes cartel finally crystalizing. It was no longer a vague thought, gossip that he and the men discussed behind the bosses back. No, it seemed that the stunningly beautiful blond woman that their leader had been pursuing with relentless determination would be going home with them. As long as they could ensure her survival.

"She will live, Reyes," Alejandro assured him. "You have my word."

Reyes grunted as Alejandro pledged his loyalty to the pale, somewhat weak woman that would stand at his side and lead their organization; their people. Fuck, he hoped he wasn't making a mistake. But he couldn't imagine letting her go now, not after having a brief taste of her. Touching her petal soft skin, tasting her sweetness and learning each fascinating new fact that just made him want her even more. She would become his and she would rule at his side.

"I'm going to see her one more time before we move," he told Alejandro.

It was Tuesday.

CHAPTER TWELVE

C asey tried to check out. She honestly did. She hated these women almost as much as she despised the men guarding her gilded cage. These were the birds that happily flew back into their cages and ate from the hands that fed them. But for some reason she couldn't zone out the way she usually did during these godawful lunches, possibly because she'd started flushing some of her daily pills instead of blindly swallowing them.

She felt the burning hatred welling up inside her as they talked about the most useless things she could conceive of. She only dined with them because Elvira Montana was among the set. Beautiful, blond and coolly distant, Elvira barely took part in the conversation either. But Ignacio insisted that the two women meet and get to know each other.

Probably because Elvira was an older version of what Casey was to become. A coked-out mob wife whose husband had bought her way into this elite company of women. And her husband could maybe get Ignacio some deals on overseas product Ignacio wouldn't otherwise be able to get his hands on. The others at the table included politician's wives and daughters, a Spanish telanovella actress and Dahlia Paxton, a high-priced lawyer to the rich and famous.

Dahlia was talking about an awkward encounter she had at a gas station when she'd accidentally pulled up to the wrong pump and been expected to fill her own tank. "I mean, what did they think," she laughed, flicking her wrist over her shoulder and reaching for her wine. "That I would get out of the car or something? Ugh, I would've gone to my meeting smelling of noxious gas fumes, or worse, I could've gotten cancer or something. I mean, isn't it dangerous to pump your own gas? I could've started a fire or something! So, I just sat there and waited until someone came out and helped me. I out-stubborned those blue-collar assholes."

Casey opened her mouth to make a comment about Dahlia's ability to go to law school and pass the state bar, yet her surprising inability to pump her own gas without dousing herself in the noxious liquid and setting herself on fire, but Elvira put a restraining hand on her wrist. Casey glanced at the other woman with a raised eyebrow, but Elvira just shook her head and sighed.

"Not worth it," she whispered for Casey's ears alone. "Just go back to sleep darling."

She patted Casey's arm with long, manicured fingers and withdrew back into her own seat, settling in to ignore the bulk of the conversation once more. Though Casey was mildly surprised by Elvira's intervention, she took it to heart. The older woman was right. There wasno point in lambasting their entitled company. For several reasons. They wouldn't thank her for it and in their elite society a snub could go a long way toward social suicide. Not something she could afford with the current state of her marriage. Casey shuddered and withdrew any further comments, instead contemplating Elvira's cryptic message, 'go back to sleep.'

Those four words had unwittingly struck right through to the heart of her, cutting deep into her soul.

"Excuse me," she murmured, placing her napkin on the table and abruptly standing.

Elvira looked startled and asked, "Do you want me to come with you?" No doubt she was worried that she'd pushed the delicate young woman closer toward some invisible edge with her kindly intended words. Theirs was a small world where gossip travelled freely among the mob wives. Just like Casey knew Elvira was a frequent user of her husband's product, Elvira knew that Casey had tried to kill herself a few years earlier to escape an unbearable marriage.

Casey managed a believable smile and said, "No thank you, Elvira, I'll be fine."

She made her way swiftly to the ladies' room and was about to lock the door when it flew open, shoving her to one side. "What...?" she gasped, stumbling back, reaching out for the counter.

Reyes strode into the small space, slamming the door and locking it. He swept her with a single look from the bottom of her feet to the top of her head, encompassing each part of her, taking in her slim black high-waisted pencil skirt and bright pink silk blouse. She shook her head and edged along the counter, eyeing him warily.

"No," she told him, trying to make her voice as stern as she could.

He ignored her, stalking closer, devouring every inch of her, his eyes lingering on her bare arms and face. "You got my gifts, *cariña?*"

"Yes," she acknowledged, gripping the granite edge of the vanity behind her until her knuckles strained. She knew it was to stop herself from flinging herself at him. God, he looked so good! He was dressed casual in dark pants and a short-sleeved shirt that strained at his biceps.

"And?" he prompted.

She couldn't help the reluctant grin that spread across her lips. "Thank you, Reyes, they were beautiful. I loved them. The flowers, the books... everything. Truly, I can't even say how much they meant."

He smiled at her, a real smile that softened his dark, scarred face for just a moment. She felt a ripple of gratitude that he would share the rare intimacy of that smile with her. This moment was special. That he was pleased his gifts meant something to her. That she'd appreciated him the way he wanted her to. His obsession for her was becoming mutual and she was tipping her hand.

They stared at each other for a few long, heartrending moments until she looked away and shook her head, a stray hair from her carefully coiffed updo trailing across her cheek. "Don't do that, Reyes. Please just stop doing this to me," she begged.

To his credit he didn't pretend he didn't know what she was talking about. His face resumed its usual hard lines as he stared her down, showing her that he didn't care how much she begged, he could and he would do whatever he liked with her. That she was at his mercy and with every encounter falling further prey to his seduction.

She held a shaking hand out, palm up and whispered, "I need you to be stronger than me." She put every ounce of pleading she could into her voice as she begged him to leave her alone. "We both know I'm weak, Reyes. That I'm the pathetic, cracked wife of a powerful man who has spent years climbing his way into the Miami underworld. He won't let go of his position and he won't let go of me."

She flipped her hand over and showed him the scar on the back then lifted her eyes to see his reaction. Fiery rage lit his gaze as he stared hard at the shiny, raised "H" before meeting her eyes. "Ownership," she told him in a shaky voice. "He will hunt me to the ends of the Earth."

He said nothing for a moment, but when he spoke, his voice was filled with such fury that she wished she had more room behind her so she could take a step back. "You think I would let him?"

Her eyes filled with tears and she shook her head again, dropping her hand in despair. "I think it's my duty to go back to him no matter what, Reyes," she said in a quivering voice. "We've been over this and I just don't think I can do it with you again." She turned away from him and reached for the door.

He grabbed her from behind and shoved her into the door, pushing her until she was flush against the wooden panel with him hard at her back. He leaned in and growled in her ear, "You go when I tell you to go, *nena*. Never before."

He swung her around and pushed her shoulders back against the door. Before she could beg him to leave her alone he crushed her lips with his own, stealing the words from her. She sobbed into his mouth, accepting the hot embrace with despairing enthusiasm. A moan escaped her and she gripped his arms tightly, holding onto him while he shoved himself hard against her, knocking her hips and ass back into the door.

He didn't give her a chance to reject him, shoving his tongue into her mouth and sweeping the recesses within, memorizing her, feeling her. He gripped her jaw and held her open for his dark caress, while his other hand swept her body, both holding her to him and testing her softness. Casey tried to still herself beneath the scorching heat of his caress, but her body clamored for attention, seeking the warmth he was providing. She arched into each sweep of his hand and began to enthusiastically meet each sweep of his tongue with tiny caresses of her own.

He pulled back just enough to mumble, "Fucking *caliente*, Casey," against her lips, before devouring her once more. His hand dropped to the edge of her skirt and yanked upward, bunching it to her waist. She cried out against his mouth, but he swallowed the sound in another hard kiss.

"It's okay, *nena*," he murmured soothingly against her lips.

She whimpered as he tore her panties aside and pushed long fingers unexpectedly deep into her pussy. She widened her legs to ease the pressure, but he took advantage by pushing further up into her body. The breath shuddered out of her and she gripped his arms so hard she thought she might leave bruises. She knew she was embarrassingly wet for him. He did this to her. He made her body drip just for him. She'd never been this way before. Oh, she'd been turned on before. Usually alone in her room reading erotic romance novels or watching sexy movies, but nothing like this.

Then he flicked his thumb across her clit and she thought she was going to die. She flung her head back against the door, knocking the back of her head into the wood and closed her eyes tight. "Stop," she whispered.

"No fucking way, not until you're mine," he snarled, leaning against her to bite into her shoulder. He shoved his fingers impossibly deeper into her. She knew she was going to be sore after this, but... fuck... it felt so good.

"Please... I don't want to do this," she whimpered.

He snarled something in Spanish so rapid and so vile she didn't quite catch it. Reyes pulled his fingers from her body with a suddenness that left her gasping, then he shoved his fingers into her mouth and swirled them around her tongue and teeth, forcing her to taste herself. When she would have turned her face away he gripped her jaw hard, leaned in and shoved his fingers in and out of her mouth a few times.

"Taste what I do to you, Casey," he growled, his dark eyes

so wild she thought he was on the razor's edge of violence. "We both know he doesn't fucking do this for you."

Then he leaned in to kiss her, shoving his tongue in her mouth, stretching her lips and joining his fingers to taste her. She moaned at the eroticism of the act and wrapped her tongue around his fingers. The kiss went on and on until she finally pulled back blinking rapidly. She turned her head sharply to the side, pushing his hand away. The moment was so intense it brought tears to her eyes. She'd gone years without crying over a man, yet somehow this man brought her to tears over and over in a matter of weeks. It was like he'd broken something inside her. Or maybe he was shaking up the already broken pieces.

A sob escaped her lips and she whispered against him, "Please, Reyes, please just push me away. I'm not strong enough for this. Tell me to fuck off before I break my vows. If you take away that part of me... I'll have nothing left of myself. J-just make me go." She clung to him, digging her nails into his flesh. She blinked rapidly and stared at her hand on his arm. Even though she couldn't see colours she could see that her skin was light against his.

He looked at her for a moment, debating whether or not to continue, knowing he could easily fuck her up against the door and she wouldn't murmur a single protest. But he also knew that if he did that, he would be taking something from her. Something extremely valuable. So, instead he pushed himself away, slamming a hand over her shoulder next to her head. She flinched, but stood still, breathing heavily. After a moment, he dropped his hand to the lock and twisted it. He pulled her back, smoothed her skirt down her body, opened the door and pushed her through with a growled, "Go."

Casey ran into the corridor without looking back. She refused to turn around as she heard Reyes leave the washroom and stride away from her. Elvira rushed quickly toward her from the other direction and reached for Casey's arm, steadying her. "Everything okay, hon?" she asked, her voice sharp with concern. She glanced behind Casey as though expecting to see someone in the shadows.

Casey nodded swiftly and lifted a hand toward her hair. Elvira reached up and tucked a few strands behind Casey's ear with swift efficiency. "You look beautiful. Don't worry that the bitch squad'll think anything's wrong. They don't have time for anything but their own selfish selves anyway."

Casey laughed shakily. "Thanks, Elvira."

"Come on. Let's go get a drink in the lobby bar," she murmured huskily, linking arms with Casey and pulling her toward the front of the restaurant.

Casey glanced back toward the Tuesday table. "Won't they miss us?"

"Who the fuck cares," Elvira said. "I'm more interested in hearing what kind of wild animal attacked you in the washroom and where I find can one of those."

Casey laughed, beginning to feel some of her tension ease and allowed the older woman to pull her toward the bar.

CHAPTER THIRTEEN

"Where are they...?" Casey mumbled, rummaging through the drawer in her washroom. She could barely see through the terrible throbbing behind her eye socket. She'd crawled from her bed to the toilet several minutes earlier where she'd emptied her stomach. Now that the horrific nausea had passed she was searching for the migraine pills Ignacio's doctor had given her. Sometimes they worked and sometimes they didn't.

Her hand closed over the box and she pulled it out with a relieved sigh. She collapsed sideways onto the bath mat and lay still for a few seconds, one hand clutching the small white box and the other pressed tight against the side of her head. Tears streamed unchecked down her cheeks. She bit back sobs of pain, knowing they would only echo in the small space around her and make the throbbing in her skull that much worse.

She cringed when something thumped against the washroom window and a loud howling sound heralded an end-of-summer Florida storm. She hadn't realized one was coming, but if her head was any indication, it was going to be brutal.

Sometimes she got really bad migraines when the weather was stormy. She wondered if they were due for a tropical storm or worse. She'd been so preoccupied with Ignacio's and Reyes' drama that she hadn't been paying any attention to the news.

When she finally managed to get her breathing under control, she squinted her eyes at the packaging in her hand and used the dim light from a lamp in her bedroom to peel back the foil. With shaking fingers, she pushed the pill into her mouth and used her tongue to press it against the top of her mouth where it slowly dissolved. She'd already taken several Tylenols and one Advil. They hadn't lessened the pain and anything that hadn't yet broken down in her stomach had been thrown up a few minutes ago. She knew from the intensity of the headache that she was past the point of over-the-counter pain meds helping her now anyway. She would just have to wait this one out.

Casey slowly pushed herself up onto shaking hands and knees. Whimpers of pain escaped her and she nearly collapsed back onto her side. She leaned forward for a minute, pressing her forehead into the cradle of her arms for relief. She used her the back of her hands to wipe the tears from her cheeks before pushing herself back up and taking several deep breaths. Fuck, it even hurt to breath. She was fast approaching the point where she was going to curl up in a ball wherever she landed and just cry and beg for death until the migraine passed. She just wanted to make it to the bed before that happened so she could wake up on the other side of this bitch in relative comfort.

"Casey," a deep voice reached softly out to her.

She cried out, startled and then nearly vomited from the sudden movement. She slammed her swollen eyelids shut and took several gasping breaths as she tried to control the nausea that threatened to overwhelm her once more. After a few more moments, she was able to peel her eyes open into slits and see the man crouched in front of her. Alonzo was looking at her with that usual mix of resigned concern. He was used to these godawful headaches.

"Crawl to me, Casey," he said patiently. "I'll help you get into the bed."

They both knew he wouldn't touch her. He never touched her because he always followed Ignacio's instructions to the letter. But he would help her as best he could. Some small part of him cared about the frail mistress he'd been tasked to care for over the years. Slowly she did as he bid her and began to crawl painfully toward him, biting back a moan. He coaxed her with gentle words of encouragement until they reached the bed where she was forced to pull herself up before collapsing onto her side.

He leaned over her placing his beefy arms next to her and asked, "How many pills did you take, Casey?"

She closed her eyes and whispered, "Not many. Three maybe."

It was the truth as far as she could remember, but they both knew he didn't believe her. Because she'd lied to him once in the past and almost managed to kill herself. Plus, she had a tendency to forget how many pills she took or how often she took them when her head hurt this bad. She heard him sigh and move away from her. Then she heard him run a glass of water before returning to the bed.

"Sit up and take this," he urged her.

She knew what Alonzo was giving her. "I don't want it," she told him. She'd promised Reyes she wouldn't take any more sleeping pills. A tiny sob escaped her as a fierce longing hit her hard in the chest. She wanted him with her so badly it took her breath away. She desperately needed his comfort, the savage protectiveness he seemed to feel toward her.

"You don't have a choice, Casey. Bosses orders. When you

hurt like this you take the pills," Alonzo said, his voice hardening. "Now sit up and take the pill."

There was no point in arguing. If she resisted Alonzo he would tell Ignacio and she would have to deal with her husband's anger and possibly a punishment. Which she absolutely couldn't handle in this weakened state. She pushed herself up into a semi-sitting position and reached for the pill and water, taking both from him.

"Thank you," she murmured and tried to palm the pill instead of putting it in her mouth.

Of course, she didn't fool his sharp eyes. Not when she was half blind and clumsy in her agony. He caught her hand, touching her for the first time in years. She gasped and tried to pull away from him, but he held tight. She forced herself to look at him, trepidation clear in her pain-dulled eyes. His dark, remorseless gaze met hers without flinching.

"You need to take the pill, Casey," he said in an even voice.

Her heart pounded in her chest, the blood in her head throbbing in tandem. She swallowed hard, trying desperately not to throw up on her lovely bedspread. Slowly he pried her fingers open, pulled the smooth, round pill from her hand and lifted it to her lips. She opened her mouth and let him feed her the sleeping pill. She had no choice. She could fight him, but she was in too much pain and she wouldn't win. If Alonzo was willing to touch her to get her to take the pill then something significant had changed in their relationship.

He wrapped his hand around hers over the water glass and lifted it to her lips, urging her to take a drink. She sipped, swallowing both the water and the pill. Tears leaked from her eyes. She'd tried to keep her promise to Reyes. She'd wanted to, but she wasn't strong enough.

Alonzo took her jaw in his giant hand and squeezed, forcing her mouth open so he could see for himself that she'd swallowed the pill. She was too frightened, too overwhelmed by the meaning of his touch to protest. Nodding, satisfied, he let her go, took the glass from her and set it on her night table, then he drew the covers back and waited for her to slide under. He treated her as though she were a child, with careful efficiency. But she felt more from him than she had before. She felt something that made her heart stutter in her chest. He was allowing himself closer access to her than he'd ever allowed in the past. He'd always kept that careful distance. She was never entirely sure why. She suspected it was partly to keep himself safe from Ignacio's wrath and to keep his post as her bodyguard. To make sure he wasn't replaced with someone else.

She kept her eyes on him, watching his every move as he pulled the quilt back up her body and tucked it lightly around her. She tried hard not to flinch away from him when he ran his knuckles down her cheek; she was so used to him never touching her. She simply couldn't wrap her head around why he was suddenly touching her now. He reached over and flicked the lamp off, throwing her bedroom into shadows except for the dim lighting from outside her bedroom, caused by lanterns from the patio leaking in from outside her window. The throbbing in her head eased slightly and she let out a grateful sigh.

She stared after him as he moved in the darkness to sit on her vanity chair and face the bed. He bent so his elbows were on his knees and he watched her. He'd done this in the past. Watched over her when she had a migraine and he didn't trust her word on how much medication she'd taken. Somehow, she thought this was different. She felt he was watching and waiting for her to fall asleep. He was waiting for something.

She desperately wanted to stay awake. She didn't trust those eyes, gleaming black in the darkness. Her head pounded in rhythm with the outside elements, battering her bedroom window with stormy fury. She couldn't seem to stop the waves of fatigue from overtaking her and gradually her eyelashes fluttered shut, no matter how hard she urged them not to. As she finally succumbed to a deep, unnatural sleep she wondered if the man watching over her was her friend or her enemy.

CHAPTER FOURTEEN

C asey wasn't sure exactly what woke her up, but she was suddenly awake and in the middle of Armageddon. Her head was throbbing so viciously her first thought was that someone had embedded an axe in her skull while she was sleeping, which was both unrealistic and not a very nice thing for her imaginary attacker to do. Then she registered the dull sound of bullets and men shouting, though the sounds were coming from a distance. Next, it occurred to her that she was in someone's arms and that the someone holding her was running at top speed through the downstairs corridor of her home.

Casey forced her eyes open, but piercing light penetrated her sensitive vision throwing a shard of imaginary glass straight through her already splitting brain. She let out a strangled scream and automatically clutched at whomever was carrying her and buried her face in his broad chest. His arms tightened around her as he ran. She heard his harsh breathing thundering above her head and felt his heart thump against the side of her face. She wondered if it would be impolite to ask him to either put her down and let her die in peace or to stop breathing and beating so loudly until her migraine had passed.

Then something exploded next to them and she felt fire rip down her arm as shards of marble flew through the hallway they were running down. A trickle of blood ran down the back of her arm and dripped off her elbow. Casey whimpered quietly and held onto for dear life. She was certain now that it was her Alonzo who was carrying her. He swore, shifted her against his side, allowing her legs to slide to the floor and reached for his gun holster.

Casey clutched him, attempting to hold herself upright while he covered them and edged around a corner holding Casey tight against his solid body. Her legs refused to hold her up and every time she closed her eyes fatigue threatened to overtake her. Why the fuck had he forced her to take that sleeping pill? It was going to get them both killed because she couldn't even work her own damn legs. Slowly she sank to the floor, her knees bending under her weight, her eyes firmly closed against the light and her fingers clinging desperately to Alonzo's shirt. He kept one hand on the top of her head while she huddled against his legs.

Alonzo shot down the corridor a few times then scooped Casey back up in his arms and began running toward the back of the house again. They raced out the back door so fast the door banged against the side of the house shattering the glass in the window next to it. The driving rain from the raging storm pelted down on them, soaking Casey in a matter of seconds. Alonzo didn't slow down. He flung Casey over his broad shoulder where she was forced to brace herself against him if she didn't want her already intensely splitting head to bang against his back. She lifted her face and tried to see through the fall of her tangled hair, the pouring rain and howling wind, but it was a blur. She had no idea how Alonzo knew where they were going and prayed they didn't end up in

the pool. She was pretty sure she would happily drown right
at this exact moment.

Alonzo crashed through another door and straight into
the pool house smashing into the far wall. The entire structure shuddered under his weight. He'd turned before hitting
the wall, taking most of the hit against his shoulder, but her
head jarred so badly that Casey felt bile rise up in her throat
and had to swallow several times so she wouldn't throw up on
him. She clung weakly to his soaked shirt as he strode
through the pool house with her still slung across his back.
She wondered what his plan was, there were no other exits
that she knew of, when he crouched on the concrete and set
her down. She moaned and curled onto her side, holding her
head with both hands.

Casey watched as Alonzo used his bulk to move a massive
shelf holding soft white towels and shoving it aside. She
curled tighter into herself as it crashed sideways, smashing
into the wall across from them, littering the floor with towels.
Without pausing he reached down and wrenched open a trap
door in the floor. Casey stared in open-mouthed astonishment. She had no idea there was an escape route in or around
the mansion. She supposed it made sense though.

When Alonzo reached for her she went eagerly into his
arms, recognizing now that he was trying to get them the hell
out of whatever shit-storm was raining down upon Ignacio's
head. And while Casey was smart enough to know exactly
who was storming the compound, intent on killing her
husband, she didn't have the capacity to work out her own
part in Reyes' plan. She felt better off going with Alonzo and
working out the rest later.

Alonzo scooped her up and plunged them through the
darkness of the hole in the floor of the pool house. Casey hid
her face against his shoulder, crying out when his feet hid
solid ground and her head smacked into him. She knew it was

a shallow wish, considering men were dying all around them, but she wanted her head to stop fucking hurting until they were safely away from the danger so she could just think straight.

Alonzo strode easily through the damp darkness of the underground tunnel with Casey held firmly in his arms. He seemed to know exactly where they were going. Silence surrounded them now that they were away from the mansion. She desperately hoped he was taking her to a car where they could drive away from the deadly chaos aboveground. Where they could wait out the storm until news of its outcome trickled their way and she was able to figure out what to do next.

Casey expected them to continue until they emerged from the tunnel but the eerie echo of Alonzo's shoes dully hitting the rough concrete abruptly ceased. He stood still in the darkness holding her, his breaths puffing in and out of his mouth above her head. Casey tilted her face back and tried to see him in the inky darkness, but she couldn't see a thing. Her skin felt icy and shivers wracked her body.

"Al-lonzo..." she whispered. "Wh-where are we?"

"End of the line," he whispered back.

He crouched to set her down and she stiffened expecting to feel the hard impact of concrete, but was relieved when she felt the softness of a blanket against her body. She heard him reach for something in the darkness and sat in confused silence until a bright light flared up in front of her. She flinched and closed her eyes against the sudden glare and the stab of pain it created in her skull. She squinted and realized he was lighting candles. After a moment, as her eyes adjusted, she was able to open them and look around. She let out a moan of despair. They were in a room with no exit. He wasn't trying to escape the carnage happening in the mansion, he had just relocated them.

Then, as she continued to search the room, despair turned gradually to confused fright. Not only was she sitting on top of a blanket, but she was surrounded by rose petals. Hundreds of rose petals. She tried to force her throbbing, drugged brain to work through the problem at hand and what she was starting to suspect was a horrible truth. Finally, she turned pleading eyes up to the man that had been her body-guard for almost a decade.

"It was you?" she whispered.

He nodded, his dark eyes bleak in the flickering light of the candles. "That Bolivian guy sent you the roses. I took the opportunity to finally show you how I felt with the petals. It was as close as I could get to touching you."

"Why?" she whispered, the word torn from her as though it hurt to ask. They'd known each other for many years. Had spent nearly every day of every one of those years together, yet never once had he indicated that he thought of her as more than an annoying child-like mistress of the manor.

He laughed grimly. "Knew our time was coming to an end. That Ignacio was about to give the order. Wanted the chance to tell you how I felt, even if you didn't know it was me."

"Alonzo..." she breathed, her heart breaking a little. How long had he felt that way? Maybe he was as fucked up as she was. "What order, Alonzo?" she asked, trepidation speeding the blood in her veins, making her head pound even harder in both pain and fear.

His terrible gaze told her everything she needed to know, a mixture of resignation, pity and love. "You know what order, Casey. His orders must always be followed. We both know that."

She shook her head, a sob crawling up her throat and escaping her lips. "No, Alonzo, they don't need to be followed, not this one. We can leave here together, try to run away. What if Reyes takes him out? Then he'll never know that you didn't follow this order. We can slip away during the fight, he'll never, ever know."

Alonzo just stared at her until she knew she was begging in vain. He wasn't going to save her. He was as broken as she was. Maybe worse. He was a soldier incapable of ignoring the orders of his superior officer. Either that or he truly believed she was better off dead and he thought he was doing her a favour. Tears trailed down her pale cheeks and more sobs leapt up her throat. His gaze turned truly agonized as he watched her cry. This was the most emotion she'd ever seen from him.

"Please don't cry, Casey," he said, reaching out to brush the tears from her cheeks. "Trying to make this special for us. You won't be alone. I love you too much to let you go by yourself, baby. I'll be there the whole way and then I'll follow you into the other side so we can always be together."

She stared at him in horror as she realized what he was saying and then her stomach lurched. Murder-suicide. He was going to kill her and then kill himself. Her teeth chattered as she begged for mercy for both of them, "Alonzo, d-don't do this. Please just think about it! P-please, for the love of god!"

"Shh, baby, it'll be fine. Just lay back and rest," he told her huskily and pressed her shoulders until she was forced to lay back on the blanket.

Casey let out a small scream and tried to fight him, surging up against him, but he easily held her down. "No, no, Alonzo, just listen to me!" she cried out hysterically, almost blind from the pain rising up in her head.

"Don't do this to yourself, Casey, baby," he said soothingly crawling over top of her and pinning her down with his big body. He gripped her throat and squeezed until the breath left her lungs and she was forced to stop fighting him. She let her fingers rest on his arm, but she stopped thrashing. She just pleaded with her eyes, knowing it wouldn't make a difference.

"It's okay, love," he said gently, sitting over top of her, making sure he wasn't crushing her with his weight. She wanted to laugh at the ridiculous concession. He was practically strangling her and about to murder her, but he wanted to make sure she was comfortable while he *fucking killed* her! "It's time. You've been in pain for so long, drifting along like a petal in the breeze. Never knowing where to land. I'm going to carry you home in my arms. We'll go together."

She really wanted to tell him that he sounded like a psychopath, but thought it wasn't the best time to mouth off while his hands were wrapped around her fragile neck and he was talking poetically about murdering her. "Just close your eyes, baby, and let the sleeping pill take hold again. Just drift back to sleep and I'll take care of everything."

A bitter laugh escaped her throat and she rolled her eyes. Because she was definitely going back to sleep under these circumstances. Her skimpy clothes were soaked through and she was in some kind of underground hideout with a splitting headache while a gun battle raged above. Oh yeah, and the guy she was hiding out with planned on offing her as soon as she closed her eyes. Then he made things even *better* by pulling his gun from the holster at his side and pressing it against the side of her head. The laughter died on her lips and she knew that this was it, she was about to die. Would their bodies ever be found or would they just rot here in this dingy room somewhere underneath the garage or the pool house?

"I've always loved you, Casey. I'm sorry I couldn't be a better man for you," Alonzo said, his voice taking on a tortured edge. He leaned down and pressed his cool lips to hers.

CHAPTER FIFTEEN

"Well this is touching," a voice drawled out of the darkness.

Alonzo jerked back from Casey bringing his gun arm up, exactly as the voice had been hoping. The moment his head was clear of hers and his gun away from her head a shot rang out. Casey screamed as blood sprayed across her chest and face, soaking her in in its sticky wetness. The noise of the gun echoed through her head and she nearly passed out from the agony it caused. She flung an arm across her face and moaned. Dead weight fell across her legs and she couldn't restrain another hoarse cry from escaping her lips.

"Alonzo?" she whispered tentatively, moving her arm away from her face and searching for movement in the shadowy lump across her legs.

"He's dead," Diego's cold voice reached out of the darkness, and she flinched as he drew nearer to her. Terror welled up, as a boot came out of the shadows and shoved Alonzo off of her. "Or didn't you feel his brain splatter all over you?"

"Oh god, oh my god!" Casey muttered, panic swelling. She scrambled backwards, crawling rapidly away from Alonzo's dead body. Once she was a few feet away she started clawing at her own chest and face looking for bits of brain and skull.

She watched in horror as Diego crouched in front of her, his face visible now in the flickering candlelight. His lips stretched in a ghoulish grin as he watched in sadistic amusement while she frantically wiped at the blood on her face, whimpers erupting from her trembling lips. Finally, her head got the better of her and brains or not, blood or not, she turned on the spot and began heaving, her fingers digging into on the concrete. Her stomach was already empty so she could do nothing but vomit a little bit of saliva and stomach acid, burning her mouth and throat as it came up.

She scraped her knees on the ground, pulling them into her chest in an attempt to curl in on herself. After a moment, the godawful heaving stopped and she dropped her head onto her knees, the tangles of her hair falling around her. Then she felt Diego's hands slide up her back and curve over her shoulders. She curled harder into herself as shudders wracked her trembling body and stinging tears straggled down her cheeks. She pulled in choking gasps of breath, attempting to force her burning lungs to work.

She tried to shrug Diego's vile touch off, but he just leaned over her, his hot breath in her ear. "While I wish we had more time down here, the boss is waiting. Time to go, princess."

He stood up behind her, dragging her to her feet with a firm hand around her arm. Casey's legs refused to hold her weight and she immediately buckled, collapsing against Diego. He grunted in annoyance and looped an arm across her back, hauling her up against him. Though she hated the idea of needing his assistance she clutched his shirt with the last reserves of her meagre strength and leaned against him. She comforted herself with the thought that she had no other choice. He was taking her back to Ignacio and she'd much rather go to her husband alive than dead, which had clearly been Alonzo's crazy plan. And since it appeared Diego had no intention of killing her, she was happy to go with him for now.

"Okay, let's go," she whispered.

She shuffled alongside him as best she could, trying to match his longer strides as he strode down the chilly, damp corridor back toward the entrance to the pool house. Now that she felt safe the effects of the sleeping pill began to overwhelm her once more and waves of fatigue swept over her. She smothered a yawn with her other hand and then gagged when the taste of blood touched her lips. Alonzo's blood.

She fought back fresh tears and didn't see clearly when they reached the end of the tunnel and Diego stopped abruptly, she swayed against him and was forced to grab him with both hands to stop herself from falling. He looked at her sharply and snorted in disgust before reaching for her waist and shoving her unceremoniously through the trapdoor leading up into the pool house. She tried to help by gripping the floorboards and pulling herself through, but she was too weak from the pills and the trauma. Finally, he ended up gripping her by the legs and just shoving her the rest of the way through. She lay on the ground panting and waiting for him to pull himself up alongside her.

Casey groaned when he didn't even give her two seconds to gather herself, but just reached over and scooped her up like she was some kind of wet noodle. She tried to protest when he didn't bother to set her back on her feet, but strode through the open door of the pool house and into the pouring rain with her in his arms. Her words were stolen in the fury of the storm and she was forced to turn her face into the shelter of his chest.

They made it through the shattered back door of the house where Diego finally set her back on her feet. Before she knew what was happening he gripped her by the shoulders and pushed her into the wall, holding her upright. "You're gonna want to pull yourself together before you see him. Make a good impression, babe."

She frowned at Diego as he used the edge of his shirt to roughly scrub at her face and neck. She assumed he was trying to get some of the blood off of her skin. The rough fabric abraded her skin and she flinched back from his callous treatment. She could see streaks coming away on his striped shirt and knew his ministrations must be working.

"Good enough," he mumbled, shoving his shirt down and grabbing her roughly by the arm.

"Why do I need to make a good impression?" she asked, her voice hoarse.

He ignored her and tugged her down the hallway, yanking her hard when she would have stumbled and fallen. She started to go down, her fingertips touching the hard marble but he pulled her back up and swung her around the corner. Casey lurched and narrowly avoided stepping on the dead body of one of her husband's most trusted bodyguards.

"Oh!" she cried out shrinking back against Diego who didn't slow down to absorb her shock. That was the first inkling she had that her husband maybe hadn't won the takeover battle.

Diego banged his fist against the door, waiting a few heartbeats for the cold, sharp summons that was most definitely not the voice of her husband. Casey's body felt hot and numb all at once as Diego pushed the door open and shoved her through, forcing her to stand face to face with the man that had promised he would come for her.

Diego dropped his hand, removing the physical support she so desperately needed. She swayed on the spot, her eyes glued to the dark, foreboding figure standing next to Ignacio's desk, taller and more imposing in Ignacio's office than her husband had ever been. She took a few measured breaths, forcing her frozen lungs to work, sipping air properly so her head wouldn't explode in pain again and disgrace her during this vital moment.

"Come here, Casey," Reyes said coldly.

She approached him warily, her legs moving mechanically as she rounded the side of the desk before stopping a few feet from him. He didn't touch her, just watched her every stumbling move with the sharpness of a predator. Casey turned when she heard a rough choking sound. Reyes obliged by stepping out of the way. She cried out in dismay and slapped a hand over her mouth. Ignacio lay on the floor of his own office, bloody and beaten, one of his knees completely shattered from a bullet wound at close range. She tried to rush toward him, but Diego, who had come up behind her, caught her arm and held her back. She finally looked around the office and noticed that a few of Reyes men were present, including his second-in-command, Alejandro. All held the dead, stony looks on their faces that she knew so well. Ignacio was well and truly defeated.

Reyes watched her with icy indifference as she tried to control her emotions. To sort through the bewilderment of having her home overrun in such a violent and ruthless manner. He stood in front of her and looked her over as though she were a stranger, as though he were surveying a piece of furniture he'd won during the takeover. She wished desperately that she was wearing more than a pair of soaked, bedraggled and bloody, probably see-through cotton shorts and tank top. By now her hair was such a tangled mess she wasn't sure if it was even salvageable or if she should just shave it off and start over. She was pretty sure there was blood and possibly vomit in the tangled ends of her hair. She forced her shoulders back, tilted her chin and glared at him.

His dark gaze moved past her and he said coldly to Diego, "She's filthy. There's blood all over her."

"She was exactly where Ignacio said she would be. Underneath the pool house with her bodyguard," Diego informed Reyes. "Alonzo was about to kill her, just like Hernandez admitted. I took care of the bodyguard, but he was crouched over top of her when I did it."

Casey's eyes flew to Ignacio, but he refused to meet her eyes. So, he *had* given the order for Alonzo to kill her when the mansion was overrun. And judging from the state of him, Reyes had tortured the information out of him. Casey sagged back against Diego and lifted a hand against the side of her head, the never-ending headache from hell thumping away demanding her attention.

Reyes eyes followed the movement, but his face remained dispassionate. She guessed he was doing his job. Or he never really cared about her and she was about to die with her husband. Maybe he would make it quick. *At least my head will finally stop hurting*, she thought with grim resignation.

She gathered as much courage as she could manage and asked in a faltering voice, "Wh-what happens now? Are you going to kill us?"

Reyes expression grew sharp, his gaze taking in her skimpy, soaked outfit, the blood splattered across her chest and neck and the wild tangle of her long blond hair. She must look like some kind of insane asylum escapee that went on a murderous rampage. But the sudden hunger in his gaze told her otherwise. Told her he'd never found her more desirable... or closer within his grasp. She shuddered, her body heating under that look while her heart iced over at the terrible implications of how their union was coming about.

"I told you how this was going to go, *nena*," he told her slowly. "You even warned your stupid fuck of a husband. Not my fault that he chose not to listen. Chose not to run and hide like he should have. Though I would have found him anyway, crushed him like the bug he is and stole his beautiful queen. Now he dies." Reyes strode to her, picked up her hand and kissed the "H" on the back, flicking his tongue against the scar. Then he turned icy dark eyes on Ignacio. "And we go home."

Ignacio made a pathetic sound. She thought maybe it was supposed to emulate rage, but came out somewhere around pain and fear. A rush of unexpected pity rose up in Casey and, despite the years of loathing and hatred that stood between her and her husband, she reached out to grasp Reyes arm. She'd been with Ignacio for ten years. He'd rescued her from the hospital after her family was killed and given her a life filled with beautiful things. And yes, while he'd often been cruel, maybe he hadn't known any other way. He was still a human being, she still had to try to save his life.

"Please don't kill him!" she begged. "This isn't right, Reyes. Please don't kill my husband. If you care about me at all, let me take him away from here. You'll never hear from us again. We'll go far away and you can take Miami, I promise. We won't interfere."

Reyes stared down at her, his face devoid of any emotion. He dropped her hand and pushed her away. With that one look he made it clear, this was business and she wasn't wanted. She wasn't allowed an opinion and she most certainly would not be allowed to interfere. He nodded at Diego. "Take her. Let her pack whatever she wants to take with her." He moved his malevolent gaze to Ignacio who'd moved his bloody, broken body against the far wall. "We leave in three hours."

Diego wrapped his hand around her arm and pulled her, unnecessarily hard, toward the door. Casey fought him with the little strength she had left in her. "Please, Reyes, don't do this!" she cried out. "If you do this, I won't go with you. I'll fight you, you'll never truly have me!"

Reyes swung around to look at her just as Diego dragged her through the door, his dark brown eyes pinning her, marking her. "Wrong, *nena*. I take what I want and I just took you."

The door slammed shut between them.

CHAPTER SIXTEEN

"Fuck you, Diego," Casey hissed when Diego opened her bedroom door and threw her inside. She went flying through the door and luckily was able to catch herself against the bed post before she hit the floor.

She turned toward him in time to see him stalking toward her. She tried to cringe back against the bed, but he was on top of her before she could roll away from him. He gripped her arms and swung her further into the mattress.

"You're lucky we don't have much time and this place is crawling with the Bolivian's men or I would show you exactly how good I can fuck you, Casey," he snarled in her face. "Maybe when he gets sick of your scrawny ass I'll let you crawl back here to lick my boots and eat my table scraps like the bitch you are."

She wanted to scream and rage at him, but she knew she couldn't. Knew she was in a precarious position. Diego was a sadist who thrived on the pain of lesser creatures. He would love to take her and break her down to nothing. She stared up at him, knowing it was the only power she had. Diego was superstitious and as much as he'd always loved her body and enjoyed hurting her he despised her different coloured eyes. They creeped him out. Sure enough, he looked away from her in a matter of seconds.

"Stupid bitch," he mumbled, climbing off her. "Pack your fucking bags so I can get rid of you."

Diego rolled off the bed, strode away from her and slammed the door shut with a warning of "three hours" tossed over his shoulder. Casey ignored him, pulling her legs up to her chest with a moan. She dropped her head onto her knees and finally allowed the fatigue she'd been battling with all night to overtake her. Intense shakes swept over her tired, beaten body. She found enough energy to lift an arm and tug her thick quilt over herself, burrowing into some desperately needed warmth for the first time in what felt like days, even though barely an hour had passed.

She stared sightlessly, her mind blessedly blank. She simply couldn't process. Her brain never really functioned properly anyway. Since the car accident, the whirlwind marriage that followed, and the barrage of medications, she was able to drift in a world of her own, especially when she was experiencing a particularly vicious headache. And now that she was in shock she thought she had even more of an excuse to check out.

Casey wasn't sure how long she lay there but her shakes gradually subsided and she became aware of the uncomfortable sensation of laying in a giant wet spot on her bed. Finally, she pushed herself up on wobbly arms and sat up of the edge of her bed. She tried to force the gears in her numb brain to work, decide what to do first. It was easier to concentrate since she'd gradually stopped taking her some of her meds, the ones she knew weren't for pain, over the past few weeks. She was less fuzzy. Maybe forty-five minutes had passed since Diego had left the room, but she wasn't sure. The concept of time was eluding her right now.

For one wild moment, she thought seriously about fleeing. Attempting to get to get to one of the cars and driving as far and as fast as she could. She could start a new life. Become a whole new person, uncorrupted by this type of life. One that was untainted by bodies, blood and men that wanted to control her every move. She glanced down at her chest and the blood stains covering her top. Then she sighed heavily and rubbed her forehead. How far would she get? Two steps maybe, if she tried to go out her bedroom door, and probably as far as a broken neck if she tried the window. She already knew that path was useless. Ignacio had ensured that. So, what now?

What would Elvira Montana do? She was an honest to goodness mafia wife and probably the closest thing to a friend Casey had. What would she do if she'd just survived a takeover bid by hostile forces?

"She'd probably be nose deep in her own product," Casey said out loud and then laughed bitterly. "Aren't I the judgmental bitch." She looked down at her bloodied clothes. "Okay Elvira, I don't have any coke, but I do have the next best thing."

She stood on aching feet and winced, feeling the bruises and cuts from running barefoot through battle zones and underground tunnels. She lurched toward her makeup table and opened the drawer, pulling out a bottle of rum that had been a gift to her from one of Ignacio's Cuban business partners. She flinched at the thought of what was happening to him in his office and then quickly forced her brain away from the grisly thought. She unscrewed the cap, lifted the bottle and took a long drink allowing the liquid freedom to slide and burn down her throat until she was coughing and spitting it up.

"Fuck," she gasped. "Elvira would probably call this amateur hour."

She waited a beat and then tilted the bottle again, downing another shot. She didn't stop until she felt some heat in her belly and the paralyzing numbness that had dogged her since seeing Reyes standing in Ignacio's office begin to subside. She swiped at the tears that suddenly appeared on her cheeks, she wasn't sure where they'd come from. Either the sting from the alcohol had caused them... or maybe they'd never stopped.

"Now what, Mrs. Montana?" she asked her imaginary friend. She took a look at her haggard, bedraggled appearance in the vanity mirror and answered her own question. "A shower, Mrs. Hernandez. The etiquette guide says you must always look your best when you find yourself viciously widowed and about to be kidnapped all in the same evening."

She grabbed the rum bottle by the neck and made her way painfully to the washroom. She stripped off her damp, bloody clothes and crawled into the shower with the bottle clutched against her chest. She hissed in pain when the water spray hit the shallow cut on the back of her arm. She sat on the floor of the shower stall, drinking straight from the bottle and scrubbing blood and dirt from her skin while tears poured faster and faster down her face until finally she couldn't stand it anymore. She curled up on her side and sobbed for all she was worth. She cried because she'd lost her loyal bodyguard and it left a jagged hole in her heart. He'd been a constant in her life for so many years, taken care of her when her husband should have but didn't, and though he was messed up in the head, Alonzo had loved her in his own way.

And even though he didn't deserve her tears, she cried because her husband of ten years was being horrifically and painfully murdered under the roof that they had lived, but not loved, together and there wasn't anything she could do about it. He was being tortured by the man she thought she could have feelings for, but now she didn't think that was possible because Reyes was staining his hands with Ignacio's blood, ensuring she would forever hate the sight of him. How could she possibly love a man that showed no mercy when she'd begged him so pathetically to spare her husband in a room full of his own people? He said he wanted to make her queen, but threw her out like garbage.

Fuck him.

Finally, after her tears ran out and the water became cold she dragged herself out. She took another set of pills for her headache, which thank goodness had subsided to a dull throb. With a short laugh and another nod to Elvira, she washed the pills down with another shot of rum. Then she changed into a white silk robe and began packing a suitcase with the few things she wanted to take with her.

There weren't many things Casey loved enough to want to keep. She had a few keepsakes from her family. Some pictures and small items that held memories. She had her parents wedding bands and marriage certificate. It always seemed strange and inexplicable to her that there wasn't anything more left of her family, but Ignacio had insisted that the estate and everything in it had been sold after their deaths to pay off her parent's debts. He'd become angry when she'd pressed for more details and, at the time, she hadn't been in any condition to push the subject.

Casey added the few gifts Reyes had given her to the suitcase as well. She hastily tossed some clothes and shoes on top, not wanting to examine too closely why she wanted to keep his gifts. She knew she should get dressed and wait for someone to come fetch her but her eyelids were drooping, a combination of the residual sleeping pill and the near constant adrenalin rush of the evening. She settled on the bed with a yawn, away from the wet spot she'd created earlier, and was instantly sleep.

She wasn't sure how long she slept for, but she felt his

presence before his touch. It was like the heat of his regard woke her. Like the warm rush of a blanket being pulled over her body and tucked around her. She opened her eyes and rolled into her side to look at him. He was gazing down at her, the burning heat that was missing in his eyes before in Ignacio's office now present in full force. She couldn't help the slight smile that curved her lips before memory rushed in on her and happiness faded away.

Her eyes fell to his hand as he caressed her hip. His hand was covered in dried blood. Her husband's blood. Her heart beat faster and she froze. "Reyes..." she whispered.

He looked down at her, his dark eyes so filled with triumph and need that she knew there would be no pleading or begging him. Ignacio was dead. She belonged to Reyes now, he'd ensured it through death and destruction. By conquering her master and taking what had belonged to him. He slid his hand down her hip, across her waist and over her breast. His dark, bloodied hand looked so barbaric sliding against the silk of her robe. The fabric parted, revealing the edge of her breast. She held her breath, wondering if he intended to consummate their relationship right there in her bed, in her husband's home, moments after making her a widow.

Instead he picked up her scarred hand and drew her up until she was sitting. "Let's go home, *cariña*."

CHAPTER SEVENTEEN

He watched her every move with such sharp impatience, she was surprised he allowed her enough privacy that she was able to dress in the walk-in closet with door closed. Casey slipped on a pair of her favourite skinny jeans with rips in the thighs and topped it with a T-shirt that had a bloody rose and skull on it. She pulled on a short leather jacket with buckles on the side and tugged her hair free. She examined her shoes and briefly considered her flats as the more comfortable option for a kidnapping, but decided she preferred the height of four-inch black heeled boots that zipped up the back and fitted perfectly over her jeans. She glanced at her reflection in the standing mirror on the wall in the closet and decided she looked almost perfectly armoured.

She had a nice selection of makeup in her favourite purse, which was on a shelf with her other purses. She was relieved that she didn't have to use her vanity table. Casey swiped on a coating of dark smoky eye shadow, smudging it until it was perfect. Then she added a thick coat of black mascara to her blond lashes and thickened and darkened her eyebrows. A coat of lip gloss and she was ready to go.

Backing up, Casey surveyed her appearance. Excellent, she looked perfectly untouchable in expensive biker chic. Exactly what she was hoping for. Exactly opposite of her bloody Bolivian captor. She was dressing how she felt, he could deal with it.

"Casey," he called to her, banging impatiently on the door with a fist. "Open the door now or I'm coming in."

She pulled the door open and gave him the coldest look she was capable of, tossing her hair back over her shoulder and standing as tall as she could, which was a touch taller than him. The heated look he gave her told her he didn't give a fuck what she was trying to pull. He swept her from head to foot, his eyes turning darker by the second with a lust so intense that she stumbled back into the closet out of self-preservation. Stupid plan because there was no place for her to run.

He chuckled darkly, stalking her into the closet. "You dressed this way for a reason, Casey? Why? To put me off? To put me in my place? You seem to think the height and maybe the leather might put me off, *nena*."

She whimpered as she stumbled back into a shoe rack. He didn't stop until he was standing right in from of her. He slammed his fist down next to her head, crashing it through the shelf. Shoes and splinters of wood flew everywhere. She cried out and flung herself sideways, but his other arm stopped her. When she dared look back at him she thought she'd see anger, thought she'd face his wrath, but she saw only hunger and raging lust.

"I fucking love being able to look into your eyes, Casey," he growled at her, leaning in until his hips were pressed against hers and his lips were inches from hers. "You keep standing up, you keep going toe-to-toe and maybe you'll survive me."

Her mouth opened in surprise and he slanted his lips

over hers in a quick, hot kiss that stole the breath from her lungs. She was too shocked to even close her eyes. It didn't matter. The kiss was over before she had time to either protest or participate. Before she could form any kind of thought he reached for her hand and tugged her from the closet and out her bedroom door for the last time. She glanced over her shoulder, but the room that had been her sanctuary for such a long time was a blur as he pulled her down the hallway.

They walked swiftly to the mansion's foyer, which was still littered with debris and the body of one of Ignacio's guards. She forced herself not to cringe into Reyes' side. Instead she stood tall and cool next to him when he stopped to survey his men and Diego who were all standing around clearly awaiting some kind of instruction from Reyes.

He maintained his hold on her arm, though he manoeuvered her so she was standing next to him when he spoke to Diego. His voice was clipped and impatient, as though he were eager to be done with his business. "Alejandro and a few of my men will stay behind for the next few weeks to help you establish contacts and set things up here. I trust you will make sure they are comfortable?"

Diego nodded shortly, though Casey knew him well enough to know he was anything but pleased with the idea of Reyes leaving behind babysitters. So, it would seem Ignacio's second had betrayed him in order to secure himself a prime position. She wrinkled her nose in disgust. Diego's gaze flicked to her for a split second, just long enough for her to see the gleam of sadistic longing within. She shuddered and inched closer to Reyes. God help her if she ever found herself alone with that man again. She didn't think it would matter if they were in a mansion filled with Reyes' men, she didn't think Diego would be able to stop himself from playing out his worst fantasies.

"You have a problem, eh?" Reyes demanded, stepping in front of Casey and getting in Diego's face.

Just shoot him, she silently begged.

Damn, the years really had changed her if that was how she was solving problems now. Unfortunately, Reyes did not shoot Diego. The new Miami underboss assured his Bolivian contact that he was in perfect control and would be happy to host Alejandro and his men. Then he walked them out to the waiting vehicles, a jovial bounce in his step. He attempted to help Casey into the back of the black Escalade, but Reyes intervened.

"Never," he snarled, getting in Diego's face again, "touch my woman."

Diego held his hands up and backed away. "I get it, man. Different boss, same orders." Then he turned and strode rapidly away.

Casey breathed easier without his oppressive, sleazy presence near her. Reyes helped her into the back of the SUV, but as soon as she was clear of the doorframe she jerked her arm away. He climbed in behind her. Once they were settled into the back he studied her serious face. "What did he mean?"

She shrugged one shoulder and sighed. "Ignacio had standing orders that no one was allowed to touch me."

He frowned. "Ever?"

She shook her head. "Not ever. Not without his permission or his presence. Touching would result in either severe punishment or death. The last guy that touched me in front of Ignacio lost his hand and all he did was touch my arm to help me down some stairs. Ignacio is..." she stumbled over her words and closed her eyes for a second before continuing, "was a control freak."

He nodded, still frowning, absorbing her words thoughtfully. Then he said, "And this is the man you were loyal to right up to the moment of his death?" He shook his head at her, frowning fiercely in the darkness of the back seat, the occasional flash from passing streetlights, lighting up his rugged features. "I don't know whether to be disgusted by you or in utter awe of your stubborn tenacity."

She stared back at him mutinously and then hissed in a low voice, "Stop using past tense, Reyes, because I'm still loyal to my husband, dead or not. I told you if you murdered Ignacio I wouldn't touch you, and I won't! You destroyed anything we could've had with the blood on your hands." He reached for her, but she immediately recoiled back against the door. "Don't touch me, don't you ever touch me! You still have blood on your hands; *his* blood!"

He grabbed her, unbuckled her seatbelt and wrenched her across the back seat of the car, holding her struggling body firmly on his lap. He pinned her arms against her side using a brutal strength he hadn't used with her yet. She cried out in pain and gave up when the pressure on her arms became unbearable. After a moment, he eased his grip and pulled her chest to his.

"You listen good, *nena*, because I will only say this once. I will touch you whenever and however I want," he growled into her face, eyes flashing. "Not long now, Casey. The moment we arrive at my home, you will be mine. Get used to the idea."

As if her heart wasn't beating fast enough from being manhandled, his words added a few skipped beats until she thought she was going to have a heart attack at the tender age of twenty-eight. He held her that way, eyes locked with hers, hands hard on her arms until her breathing began to slow. He moved her into the seat directly next to his and buckled the seatbelt around her waist then placed an arm around her shoulders anchoring her against his side.

She desperately wished for the creeping numbness to help her cope, help her manage her emotions, but she seemed to be hyperaware of everything around her. She frowned. It was weird. She didn't usually feel things so keenly. Maybe it was surviving a gun battle and then nearly getting shot in the head by her own bodyguard. But... no, that wasn't right. If she were being totally honest with herself, she'd been waking up from her stupor for weeks now. Ever since Reyes had stepped into her life and forcibly started making her notice things.

Plus, the lack of prescription drugs in her system. She hadn't wanted to believe that Ignacio had been deliberately drugging her to keep her compliant for years, but the reality seemed more and more likely. Another thing she could contribute to Reyes; she'd hated the idea that he might think of her as a user. So she'd been flushing her pills, shame as her motivation.

She glanced out the window and a small laugh shook her, catching his attention. "What is it, *nena*?" he asked.

"It stopped raining," she pointed out. "I hadn't noticed." Apparently, she wasn't ready to start noticing everything yet.

"So it has," he agreed. "The weather is cooperating with my plans to fly out immediately."

The breath caught in her throat and she looked at him sharply. She knew he planned on taking her back to his home, but somehow, she hadn't though it would be this soon. If she were being honest a part of her believed she might somehow get out of being taken to Bolivia, either by talking Reyes out of it, or possibly by escaping. But now, glancing out the window, she saw that they were indeed on their way to the airport.

After 20 minutes, they arrived at the airport and parked the vehicles near a private hangar. Reyes escorted Casey from the vehicle and led her to the side of a building where she stood watching in shivering fascination while he and his men talked to a pilot that clearly worked for Reyes about take-off preparations. One of the men used a water bottle to soak a towel and handed it to Reyes. Reyes rolled up the sleeves of his shirt, took the towel and absently washed the blood from his skin without once breaking conversation with the pilot.

Casey shivered at his callousness, his ability to take a life one moment, steal the dead man's wife the next and then continue as if nothing had happened. And yet... there was something undeniably attractive about him. His scarred face and thick, black hair woke something within her. Called to her with a wildness that frightened her because she knew the things she felt for him were nothing like anything she'd ever felt for her husband. And that if she wasn't careful she could find herself in danger of becoming obsessed with her husband's killer.

As if sensing her stare, he turned his head to look at her, returning the intensity of her regard with interest. She knew she wasn't alone in her feelings. Not even close. He abruptly finished his conversation with the pilot and turned to her, taking her arm once more. "We're in luck, *nena*. Hatcher assures me that the weather has cleared enough that we can maintain my original schedule. We will be able to leave within minutes."

Her mouth felt suddenly dry and all she could do was nod. She was going to Bolivia.

Moments later she found herself bundled onto the plane and buckled in. She looked around in wide-eyed awe. She knew she'd flown before, when she was a child, or a teenager, but the memories were fuzzy and hard to grasp, not concrete. Somehow, she knew this was much different. The plane was some kind of smaller commercial carrier with passenger seats. It didn't look very comfortable for a trip that she knew was going to be as long as a flight to Bolivia would take. Then she frowned, a thought occurring to her as the men shuffled past her and began taking seats in the back.

"No one checked our passports," she mumbled.

Reyes crouched in front of her and checked her seat belt, tightening it across her lap. He chuckled at the annoyed look on her face. "You don't need to worry about that, *cariña*."

She gave him a scornful look as he took the seat across from hers. "You are such a criminal, Reyes."

He ignored her scathing condemnation.

She turned in her seat and clutched the window frame, watching the goings on of the crew as they prepared the plane for takeoff. Within minutes the plane was taxiing down a runway and she was bracing her back against the seat. She could feel Reyes' eyes on her face, taking in every minute expression, but she ignored him. With each mile that passed between her and her home, her anger climbed.

She watched as the plane banked and soared higher, taking her from the only home she'd ever known. As the airplane rose and the city gradually receded, giving way to ocean the reality of her situation hit her. Panic and rage flared up in her chest and she swung her head away from the window. She glared at the source of her angst, the man who had entered her life like a bulldozer, smashing everything within, figuratively and literally.

"How could you do this, Reyes?" she hissed, and then raised her voice to be heard over the airplane noise. "How the fuck could you do this to me?"

He watched her, his eyes roaming over her stiff body, branding ownership with every heated touch. She wanted to strike out at him, to say or do something to cause the type of turmoil she was now feeling. She hated that this was her life. That she was forever bound by the unspoken laws of the mafia women. Shut up and wait for your orders. He confirmed her thoughts with his next words.

"Don't worry your pretty head over it, Casey. Just relax and do your job," he said.

"And what is that?" she demanded.

"Stay gorgeous and fuck me when I tell you to."

"You know what, Reyes?" she snarled, gripping the edge of her seat to stop herself from launching at him. "You can go fuck yourself, I'm not touching you!"

His eyes glinted with humour and she heard several of his guys chuckle around her. She whipped her head sideways to glare at them. They looked away quickly, not wanting to get caught staring at the boss's new lady while she stepped dangerously close to the edge of mouthing off to the big guy. Everyone sat in breathless anticipation as Reyes leaned forward and took her chin gently in his hand, tilting her face so she was forced to look at him.

"There is the fire I want from you, *cariña*," he said softly, for her ears only. Then he pushed her back, double checked her seat belt and tucked a blanket around her legs so she wouldn't get cold. "Sleep if you can. It's a long flight to La Paz and you'll need the rest."

Casey subsided and watched warily as Reyes settled into the seat next to hers. But he did and said nothing more to her. She couldn't really believe he had allowed her to have her small temper tantrum in front of his men. Confusing fucking man. One minute he was acting like a caveman telling her he could touch her whenever he wanted and the next he was telling her to fight him. What the hell did he want from her?

CHAPTER EIGHTEEN

They stopped once to refuel the airplane in a mountainous region about four hours into the flight. Neither Reyes nor any of his men told her where they stopped, but they seemed relaxed enough as they disembarked the plane to stretch their legs at the private air field. Reyes helped her off the plane and walked with her toward a building where she was able to use the facilities and grab a sandwich.

When Casey emerged back into the morning sunlight she was keenly aware of the intense perusal of several armed men wearing military uniforms. Reyes joined her again, sliding his arm possessively around her back. The eyes that had been on her fell quickly away as though they knew exactly who he was. Apparently, his claim on her sealed her position. Not having any clue where she was, she wasn't going to fight him on it. He handed her a pair of large, aviator style sunglasses that covered half her face when she slid them on. She was grateful for the coverage. They boarded the plane as soon as it was ready to go.

In less than three hours they were landing in Bolivia at a

private airstrip just outside of La Paz. Reyes spent most of the flight either lightly napping or in low-voiced discussion with one of his men, who seemed to replace Alejandro when the second-in-command was left behind. But Reyes also talked to her about her new home just before they landed, perhaps sensing her rising trepidation as they flew over the sprawling city of La Paz, surrounded by the high mountains of the Altiplano. She already knew from the guidebook he'd given her that La Paz was the highest capital city in the world, located in a canyon Southeast of Lake Titicaca. She swallowed hard, allowing her ears to pop as the airplane banked through the thin clouds and went in for a landing while Reyes explained that the next part of their journey would be taken by helicopter as his home was accessible through no other method.

She stared at him with a mix of dismay and astonishment when he told her this, and caught the deliberate satisfaction he clearly wanted her to see on his face. He wanted her to know that she was trapped. That he was taking her to a new cage. He leaned against her, his arm across her back as he pointed out different aspects of the city they were flying over. She was excited despite herself. She'd lived in Miami her entire life and rarely travelled. Having been under Ignacio's roof and sole control for the past decade, she hadn't even considered a different type of life for herself. A gentle thrill started to ripple through her, starting in her belly and swelling up through her chest.

Reyes leaned in and spoke low in her ear, "I like that smile, *cariña*. You are uncommonly beautiful without it, but when your lips curve like that, fuck, it makes me want to conquer the world for you and hand it over on a silver platter."

Startled, Casey touched her lips, not even realizing she had been expressing joy. So much had happened in the past twelve hours it didn't even seem possible. But... a part of her *was* happy and excited. She was in a new place. And despite being caged once more in a new type of prison, it wasn't Ignacio's prison. She dared a glance at the man watching her so intently as she surveyed his city, the city that was rushing at them faster and faster. She was now the property of a man that she knew deep in her soul could be as much of a monster, if not more so, than her late husband. But Reyes was also capable of great passion. He said beautiful things to her and gave her meaningful gifts.

She turned away from him, unwilling to examine their connection further. She just wasn't in the right state of mind to deal with everything that had happened to her. Ignacio's body was barely cold and she was being escorted to a new home by his killer, a man who was going to claim her as soon as they arrived at their destination.

His arm tightened around her when the tires of the plane touched the ground.

Casey was allowed to once more freshen up in a hangar washroom at the airstrip before she was rushed to a helicopter. There were two helicopters waiting for them. Reyes and his men split into two groups, Reyes leading her toward one of the helicopters with a hand at her back. They seemed to have organized already as no words were spoken. Casey slid into the seat Reyes pointed at and lifted her arms while he buckled her in. He placed a headset over her ears and adjusted the pieces until they fit her. She clearly had a smaller head than the person who'd used the headset before her. She also had zero experience with such things and made no fuss about his taking over for her. Reyes placed one over his own head and tested it to make sure she could hear him. She nodded, staring at him seriously.

This was it. There was no going back home after this. No way she could get away from a mountain fortress high up in the Bolivian Andes. Not that she had much of a chance of escaping in La Paz, but she had a better chance of hiding out in a city of over two million people than she did in the wilds of the mountains. As the helicopter lifted off she watched her last hope of escape recede and wondered if she shouldn't have at least tried. Then she forced her body to relax into the cushioned seat.

Of course she shouldn't have tried. It was an absurd thought to begin with. Where exactly was she going to go at a private airstrip surrounding by a dozen of Reyes' armed men? And if she had managed to get away, she'd be the only pale, blond woman for miles attempting to catch a lift into a city filled with unknowns. A very unhappy Reyes would've been on top of her within minutes. Which would have made the intimacy of their first moments in his home that much more worse.

No, she was doing the best thing for herself in the long run. Measuring the situation and taking the best course of action open to her. One day, eventually, there would be an opening and then, on that day, she would seize it with both hands and start running. Until then, she would take in as much information as she could about her new home and her new jailor.

CHAPTER NINETEEN

The final flight to Reyes' home took about forty-five minutes by helicopter through treacherous mountain passes and valleys. Occasionally he pointed out volcanoes to her, glaciers and lakes. She shivered and craned her neck, staring in open-mouthed awe at rugged scenery she had never even thought to hope to see in her lifetime.

When they finally landed, Casey was surprised at how energized she was despite her lack of sleep. Her body felt as though it were on some kind of high. She managed to unbuckle her own belt while Reyes tugged the headset off her head, careful not to catch the long strands of her hair. She turned her head this way and that trying to catch a glimpse of his home, but she was frustrated in her efforts when she only saw more mountain peaks.

"Patience, *nena*," he chuckled, catching her chin and forcing her to look at him. "The house is lower into the valley. I keep what is mine well protected." She easily caught both the innuendo toward herself and the implied criticism of her late husband.

He took her hand and helped her step down off the helicopter. The other one was still landing, but he didn't bother waiting for it. He tugged her toward a rugged looking SUV, followed by two of his men. Another man stood next to the vehicle, opening the back door as they approached. He cast a curious glance toward Casey, but looked away immediately when Reyes gave him a hard look.

As soon as they were buckled into the back of the vehicle, Reyes snapped at the driver. "Take us home. Now."

She blushed at the impatience in his voice, hoping she was the only one that knew the reason for it. Then she forgot her embarrassment in her eagerness to catch sight of her new home as they crested over the top of the landing pad and took the winding road down into the valley. She had no idea what to expect and was completely shocked by the sprawling size of Reyes estate. It looked more like a town than a home with the amount of buildings nestled within the valley. She could easily see from the way they were structured that they'd been designed with fortification and security in mind. But the overall architecture was beautiful.

As the vehicle drew closer to the main gates she was able to discern which was the main house; it was a truly stunning structure. It was a classic two-story mansion with historic columns and arches. It could have been gaudy, but instead had a truly elegant feel to it. Somehow, she hadn't pictured a man like Reyes, such a tough, sinister man, in such a lovely home.

She wanted to say something, to tell Reyes how beautiful she found his house, but she couldn't find the words. It didn't matter. When she turned her eyes to his, she knew he saw everything he needed in her expressive face. His own transformed into easy lines of satisfaction, the scars easing as his face softened. The vehicle curved around the driveway and stopped in front of the house. Reyes got out first and reached in to help her slide out after him.

They walked through the front doors of his mansion

together, past the many watching eyes of his security and staff. For Casey, the entire scene felt both eerily familiar and entirely foreign. She was tempted to cling to Reyes as a source of comfort, but knew she needed to ignore that impulse. It would be like reaching for the tail of a lion, hoping the lion might lead her to safety rather than turn around and devour her whole. Reyes was not her savior; she must never forget that.

"Come, *nena*, it's time for us to get some rest," he said, his voice a deep rumble for her ears alone, though she knew he didn't care who overheard.

He turned and snapped several orders to a man standing beside him. He spoke in rapid Spanish, but Casey knew the language well enough to catch the general idea of what he was saying and became quickly aware that the man, named Nicolas, was Reyes' head of security for the compound. Reyes was arranging a time later in the evening when they would meet to discuss anything that had happened during his absence. They would also discuss a security detail for his new... wife? For a moment Casey went ice cold and then hot with fury when she thought he was married and bringing her into the mansion as a mistress. Then it hit her, he was referring to *her* as his wife. Casey's mouth fell open in shock.

Reyes finished his conversation with Nicolas and turned to his housekeeper, Serana, and ordered food and drink sent to the master suite. Then he took Casey's hand in a firm grip and strode impatiently through his home with her in tow. He walked so quickly, she barely had time to register any of the beautiful furnishings or the people who gaped after them and jumped quickly out of their master's path as he progressed toward his bedroom with her hand held firmly in his grasp.

"Reyes!" she gasped, digging her heels into the carpeted hallway as they approached a set of beautifully carved double doors on the second floor that could only lead to the master suite.

"What?" he snapped, shoving the doors open and flinging her inside by the wrist.

She stumbled into his bedroom and turned to look at him, eyes widening in dismay. She backed away from him as he advanced slowly toward her his eyes gleaming with dark, predatory lust. She licked her lips nervously. "I-I'd really like my own bedroom, Reyes. P-please get someone to show me where I can sleep. I'm very tired."

"I told you that you wouldn't be leaving my bed once I had you, Casey," he said, drawing the words out slowly as he stalked her around the bed. "You need to start believing the things that I tell you. It will be better for you in the long run. More... comfortable, perhaps."

She turned to look at him warily, tearing her eyes away from the bed that seemed nearly as barbaric as he, huge and piled high with dark coverings and pillows. "I didn't think you meant quite so literally, Reyes. People in our positions don't share bedrooms. Women like me... they get summoned when they're wanted."

He stalked a few steps closer, his eyes taking on that dark glow when he was pissed off. God, why did she always have to let her tongue have free reign?

"Women like you?" he asked, his voice menacingly quiet.

She nodded miserably. "Yes," she whispered. "The wives and the whores. The women, Reyes... we're nothing to men like you. Men with power."

He stared at her and she could see something moving behind his eyes, a creeping darkness. She desperately wished she knew what it was. He clearly didn't like her talking about herself this way, but if she had to guess... she'd just hit the nail on the head. She'd described a world that he was used to living in just as much as she; and he didn't like it. Not one fucking bit. And if she had to guess again, she'd guess that no woman had ever been summoned to share his room for longer than a few hours at a time, if even that. His room was probably his sanctuary. He likely fucked his women somewhere else.

"Come," he finally bit out. "We had a long flight and I want to wash your dead husband's blood off my body before I fuck you for the first time."

Casey's mouth fell open and she couldn't help the look of horror that passed over her face at his blunt words. She knew the harshness of that statement was meant to shock her back into her place. To tell them both exactly where she belonged. Maybe her little speech had reminded him that he shouldn't be elevating her beyond what she actually was. The pathetic widow of a dead, degenerate ex-business associate.

Reyes grabbed her hand and pulled her forcibly behind him toward a massive open doorway off the bedroom. It was a huge tiled washroom filled with gorgeous frosted glass and light furnishings. She was used to luxury but nothing like this. She would have taken more time to stare around her in awe and touch the things in the lovely room, but Reyes began undressing right there in front of her, capturing her entire attention.

Casey started to back away from him toward the bedroom, but he snatched her wrist and swung her around until she was trapped between him and the rest of the beautiful bathroom. "I don't think so, *nena*, we shower together so I know you won't run away on me."

She wanted to protest, to tell him she would do no such thing, but her ability to speak fled when his shirt dropped, revealing his upper body. She'd known his strength, he's used it on her before, but seeing him without his shirt, the hot, chiseled muscles that rippled down the front of his body in flat ridges and flexed over his stunning arms gave her a reality check she was not expecting. A deep gouge, long since healed, but badly, now left a puckered slash down his side. She thought it had probably been deep enough to reach his ribs. Her fingers twitched to touch and sooth, but she smothered the impulse.

Then his belt buckle and pants hit the floor. He was *not* wearing underwear. Sadly, her first thought was that he'd taken over an entire mafia operation and kidnapped her, all while commando, and that took some serious balls. Then her brain caught up to her eyes and she slowly started backing up again. The only man she'd ever been with was her husband and the last time had been well over a year ago. And sadly, Ignacio had not been built like this man. Not even close. Not in any way. She didn't even know men came this different. Well, she'd suspected, given some of her reading material. But she didn't *know*, know.

She nearly jumped out of her skin when he closed the space between them and without hesitation, reached for the hem of her shirt and pulled it right over her head. She was still gaping at him when he unsnapped her bra and made short work of that too.

"Stop it!" she gasped, pulling away from him and covering her breasts with her palms. "Leave me alone!"

He used her momentum to knock her off balance and force her into a sitting position on the edge of the tub where he bent in front of her and swiftly unzipped and removed her boots. She just gawked like an idiot at his easy handling of her. Without thinking she smacked him in shoulder, the heel of her hand thumping against the muscle.

He lifted his head to give her a warning look but he didn't make a move to stop her. He only said in a low voice while reaching for the fastening on her jeans. "Strike me in anger again, *nena*, and I will retaliate. I'm not a patient man or an easy man. You want a war, I can give you a war. But be careful what you ask for."

Her hands fell to the edge of the tub and gripped so she wouldn't be tempted to do anything stupid again. She didn't know what he considered retaliation and she wasn't sure she was ready to find out. He unzipped her jeans and maneuvered them easily down her hips while she sat in silence. Then it occurred to her how he was handling her with such ease. He was probably used to pushing people around physically as part of his every day existence. She guessed she was just lucky he was being so gentle with her. She shuddered.

Fear and embarrassment crashed through her once he'd pulled off her panties, the last item of clothing from her body. There wasn't even an ounce of the usual lust she felt when she was around him. She was too unsure of him and the situation to be responsive.

As if sensing her trepidation, he sighed, almost tiredly and held out his hand. "Come on, Casey," he said in a low voice. "You'll feel better after you shower."

She stared at his hand and then looked up at him and shook her head. "I would feel better if you took me back home and stopped pretending this is something that I want."

His eyes hardened and he let out a growl. He grabbed her arm and pulled her off the edge of the tub. She slammed into the heat of his rock-hard body. She brought her hands up to catch herself and then thought better of it when they slid along the warm steel of corded muscles. She tried to drop her hands but he jerked her closer and snarled in her face, "You don't get it. What you want doesn't matter anymore, if it ever did, Casey. You belong to me now, *nena*. 'Spoils of war' is how I believe you so inelegantly put it. It's up to you whether you come to me as my queen or my slave. Now we will get in that shower and rinse off and then I'm going to fuck you, willing or not."

He didn't give her a chance to respond, instead he dragged her toward the big beast of a shower stall and stood with her arm gripped tightly in his fist while he messed with the settings. Once he seemed satisfied, he hauled her in with him and shoved her under the spray facing away from him.

She gasped as he set about soaping her without any finesse or gentleness. She squirmed and cried out when his fingers violated every part of her body with quick firm strokes. She would have called the cleansing impersonal, but when she looked over her shoulder at his face she could see the lust blazing through his anger. His fury seemed to fuel his desire for her.

"Stop!" she begged when his soapy fingers slid between her legs, but he didn't. He turned her around to face him, pushed her against the shower wall and then shoved a finger inside her. Casey tried to stop the whimper that erupted from her throat but it was useless. She was past the point of being able to control herself. Either physically or emotionally. Then his fingers slid through her folds and without warning he pushed the tip of his soapy finger into her ass. She screamed in surprise and jumped up onto her toes, trying to squirm away from him.

"Fuck, Casey," he grunted. "So fucking tight."

She wanted to die of embarrassment but he removed his hands, turned away from her and began soaping himself in quick, efficient strokes. She crossed her arms over her wet breasts and just stared, caught somewhere between the pleasure of watching an extremely masculine, good-looking man wash himself and the terror of knowing what that man intended on doing to her when he was done.

He finished, turned the taps off, took hold of her arm once more without even looking at her and hauled her out of the shower. Casey followed him, the picture of docility, while attempting to cover herself with her remaining arm. Inside, she was beginning to both panic and seethe, the prospect of his bed looming closer and closer. When he picked up a towel off the vanity, shook it out and began drying her off, she got the sudden urge to bite him.

Instead she took hold of the edge of the towel, stepped quickly back and snapped, "I can dry myself."

His head came up along with one thick, black eyebrow. A clear warning was evident in his gaze and she thought he was about to back it up verbally or physically but some of her panic must have leaked through in her eyes, because he closed his mouth, gave her a quick nod and let her have the towel. She breathed easier and dried herself while simultaneously exposing as little of herself as possible, though he'd already seen everything. She wrapped the large towel around herself and allowed him to escort her back into the bedroom.

As they approached the bed, she shook her head and dug her feet into the thick carpet, pulling her arm away from him. She clutched the towel tightly over her breasts with her other hand. "Not happening, Reyes," she said with as much authority as she could manage given her lack of attire or position within his household. He turned to her with a complete lack of modesty over his own nudity and stared, his gaze both icy cold and intensely heated at the same time. She shivered, sparing a thought for the talent it took for these mafia bosses to perfect those kinds of intense stares.

"Explain yourself. And do so carefully, *nena*," he said with deadly calm. "This is your only chance."

She shivered, but lifted her chin and gave him her best mob wife stare. She knew how to give as good as she got. And so far, she'd negotiated herself out of sex with him twice. She could do it a third. She knew she wasn't going to escape him forever, but she just couldn't bring herself to hop into bed with the man who had killed her husband only a few hours earlier. No matter how much she'd despised Ignacio, his memory just didn't deserve that kind of cold disrespect.

"You may have made me a widow, Reyes," she said, ice dripping from each word, "but I'm still married to Ignacio Hernandez in my head. You haven't given me any time to process this brutal situation. I am still Casey Hernandez until the moment you take that away from me too. And you are the man that murdered my husband in the only home I've known for ten years. You are the man that tore me away from that home, abducted me and took me to a new fucking continent! Now you want me to just crawl into your bed and spread my legs. No thank you, Reyes." She thrust her chin out and glared at him for all she was worth. "No... you can go fuck yourself. I don't care how many showers you take, you still have Ignacio's blood all over you and I won't forget that."

He stood silent for a moment, just watching her. Absorbing her blatant disrespect and refusal to give him what he demanded. It took her several heartbeats to realize he was containing the rage that her words had provoked within him. She saw it in the clench of his fists and the ripple of his muscles. She saw in the impassive mask he struggled to maintain. She would stand her ground though. She reminded herself of who she was and why she was there.

"You want to see what I'm capable of?" he said, his voice grimly quiet, when he finally spoke. "Say his name again, Casey. Tell me you belong to a dead man one more time."

She glared at him and smacked her chest over her heart with her fist and snarled in his face, "I am the wife of Ignacio Hernandez!"

CHAPTER TWENTY

Without warning he grabbed her by the neck with one hand, his fingers wrapping around the delicate column. She stumbled back. He followed, pushing her until her legs hit the bed and she fell backwards. He tore the towel away from her body with his other hand, baring her pale body to his sweeping gaze and ruthless touch. He kneeled next to her, throwing his weight across her body. She brought her hands up, bracing them against his hard chest.

Her terrified eyes met the steely determination in his. "Say his fucking name again," he snarled, leaning down to speak in her face, his lips hovering above hers. His fingers tightened around her throat, cutting off her ability to speak and most of her ability to breath. "Speak that man's name again in my home, in my very bedroom, I dare you, *nena*. Push me further, find out what will happen."

The elemental threat of his hand on her throat, controlling her very life both terrified and exhilarated her. She lifted her chin in defiance, her tongue darting out to lick her lips. His eyes followed the movement, heat flaring before meeting her gaze. Her eyes dilated in response. He eased his grip and leaned down to taste her lips, to follow the path of her tongue. Her eyes flashed up at him, giving him only the briefest of warnings before she sank her teeth into his lip, biting down hard enough to drawn blood.

He jerked back in surprise and then immediately reached for her, but she was gone in a flash, rolling out from under him and across the bed. Casey lunged off the other side of the bed, fueled by adrenaline, much faster than she thought herself capable.

He growled in annoyance, touching a finger to his lip and giving the bloody evidence on his finger the barest of glances. "Stop playing games, *nena*. You know this is inevitable. Act like a real woman and get your ass over here."

"Act like a real man, Reyes," she taunted from across the bed, grabbing up the edge of a blanket and holding it against her naked body, "and go find a woman that wants you."

She saw pure, unadulterated rage flash through his eyes right before he struck, lunging for her. He was so fast she didn't stand a chance of getting away. She dropped the blanket and ran for all she was worth. He caught her by the ends of her hair as she tried to streak past him, yanking her back against his bare chest. She screamed in pain, but he eased his grip the moment her struggling body was in his arms. He picked her up and slammed her down hard on the bed, knocking the breath from her.

He fell on top of her, squeezing her until she was forced to give up the fight or lose what little air she had left in her lungs. He leaned over her and said in her ear, "You need proof that you want me, Casey? I will be happy to show you this, over and over again until you beg me to stop. There is more than one way to torture a person and I'm happy to introduce you to this method so you will be more careful with your words to me in future."

He rolled off the bed, dragging her with him. She cried

and begged him to let her go, but he completely ignored her pleas. She was terrified now that her defiance had brought out a monster in him. Years of punishments welled up in her, terrorizing her mind until she could think of nothing but getting away from Reyes. She fought with every ounce of strength she possessed, but it wasn't much. She was the pampered trophy wife of a dead man with more issues than she could throw a stick at.

Reyes had her subdued and helpless with her arms tied tightly over her head with a belt quickly and efficiently. He didn't bother tying her legs, growling down at her that he'd rather have free access to stretch them wide and pull them over his shoulders. She opened her mouth to shriek at him, but he slammed his lips over hers, swallowing her protests in a bloody kiss. He shoved his tongue deep into her mouth as if daring her to bite him again, but she didn't have it in her to taunt him further. His retaliations were proving painful and humiliating.

He kissed her over and over, stealing her breath, and drugging her with heat and need until she was meeting him kiss for kiss. Her baser instincts were taking over, giving way to the intense attraction that blazed within her whenever he touched her. The desperate desire to give this man exactly what he craved. Something inside her broke every time he touched her. Broke and woke up, clawed its way up her chest to meet him, reaching desperately for him, begging him for more. Clinging passionately to the man she recognized as her equal, even if her logical brain couldn't do it yet.

A sob tore from her throat and she arched toward him in abandon, her lips wet with his blood and saliva. He slashed a grin down at her. "There's my girl."

She pulled on her wrists, but the binding he'd tied her with held tight. She whimpered and twisted against it, tossing her head and looking at him imploringly, wanting to touch him back. He shook his back. "No," he growled. "You were bad, *nena*. Tried to fly on your own. And I will never allow that. Now you can suffer this lesson."

He moved down her body, worshipping her breasts, leaving a trail of blood in his wake. She couldn't see the colour, but she could see the difference in shades against her skin and it was beautiful to her eyes. He lavished her breasts and nipples with such tender attention that it made her wild in her need to be closer to him. She arched her spine upwards, pressing herself into his hot possessive mouth. She'd never felt anything like the lash of his tongue against her sensitive nipple as he sucked it into his mouth and played with the engorged bud until she was screaming with pleasure, spreading her legs against the plush bedding and begging him for more.

"*Más?*" he questioned her. "You want more, Casey?" he growled against her body, tearing his mouth away from her flesh and climbing lower while she cried and whimpered, thrashing against her bonds.

"No!" she screamed as he pressed one hand between her breasts and forced her heaving body back into the bedding, then with a heated look, pressed his thumb against the core of her, sliding it along her pussy until he was pressing fully against her clit. "Fuck, yeeeesss!" she screamed, her head arched back into the pillows, her throat straining with tension.

He used his shoulders to force her slim, shaking legs wide and flicked her clit with his thumb until she was crying and begging him to both stop and continue. Sweat beaded against the hollow of her throat and she pulled weakly on the belt he'd wrapped around her delicate wrists.

He leaned in and inhaled her scent growling, "Fucking

caliente," against her flesh before devouring her with his tongue, driving her to the edge over and over again without allowing her to fall over. True to his word, Reyes tortured her in the most delicious way until she was writhing and crying underneath him, begging for release.

"Anything... please just stop," she panted when he eased back again, stealing her release.

Tears leaked from her beautiful eyes where they were fixed on the ceiling. Despite the pain of an over sensitized body, she refused to look at him. She refused to give in entirely to the man who wanted to own her body and soul. He climbed up her body and took her jaw in his hand, forcing her to look at him, allowing her no escape from his world of deprivation. Her lips trembled as she met his eyes.

"Give me what I want," he rasped, lust, rage and admiration for her clashing and warring within, telling her he was as affected by her as she was by him.

"I-I will never speak his name under this roof again," she whispered weakly.

Triumph blazed bright and with her jaw still tight in his hand, he took her lips in a passionate kiss filled with the promise of what was soon to come. She moaned into his mouth as she tasted herself on his tongue. He reached between them and positioned himself between her thighs, shoving her legs back until he was poised to take her. He leaned down over top of her until his lips were inches from her own. "Who do you belong to, Casey?" he demanded.

She didn't say anything for a second and then she met his eyes, one amber and one green clashing with his dark eyes. "You, Reyes," she whispered. "I belong to you."

He dropped his head until his forehead touched hers and he thrust foreword, burying his full length within her. Casey cried out at the intrusion and bucked against the bed, arching her neck in protest. Tears of pain escaped her eyes and she squeezed them shut while she tried to adjust to the fullness of having a man in and on her body once again. Especially one as large as Reyes.

He framed her face with his hands and dropped a kiss on her trembling lips. "Shhh, *nena*, come on. Open your eyes," he urged her.

A sob escaped her lips, but after another moment of adjustment she did open her eyes for him. She was afraid she would see triumph, but she didn't. She saw concern. Just... raw worry as he searched her face for passion. She couldn't deal with that. She couldn't handle her own emotions let alone anything he might feel for her. Nothing about this situation was okay. She blinked again, closing her eyes and allowing herself to drift the way she used to when things got too overwhelming.

"No," he said sharply, shaking her. "No, Casey. You come back to me. Look at me, *cariña*."

She blinked again and then he was in focus once more. Then he moved within her, withdrawing before plunging back in. She was tight, but she was also so very wet ensuring that it no longer hurt. It felt... fucking incredible! She gasped and lifted her hips to meet his thrusts. His eyes blazed with pride when her primal nature took over, rising up and meeting him.

"Yes, Casey, fuck yes," he growled, swooping down to kiss her hard on the lips again. She licked her lips, tasting herself in his kiss, sinfully spicy and erotic. "Good fucking girl."

He set a hard, fast pace, fucking her with intense strokes that made her cry out and grip the leather belt above her head. He rode her hard, his cock bottoming out deep within her, slamming ruthlessly into her cervix. She tried to bring her knees up, to force him back, to slow him down, but he gripped her thighs and held her wide, stretching his body over hers.

Her face twisted and she begged him to slow down,

"Please, Reyes, the pressure... it's too much, it's been too long for me."

He gripped her jaw and forced her to look at him, his eyes blazing into hers. He adjusted his hips, fitting himself closer in the cradle of her hips and then slamming himself home. He shook his head, his dark eyes tender and brutal all at the same time, "No, *nena*, you can take me. Always." The moment was so private, so barbaric, she felt like something in her was clinging to a rope that he was gripping with his massive strength. Something he was refusing to let go of. She stared back at him and relaxed the muscles in her legs.

He reached between them and glided his thumb over her slick, over-sensitive clit. She screamed, flinging her head back into the pillows. The sensations were too much after he'd played with her body, bringing her to the edge over and over again. He hovered his broad shoulders over her and leaned in so he could see her face while he continued to strum her body like a master player.

"It's time to let go, *mi amor*, *mi cariña*," he growled softly, the tender words at odds with the brutal slam of his cock in her body. "Come for me, Casey." And she did, flying apart in a world of colour that only she could see in her broken head.

"Oh fuck, woman, the sounds you make," he snarled. He bent his head and bit her neck right where her throat met her shoulder. "Do it again," he groaned against her skin and slammed himself deep into her body while continuing to stroke her clit, circling the slippery nub with hard fast strokes of his thumb.

She jerked hard against her bindings, twisting her hips to escape the second, even more intense explosion building within. She yelled and cried for him to stop and then begged him to let her come again. He watched her face the whole time with an intensity that would have scared her if she were in the right mind to pay attention.

"Oh god, Reyes!" she screamed. "I'm coming!"

"Yes, *cariña*," he hissed in her ear, slamming himself deep inside her just as she clamped down hard on his cock, anchoring him in her tight, silken passage. "Come for me." He slammed his mouth over hers and bit her lip until his teeth cut into the tender tissues and she tasted her own blood.

Her hips jerked up into his, her orgasm driving higher with the slight pain he inflicted. Her eyes flew open to meet the blazing satisfaction in his as she felt the hot flood of semen deep within her. Slowly she opened her mouth to allow his tongue entry and they kissed leisurely while he stroked his cock slowly in and out of her, filling her with his seed. He refused to let her eyes go until he was done. And even then, when she tried to break their kiss and turn her head away, he reached for her jaw and held her still, forcing her to look at him still.

Reyes swiped his thumb across the tiny bite mark he'd given her, smearing her blood. He held it up for her to see and raised a dark eyebrow. "You see this, Casey?" she nodded slowly, her heart beating faster. She knew this moment was deeply significant and she felt both elation and terror well up. He pressed his thumb against the place on his lip where she had bitten him and drawn blood. "From now until death, we bleed together. Understand?"

She nodded.

"Say it, Casey," he demanded.

"I understand, Reyes," she whispered. "We bleed together."

He bent and kissed her, sealing his blood vow. She sighed and opened her mouth to him, wishing he would freaking unbelt her already so she could wrap her arms around him. In just one good fuck he'd managed to give her two earth-shattering orgasms, shake her loyalty to her former life to its very core and crack a fissure in her heart as wide as the Altiplano. God, these intense mafia guys.

Maybe this *was* the life for her.

CHAPTER TWENTY-ONE

"Where is she?" Reyes demanded, snapping at Alejandro as he strode down the stairs toward the front doors of the mansion. He knew she wasn't inside since he had his entire staff searching for her and no one had found her.

Fuck, he hadn't taken his eyes off her for two solid weeks and once, just once he'd allowed her a moment alone. She'd asked him if she could go take a nap by herself while he attended to business and she up and fucking disappeared. He knew his obsession with her was bordering on insanity, that she needed a little breathing room, but he couldn't seem to help it. It wasn't that he didn't trust her, though he was about to revise that opinion. No, he just couldn't seem to leave her alone. Didn't want to keep his hands or his eyes to himself. Now that she was in his keeping he wanted his queen in his bed, in his presence and by his side with a fervency that surprised even him. He'd always been extremely solitary, preferring his own company. But now he wanted Casey with him; always.

He didn't give her a chance to deny him. He touched her at every opportunity, rarely allowing her to leave their bed, unless meals or business forced his hand. And even then, he decided he wouldn't be separated from his woman. He was past the point of caring to examine why he needed her so badly, he just did. The first moment he set eyes on Casey, she sucked him in like a moth to flames, burning him in the best possible way. Now that he had her in his home, had tasted paradise in her pussy, he was beyond questioning this obsession. It just existed deep within his breast.

Something within him had shifted, the man that had violently risen up to create the most powerful cartel in Bolivia and beyond was now consumed by a woman. And he would gladly share his power with the woman that obsessed his mind, body and soul.

If he could fucking find her.

At first, she had been confused and even reluctant to accompany him everywhere. She'd hesitated when he'd insisted she attend business with him, but he hadn't given her a choice, seating her at his side within constant easy reach. Even his men hadn't wanted to speak in front of a woman, especially an outsider, but one steely look from the boss had loosened their tongues. His unwillingness to compromise, combined with Casey's lighthearted, bizarre chatter had eventually won a few of his men over. Her constant presence was beginning to ease the rest of his staff into the idea of having her around as a permanent fixture.

Now he just needed to find the woman and remind her, possibly using methods she wouldn't enjoy, that she must never leave his sight. He eyed his second-in-command with icy deliberation. "You know where she is," he grunted and considered shooting the man for not offering the information the instant he realized Reyes was searching for her.

"Calm down," Alejandro urged him, holding up a hand. He yawned widely and ran a hand over his unshaven face. He'd arrived back from Miami the evening before, reluctantly satisfied with Diego's progress on that front. Apparently, he cared little for the other man, but was convinced he could pick up where Ignacio had left off until the Bolivian's were ready to make a final decision.

"Speak now or die." They both knew he was leaving the word 'horribly' hanging in the air.

Alejandro grunted and turned on his heel, mumbling something like. "I tried." Then a little louder. "If you'll follow me, I can show you where she is."

"Tell me she's safe and I may spare your life," Reyes said with deadly calm, falling into step next to his *formerly* trusted second.

Alejandro shot him a look and gave Reyes a little more space as they curved around the side of the house, skirting the majestic white columns and following a meticulously cared for hedged path down to the training grounds behind the men's barracks. Reyes' frown grew progressively blacker as they approached the buildings where dozens of his single men slept, ate and played.

"I can assure you that she is perfectly safe and in hands of a man that would rather die than allow any harm to come to your woman, Reyes," Alejandro assured him.

Reyes grunted. "He may lose his hands for touching what is mine."

Alejandro remained wisely silent as they approached the outdoor gym and weight facilities. Reyes caught sight of her right away, her pale blond hair shining like a beacon in the weak sunlight filtering through the cloud cover. He growled savagely and strode faster when he observed her take a nasty spill, his head of security having just thrown her to the ground over his shoulder. Reyes had his gun un-holstered and pointed straight at Nicolas' face before anyone could blink.

Reyes had become so protective of his American lover over her few weeks at the compound that it was almost a certainty that he would have pulled the trigger if she hadn't reacted as fast as she did, scrambling off the ground and leaping in between the two men. Luckily for Nicolas, she chose to fling herself at Reyes instead of the head of security or his life would have been forfeit no matter what she would have said in his defense. Reyes could not have stood her touching another man in that moment.

"No!" she cried out, clinging to Reyes, her fearful eyes begging for mercy. *Mercy for another man*, he thought savagely. "Please, don't hurt him!"

"Explain," he snarled in a low voice.

"Okay, y-yes, I can explain," she breathed, trying unsuccessfully to tug his gun arm down. She gave up and just wrapped her own trembling arm around his instead and talked as fast as she could. "It's just that you've been keeping me with you every minute of every day and insisting I go with you to all these business meetings. And eventually you're going to have to go off property to meet with your other associates and I assume you'll have to take me with you... I mean you as much as admitted you won't be leaving me behind. Ever. So, self-defense is a must. And I know you've been trying to teach me some stuff, like how to punch and how to duck a hit. But, Reyes, you're a... well... you're a really bad teacher."

Reyes blinked, finally releasing his head of security from the death glare he'd been giving him and turned his head to look at the psychotic blond he'd pledged his life to. A bad teacher? She could not possibly have just said that. "What the fuck, Casey?" he growled.

Alejandro took a step back and swallowed what sounded

like a choking cough. If he wasn't careful he was going on Reyes' kill list too. Fuck, he was going to have to replace his entire, very talented team of men just for touching and looking at what belonged to him.

Casey ran her fingertips up and down the arm that was still tensed and extended in case he still needed to put a bullet in Nicolas. She licked her lips, ensuring his eyes continued to stay on her beautiful face. "It's just that you refuse to actually do anything that might scare me, Reyes, and we both know you pull your punches when you try to teach me. And," she glanced over her shoulder at the two men that were now pretending to do anything but listen to their deadly boss go soft over a woman, then she leaned in and whispered, "we both know every time you get your hands on me you forget about the self-defense part of the lesson. We usually end up in bed before I learn anything about taking care of myself properly. Whereas Nicolas is actually interested in teaching me how to survive if things go south."

Reyes groaned and dropped his arm around her waist, hauling her against his taut body. *Fuck*. She had a fucking point, and he hated it. He rubbed his face with his other hand, attempting to push away some of the aggravation. "Why couldn't you just explain that you were attempting to take combat lessons instead of sneaking off, *nena?*" he asked sternly.

"Would you have let me go?" she asked seriously.

He thought about it for a moment and then gave her an honest answer. "No."

Her face fell a little and then a look he'd not seen since he brought her to Bolivia swept over her face, paling her delicate features. Her fingers clenched against his stomach muscles where she was holding on to him. "What is it, Casey?" he asked.

"W-will you punish me?" she whispered. "I lied to you a-

and left the house without your permission. I let another man touch me." Her voice rose in alarm as she recited her infractions.

He frowned at her, disliking the stiffness of her body, the withdrawal he could feel in her. As though he could feel the flinching of her soul as she curled within herself and slowly begin to drift to a place that he couldn't reach. He shook her and then squeezed her waist until her beautiful eyes jumped to his. It bothered him that for just a moment, she was right, the dictator within him wanted to do exactly that. Murder his head of security and show his mistress her place. But the lover preferred that his queen be whole and undamaged.

"Tell me why you think I would punish you, Casey," he demanded.

Shakily she lifted her fist in between them and showed him the back of her hand with the shiny scarred "H". Ah, so the truth finally emerged. He'd been waiting for her to tell him the truth of this scar. He turned and nodded sharply to his men, "Dismissed."

He started pulling her toward the nearest building, the sauna, wanting to have their conversation in private. He knew whatever she was going to tell him wouldn't be pretty. That it would be some story of mob justice against a mob wife who strayed or broke the rules. He also knew he'd need to bury his cock in the woman he loved after she told him her story of pain because he'd need to affirm that this beautiful, broken woman was still here with him. Still alive. And still in his keeping. He couldn't seem to stop fucking her. It was like he needed affirmation that she wasn't a ghost or some kind of figment of his imagination.

He quickened his strides, his dick coming relentlessly to life as his brain thought only of branding himself all over Casey once more. And he couldn't do that in a training field where one of his guys could come along. It was a poor excuse to have to remove their eyes. He was having a difficult enough time just knowing other people got to bask in her beauty when she was fully clothed, no fucking way any other motherfucker was going to see his woman naked.

He wrenched the door open and placed a hand on her back, impatiently waiting for her eyes to adjust before she entered the building. He'd quickly noticed in his time with Casey, though she seemed to have perfect vision, except for colour-blindness, her night vision was terrible. She refused to enter a room before she could properly see inside. He'd made a note in his calendar to get her examined by an eye doctor, find out if her strange vision issues were from her head injuries or if they were just a part of her.

The sauna was warm at that time of day from being well insulated, though it hadn't been used yet. He waved his hand at a bench and she sat down glancing up at him warily. He nodded at her, "Tell me about the scar, Casey."

She licked her lips and gripped the edge of the bench, wiggling a little. Then she sighed and lifted her eyes, those beautiful multi-coloured eyes that had hooked him right from the start. He had to ruthlessly calm the blood that surged through his veins and remind himself to listen carefully.

"Did Ignacio tell you much about me?" she asked. "B-before he died?"

Reyes stiffened, his gaze turning to stone. "Watch your tongue, *nena*," he said with seething intensity. "Same rules apply. You are not to speak that man's name. In answer to your question, yes, I took the... opportunity to speak to him at length about you. Whether or not he spoke the truth in his final hours remains to be seen."

She glared up at him and he could see the internal struggle not to roll her eyes at him. She finally won the battle and dropped her gaze to the floor, choosing the self-preservation of her ass over sass. *Good girl*, he thought and bit back an approving grin. He knew he was often unreasonable where she was concerned. Acted more like an unpredictable caveman than a reasonable lover. He was struggling to find a balance with this equally unpredictable woman. And truth be told, he was loving every moment of their exhilarating journey together. If their present was any indication of their future, he couldn't wait to spend a lifetime with her.

Finally, she shook her hair back, tilted her chin and snapped, "We're not in the damn house, Reyes, the don't-say-your-dead-husband's-name rule doesn't apply out here." She just couldn't help herself.

He stared down at her for a moment then roared in laughter, startling her. She let out a small laugh, joining him for a moment until they both calmed. They stopped and looked at each other still smiling, eyes shining in amusement. She took a breath and said, in typical Casey fashion, "He burned my hand as punishment because I tried to escape him."

Reyes nodded gently. "I figured that much. How did you try to escape, Casey? How did he catch you?"

Her gorgeous eyes grew cloudy, but she bravely held his. "I tried to kill myself," she whispered.

Reyes felt as though he was being plunged into a pool of ice. His body froze. He felt as though his heart stopped in that moment and then her long-fingered hands with their prominent bones, too delicate, too pale, reached into his chest and tore out his heart while it was still stopped. He'd known she was damaged. Known she was too frail for his world. And if he'd been willing to listen to his own damn subconscious, had fucking known this was coming. Had fucking known the woman he'd fallen in love with was suicidal.

In a flash his brain rewound everything, back to the night he'd made his final decision. The decision to keep Casey. Deep in his gut he knew if he'd possessed this knowledge, if he'd known his queen was capable of ending her own life he would have gone the other way. He'd have taken her out with her husband.

Now it was too late, he was in too deep. He was stuck with a defective queen.

CHAPTER TWENTY-TWO

C asey watched in silence as Reyes raged in front of her like a lion in a cage. She felt every one of his thoughts as though he shouted them at her. She knew them because they were things she'd said to herself in moments of terrible self-pity. She couldn't blame him. He'd wanted more from her, but found out the worst. So, she waited patiently for him to sort through his feelings. If there was one thing she'd learned about her abductor over the past few weeks, it was that he wasn't used to the types of emotions she was engendering in him and he needed time to process.

Also, he preferred to have her close by while he dealt with those feelings.

"Fucking hell, Casey!" he snarled.

She flinched when he slammed his fist into the wall, making the entire wooden structure shudder under the impact. Okay, time to bring the beast back under control. That was another thing she'd learned about him. While she seemed to be the cause of a wide variety of emotions in him, she also had the ability to leash his rampaging temper.

"Please Reyes," she begged. "Will you let me explain?"

He turned back to her, his wide shoulders heaving and his eyes smoldering with helpless rage at a situation he saw as something he couldn't control; the spiraling darkness of his chosen queen. She wanted to go to him, but this wasn't the right moment. Not until she'd told him her story. He nodded sharply, crossing his arms and holding himself tight until his muscles bulged against the fabric of his rolled-up shirtsleeves.

She swallowed the nervousness that threatened to erupt in her throat and sorted through her foggy thoughts and memories. "Well..." she started. "It happened three years ago..."

"Don't make it sounds like something that happened to you, woman," he snapped, interrupting her. "You tried to kill yourself, at least own that much."

She flinched at the derision in his voice. She'd grown used to hearing him speak to her with nothing but respect. She lifted her chin and emptied the emotion from her eyes. "If you want to hear this story, then you *will* listen and not interrupt again, Reyes," she said with chilling imperiousness.

He stared back at her, his own eyes challenging and then nodded sharply for her to continue.

"You may have noticed in all the time that we were married, that Ignacio and I never had children." She ignored the tightening of his body when she spoke her late husband's name again. "As a cartel guy, I'm sure you can sympathize... these mafia men, they like to spread their seed, you know? Like to produce as many sons as they can as quick as they can so they can carry on the family business and keep it in the family."

He ignored her lip. Partly because he wanted her to keep speaking and part because she wasn't wrong. In the mob, family was everything. "No kids," he grunted in an even voice. "Keep talking."

"Well, it wasn't for lack of trying..." Then she giggled.

"Okay it was, he had some serious issues in that department, but let's not get into that now. Or ever... because yuck." When he growled she pressed her lips together and moved past her momentary amusement. "Anyway, despite Ignacio's growing impotency, I did manage to get pregnant about... ummm... three and a half years ago. With a baby boy."

"Fuck, *nena*," Reyes said, his eyes softening. Obviously, he could see where this was going since she had no children.

She nodded sadly.

"I went into labour a few weeks early, but nothing too far out of the ordinary. The pregnancy shouldn't have been at risk." Her eyes fogged over and she started to drift away from him, she could feel her skin growing colder despite the warmth of the room as memories washed over her. Her voice became distant as she spoke of one of the worst times in her life, when she'd thought that she might have a family once more only to have that tiny, selfish hope flicker out and die. "Ignacio wanted me to have a natural birth at home with only his personal doctor in attendance. I was nervous, but they assured me everything was on track and I would be fine. As soon as we realized there were complications it was too late... my son... he didn't make it. There was a lot of bleeding, I was... eventually taken to a hospital to stop the bleeding."

Reyes swore viciously, his fists tightening against his arms. She thought he might ask her any one of a hundred questions about the horrific situation, but instead he asked her the one thing that no one ever bothered to care about. The one thing that mattered most to her. "What was his name, Casey?"

Tears spilled over her lashes and trailed down her cheeks. And for the first time she was able to admit that she was no longer his captive. Even if he opened the bars to her cage, she wouldn't run. First of all, there was no way off this damn mountain without a helicopter license and second of all she was falling deeply in love with the only human being that seemed capable of understanding her cracked heart.

"I called him Jack," she whispered, then a slow, sad grin spread across her face. "After Jack Skellington from the Nightmare Before Christmas. My favourite movie of all time."

He looked lost for a moment and then he asked, more gentleness in his voice than there had been, "And the suicide attempt."

"Ignacio blamed me for the death of what he knew was likely to be his only chance at a son. He was angrier than I'd ever seen him and I was in delicate condition, both physically and emotionally. I was experiencing classic symptoms of post-partum depression, yet the moment I was released from the hospital, he locked me up in my room and refused to allow me any help, either in the form of doctors or anti-depressants." Casey paused for a moment, pain clouding her face once more as she remembered the loneliness and pain she'd had to endure. "Day after day I was forced to stare at my own walls, listening to his grief in the form of raging and ranting while attempting to bury my own grief. And you want to know the worst part?"

"What, *nena*?" he asked, though she could tell the words hurt him.

"He wouldn't allow me to have a funeral for our son. Said because Jack wasn't born alive, he wasn't even a real person," her voice broke on the last word. She lifted her hand to cover her mouth for a second before gaining the courage once more to continue. "Can you imagine? I missed the funeral for yet another of the most important people in my life."

"Ah fuck, *nena*," he whispered. "You're breaking my heart."

"Broke my heart too, Reyes. So I decided it was time to take my broken heart, my broken head and finish off my broken body," she whispered, her eyes shimmering with tears.

"I swallowed a package of sleeping pills with a bottle of rum... well a bottle of Malibu rum because I didn't have the real thing. I couldn't even manage to get suicide right," she said with a short, bitter laugh.

He stayed silent and she could feel the tension thrumming within him from the few feet that separated them. Knew he wanted to reach out and touch her. She also knew from the incredible, undeniable connection that had held them in thrall since the very beginning that if he touched her they would both break apart and he wouldn't hear the end of her story. So, he stood over her, watching her, protecting her as she spoke.

"Only I didn't wake up on the other side surrounded by my family, holding baby Jack in my arms," she said, a tiny sob escaping her lips. "I woke up in another hospital bed, this time strapped down and with a raw pain in my throat because they had to pump my stomach. I was surrounded by Ignacio, Alonzo and Diego. Two days later Ignacio was allowed to take me home. We barely walked into the mansion when he ordered the branding as punishment for daring to take the coward's way out of our marriage." Her eyes flared bright with remembered pain and rage. She squeezed her hand into a fist and finished. "He was pissed enough to enact this punishment himself, despite his weak stomach. He burned my flesh while Alonzo held me down and Diego watched."

Reyes nodded, a look of utter anguish sweeping over his dark, scarred features.

"I can fix it, *nena*," he said, his voice raw. He went to his knees in front of her and took her hand in his, pressing his lips against the back, touching the mark. "Fuck, Casey, for the first time in my life I feel shame. Shame because when I first saw this mark, all I could think was that I wanted to twist it, to take it for my own. To burn this beautiful flesh with my own mark." She saw that shame deep in his soul as fury burned in his dark eyes. He looked at her from the floor, a position of significance for a man like him to take in front of a woman. "That I could ever harm my woman so brutally, strike her low, the way your late husband did, makes me sick to my soul. I swear to you, *nena*, I will take the mark away. You will never have to see it again."

"Don't do that," she whispered, taking his hand in hers and squeezing. "I earned this mark, Reyes. It belongs to me through the pain of giving birth, of having a stillborn child, of a botched suicide attempt, of having a mean bastard for a husband. I should thank you for putting him in the ground for me. No, I think I'll keep my scar."

"But it will always remind you of that time in your life. What if you look at it one day and regret keeping it?" he asked, pressing the back of her hand against his cheek.

"It won't happen. I don't believe in regrets," she smiled.

"What do you mean, *nena*?" he asked, burying his face in her lap. "Everyone has regrets."

"Well... if you were going to do something you shouldn't or something you might regret, then just don't do it in the first place. Then you'll have nothing to regret." She shrugged. "Or if you have impulse control issues like me, then just learn from the stupid thing you did and don't do it again, rather than looking back and spending your life wishing there were a bunch of things you'd done better. I have no regrets, Reyes, not now or ever."

He looked back up at her, his dark eyes shining. "You are so damn beautiful, Casey. Fucking amazing." He tugged on her hands and pulled her up until she was standing with him. "Now I need you to promise me something."

She knew what was coming, what he would ask of her. What he was going to demand. She shook her head and tried to step away from him. She couldn't give it.

He took her jaw in his hand, his hold gentle and bent his

face to hers. She was wearing flats so he was a few inches taller than her. "No, *nena*, you need to listen and you need to make this promise. Because I know you and I know when you make a vow you don't fucking break it for anything. Just like you don't believe in regrets, you don't break your promises."

She pressed her lips together and squeezed her eyes shut to block him out, her only defense now that he refused to let her drift away from him.

"You promise me you'll never try to take your own life again. Not for any reason," he demanded his eyes glowing with a fervor that promised he would do anything to extract this vow from her and then spend a lifetime ensuring she never broke it.

"Reyes," she whispered brokenly, tears falling again. "I can't give you that vow."

CHAPTER TWENTY-THREE

"You will," he snarled in her face. He took her by the shoulders and gave her a quick shake until her eyes snapped open. "Tell me why the fuck not? You plan on taking your own life to escape me, is that it?" His voice escalated as this thought occurred to him. "Because that will never happen, Casey, *nunca*. I will make you my prisoner, wrap you in chains for the rest of your life if that's what it takes to keep you safe." His voice became a vicious snarl and his fingers bit into her shoulders by the time he finished.

Casey placed her hands on his chest, splaying her fingers and ran her hands up and down from his pectoral muscles to his stomach soothingly until she saw his eyes droop in response. "No, Reyes, no baby," she breathed, stepping in close to him. "It's not like that at all. I love it here and I love being with you. This is the best time I've ever had in my life. Please, you have to believe me."

"Then why?" he demanded from between gritted teeth, "won't you make this vow to me?"

"Because I don't know what life will bring for me, what kind of dark twists it might have in store," she whispered, pleading with her eyes, trying to make him understand. "And since I don't believe in regrets, I refuse to give a vow that I might have to break if my motivation becomes powerful enough."

He stared down at her, his expression one that she was becoming vastly familiar with; admiration mixed with fury. "Not good enough," he growled. "Give me your word anyway, Casey. Promise you will never consider taking your own life."

She lifted her chin defiantly. "No."

He took the messy ponytail at the back of her head in a fist, jerked her head back and slammed his mouth over hers, taking her lips in a brutal kiss meant to punish her for her defiance. Passion rose quickly up within Casey, she threw her arms around his neck and was soon meeting him kiss for kiss enthusiastically, despite the rage simmering just below the surface of each stormy, bruising sweep of his mouth over hers. She moaned against him and opened her lips to the demanding thrust of his tongue, allowing him entry when he ruthlessly insisted.

Her workout T-shirt tore as easily as tissue paper under the angry insistence of his fist. Her bra followed and then her yoga pants and panties until she was naked under the intense assault of his stormy emotions. She stood before him, her hair tumbled down to cover her shoulders and breasts.

"Reyes, wait!" she gasped, backing up. "Not so angry, please! I don't want it to hurt!"

He growled and made a grab for her wrist, jerking her hard against his body. She shivered when he drew her in for another fierce, punishing kiss. She moaned into his hot mouth, opening for him. She was soaking wet between her thighs, ready for whatever he threw at her. But she wasn't used to such rage. His love-making to this point had been a simmering controlled passion that took her to heights she'd never known before Reyes. This was new. Exciting, but also terrifying.

"Make. Your. Vow." he snarled.

"Please, Reyes..." she cried out, twisting in his arms.

He lifted her in his arms, his hands on her ass and strode backwards until he thrust her against a towel rack. She let out a small scream and gripped him hard. He stared at her, his eyes furious and filled with dark, heated lust as he sank his fingers into her body from underneath, the thick digits eased by her body's own natural lubrication. She moaned and clung to him as she sank down onto his fingers and then arched, riding him.

"Oh fuck!" she panted, her eyes rolling back.

He leaned in and licked between her breasts before biting a path to her small, taut nipple. She gripped his head in both hands and arched shamelessly into the amazing, incredible heat of his mouth. She felt his fingers moving in and out of her slick pussy, playing with her while holding her high up off the floor. She had no idea how he managed such a maneuver and, as she built toward an explosion of epic proportions, she didn't really care.

She closed her eyes tight, thrust her head back, slid her long, silky legs along his hips and rode his skilled fingers. Whimpers of ecstasy erupted from her throat as he slid his fingers first deep inside her, massaging her, then back out to slide and flick along her dripping slit until she went wild in his arms. He barely managed to hold her up against the wall with one straining, bulging arm considering how much she was writhing against him uncaring of the weight she was throwing at him. He slid his fingers back and forth until she thought she would burst into flames, until he was wet enough from her fluids to slide the tip of his finger into her tight ass.

"Oh god, Reyes," she moaned, digging her fingernails into the flesh of his arms over his shirt. "Oh, oh, my fucking god!"

"Yeah, *nena*," he growled. "Feels good, don't it? You want to come baby?"

She nodded frantically. "Yes, yes please... please let me come," she begged tossing her head back and forth against the towel rack. She reached over her head with one hand to grab it so she wouldn't slide down the wall.

Despite the constant misfiring going on in her brain from sensual overload, she had enough awareness to wonder if this was part of a cruel plan to withhold the explosive orgasm she so badly wanted. If that was his plan then he dearly underestimated her desperation. She would do just about anything to claw her way up to that blessed orgasmic peak. She would debase herself in any way he asked. She would enthusiastically go onto her knees before him, take his cock down her throat and happily choke on him if he would give her want she needed. She would crawl, she would fuck, she would suck, she would do just about anything in that moment.

He drew the torture out even more by releasing her body further from his grip and allowing her body weight to sink her even more onto the finger he'd lodged in her ass. She moaned at the dark, slightly painful pleasure as it bit into her. She widened her knees against his hips and surged against him, crying out. Sweat beaded against her throat and he leaned in to lick and suck the exposed skin, whispering dark, sexy words of praise that drove her closer and closer to the edge.

Finally, he gave her what she wanted, he growled against her throat, "Can't hold out against you, *cariña*. Too fucking gorgeous. Come for me, Casey."

He slid his finger back and forth over her painfully engorged clit until she was shamelessly thrusting her hips against him, sliding her pussy against the buckle of his belt for even more friction, heightening the orgasm that crashed over her a few seconds later. A keening cry erupted from her throat, where her head was thrown back. His own head was bent just below her jaw. His fingers gripped her hard, tightening against her flesh as he tried to draw out the tidal wave of her orgasm while his own painful erection begged him to fuck his woman as hard as he could up against the wall.

As she started to go limp in his arms he pulled his finger from her ass, reached between their bodies and unbuckled and unzipped himself. He shoved his trousers and underwear down just enough to free his erection. Then he lifted her once more and slammed her down, sliding her soaked pussy easily over his engorged cock. She let out a scream as she was filled up with hot, demanding flesh, stretching her completely. He didn't give her a chance to adjust or get used to the fullness of his entry. He wrapped his hands around her waist, lifted her up and began slamming her down with savage intent. He gritted his teeth and let his head drop back, planting his legs apart as the intense pleasure he could only find in the body, mind and soul of this woman wrapped itself around him and refused to let go.

"Casey," he breathed, then again, louder. "Casey."

She gripped his arms, hanging on as best she could while he pounded into her, allowing no release and giving no inch. She had no choice but to take what he gave as her body helplessly built back toward another, more powerful orgasm. As though he could feel the tightening within her pussy, he tipped her back against the wall, tilting his cock within her passage so he was hitting her silken walls at just the right angle to send her skyrocketing over the edge of her orgasm with a screaming bang. She reached back over her head and gripped the towel rack so hard she spared a brain cell to wonder how it didn't pull off the wall and send her tumbling to the floor.

Casey's legs shook as the orgasm crashed over her in waves and still Reyes was slamming himself into her. She opened her eyes to watch him, to see the beautiful strain on his face as he reached for his own release. She uncurled the fingers of one clenched hand from the wooden towel bar and reached desperately for the man that stole her heart a little more with each day, each fuck and each word he spoke.

He lifted his eyes and met hers, watched her as she watched him fuck her. He shifted his body, bringing himself in closer until he was hugging her against him. The look on his face was both tender and savage. It was so... him. Reyes wasn't much of a poet. He was a cartel boss, a dictator and brutal killer. But damned if he didn't hold the key to Casey.

And if he was going to give her the gift of understanding then she could give him a gift in return.

"I... will give you your vow," she panted. "On one condition."

"Name it."

"You release me from my vow in the event of your death," she whispered, eyes serious on his. "You bleed, I bleed. You die, I die. If you want a queen, Reyes, then you take me for all that I am."

"Done," he snarled thrusting into her one last time, spilling his seed. He gripped her so tight she thought she might break apart. But she trusted him not to reach that point with her; she knew he would protect her with his life and beyond. "When it's our time, we go together, *mi reina*."

PART TWO

Rise Up, Mi Reina

CHAPTER TWENTY-FOUR

"Fix her or die," Reyes shouted, pacing their bedroom liked a caged lion. Seeing Casey flinch made him immediately regret raising his voice, so he settled for glaring death at the doctor he'd flown in from Las Pas the moment she started showing symptoms of a migraine.

Casey lay curled on the bed like a broken doll where he had placed her after she'd finished her last bout of violent sickness. She'd tried to turn away from him, push his hands from her body and beg him to leave, but he refused. He would not allow her to sink into this darkness alone. How she'd survived so many years in the hell of her own head he could not possibly imagine. This was the most gut-wrenching pain he'd ever seen another human being go through, and he'd inflicted a lot of pain on others in his lifetime. Hell, if he could somehow bottle migraines and use them for torture he suspected they would be more effective than most methods.

The doctor, a thin man in his late thirties or early forties who specialized in neurological medicine eyed Reyes apprehensively while Casey moaned from between the fingers that were covering her face, "Leave the man alone. He can't treat me if you bully him, Reyes."

"He can," Reyes contradicted her, but he lowered his voice so his tone wouldn't cause more damage. He was terrified by the change in her pallor. Her already pale features had gone stark white and there was a blue tinge to her lips and fingernails indicating lack of blood flow. He turned to the doctor and said in a deadly quiet voice, "Fix her immediately."

The doctor sighed and moved toward the bed, his hands surprisingly steady considering he was decidedly nervous. He clearly knew exactly who he was dealing with, the Reyes cartel having built a ruthless but fair reputation among the locals. His voice was shaky as he spoke, betraying his nerves. "I can't 'fix' your girlfriend…"

"Wife," Reyes cut him off.

Casey whimpered and they both looked down at her, the doctor with pity and Reyes with feral desperation. He continued to pace, every muscle in his body taut as he was forced to watch helplessly while his woman suffered. He could do nothing, torture no one, burn no cities to the ground to make her better.

"Right," the doctor continued. "I can't make your wife better, just more comfortable. Hopefully take some of this pain away."

Reyes nearly reached for the man, but he restrained himself, knowing if he lost his temper he might end up murdering the man in their bedroom while Casey lay there suffering. She still needed a doctor and if he killed this one she would have to wait another forty-five minutes until Alejandro could fetch another one. Plus, word might get out that he was disposing of doctors and they could become reluctant to come to his compound. Not that he would allow their reluctance to stop him from collecting a physician, but he didn't enjoy complications when it came to Casey's health.

He took a deep, calming breath, gritted his teeth and said in a polite voice, "Knock her the fuck out so she can't feel anything."

The doctor shook his head and pulled items out of his bag including an intravenous setup and vials of medication. "Can't do it. She needs to remain conscious or in a natural sleep."

Reyes unholstered his gun and though he didn't point it directly at the other man, the doctor froze and lifted his hands from where he was gently maneuvering Casey's arm away from where she'd wrapped it tightly around her head. "Explain," Reyes growled, his eyes filled with death.

"I'm not your wife's regular doctor, I've never seen a case file and I'm not sure why she suffers from these debilitating migraines," the doctor spoke quickly, self-preservation uppermost in his smart little mind. "I can't administer anything that will render her unconscious. I need to make sure there won't be swelling in the brain that might cause bleeding, or worst-case scenario a stroke." He held up the IV and a vial of medication for Reyes to inspect. Reyes snatched the bottle from him and read the label. "I can make her far more comfortable, *Señor* Reyes, administer something that should take the pain away and reduce any swelling. She'll be able to rest comfortably."

Reyes reholstered his gun, pulled his phone out and began researching the medications the doctor was proposing to use on his beloved. He immediately found the one he was looking for and skidded to a halt on the side effects. A vein throbbed in his forehead and the scars on his face became rigid when he read the word 'death' and he gave the doctor a look that told the man exactly what he was reading. The man held his hands up again and backed into the side of the bed, likely correctly guessing his only ally was the woman curled on her side crying silent tears of agony.

"Worst case scenario," the doctor mumbled hastily, "never happens!"

"Must've happened some time, somewhere for them to list it as a potential side effect, doc," Reyes snarled, tossing the vial on the bed and pulling his gun again.

"For fucks sake, Reyes," Casey gasped from the bed, surging up on her arms, surprising both men with the sudden movement. "Let the man work before I die just to escape this goddamn conversation!"

She collapsed back onto the bed with a pitiful moan. Reyes dropped his gun onto the side table and crouched over her in an instant, both contrite to have caused her pain and delay in relief while simultaneously still glaring at the doctor over her bent body. The doctor did his best to ignore Reyes while he set up his equipment and went to work on Casey, reaching out to take her limp hand in his and press a needle into the back.

Reyes growled low in his throat as he watched the large steel tip enter the tender skin. She looked too small and delicate in that moment to handle this treatment, but he knew he needed to shut up and just let the doctor work. He tried not to jostle her as he watched over her like a wary lion watching his injured mate. It destroyed him to allow another touch her while she was weak. Everything within him wanted to tear the doctor apart limb from limb. He satisfied the dark urges within by telling himself that if this fire continued to rage in his veins once the doctor completed his treatment, depending on the outcome, Reyes may give in to his baser instincts.

He bent over Casey and brushed his lips against the edge of her ear as the doctor hooked up a saline bag and two medication vials. Reyes listened without interruption this time when the doctor explained that he was administering a pain medication as well as an anti-nauseate. When he finished hooking her up he explained that she would get another dose in an hour. Reyes nodded and dismissed the doctor, telling him to come back when he was needed.

The doctor didn't even look back, he turned around and left, relief clear in every step that took him closer to the door and away from the psychotic Bolivian cartel boss holding him hostage. Reyes held Casey, stroking her back and neck gently when she permitted his touch and backing off when she reached over to push his hand away as even those soft caresses were occasionally unbearable.

Gradually she began to relax as the saline bag emptied and the medications dripped into her system. He felt her muscles loosen and agony began to release its grip on her. She sighed and unfurled a little from her tight ball. He stroked a hand experimentally down her thigh and was pleased when she didn't flinch away from him.

"Better?" he murmured.

"Yeah…" she moaned, relief ringing clear in her voice. "Much."

The doctor stuck his head around the door and asked hesitantly if he could see the patient. Reyes waved the man in. "She seems to be doing better," he said quietly, unable to tear his eyes away from her face where colour was beginning to seep back into her cheeks, staining them with a healthier pink glow. "Check on her," he demanded. "Give her more medication."

The doctor nodded. "Of course. I think she can take another dose and then she should sleep. This was a stressful event and her body needs rest. Her blood pressure was extremely high when I checked it."

Reyes looked up sharply. "Check it again."

"Of course," the doctor agreed quickly and immediately complied. Casey made a murmur of protest when the doctor wrapped the cuff around her arm, but Reyes held her still. "A little high, but within the normal range," the doctor confirmed.

He switched out the saline bag and gave her another dose of each medication. Casey happily drifted off to sleep under their watchful supervision now that her head wasn't at risk of exploding. Reyes nodded his head sharply toward the door. "Walk with me."

The doctor glanced at Casey as though she might wake up and save him from whatever horrors Reyes was about to inflict on him. Reyes almost laughed out loud. He'd become so enamored of her that he probably would allow her to have the doctor for a pet if she asked. But she was asleep so the good doctor was on his own. As soon as the door was firmly closed behind them he began speaking.

"I'm in touch with one of the best neurologists in South America and he's going to make time to see Casey and myself in a few weeks," Reyes said. "I understand that you have no family in La Paz. So, between now and when we fly to her appointment you will remain here and become her personal physician. Make sure she has everything she needs and does not suffer if she has another episode. Understand?"

To his credit, the doctor only gaped for about three seconds before responding in the only way he could. "Of course, señor."

"Good man," Reyes said and reached for the door, not wanting to leave Casey alone any longer than he had to. "Go see Alejandro, he'll get you set up with a room. I want you nearby my wife in case of emergency."

CHAPTER TWENTY-FIVE

Despite the rocky start to their relationship, Casey grew progressively closer to her new doctor, Miguel Garrido over the following days. She learned far more about neurology and her condition in just a few conversations than she had in almost a decade of unbearable headaches. At first Reyes had hovered over their meetings, relentlessly watching over Casey, pacing and demanding more answers than Dr. Garrido could give.

Finally, Casey turned to her lover with irritation while they were eating breakfast and snapped, "You need to leave us alone, Reyes. He can't work when he's under constant threat of death and I'm sick of your never-ending mothering."

The look Reyes settled on her promised retribution for her emasculating comment, though his dark eyes caressed her features with amusement and he raised a thick eyebrow. He bent over her chair from behind as she chewed on a piece of melon and bit her ear. He held her still with a hand on her neck when she tried to flinch away from his teeth and whispered in her ear, "Can I trust you alone with this man, *cariña*?"

Shivers ran all down her spine at the way he licked the tiny bite mark he'd inflicted. She kept her eyes on her plate, her cheeks heating from the knowledge that they had an audience. She gave her head a tiny nod 'yes' and played with her fork wondering what he would do if she stabbed him with it; just a little. Well, she knew what he would do. Retribution as foreplay before fucking her as punishment. A better question was, how fast could she run?

Reyes lifted his eyes from Casey to the doctor, giving him one of those dead stares that made the recipients desperately wish they'd never heard his name or agreed to whatever ultimately landed them in his presence. No amount of money was worth earning that glare. "But can I trust him alone with you, *nena?*" he growled in her ear, his eyes unwavering from his prey.

"O-of course you can," Dr. Garrido hastily assured him, spilling a little of his coffee as he put his cup down hard on the table. "I have no designs on your wife!"

Reyes' nostrils flared and his body hardened against Casey's back. He removed his gun from the holster at his side and placed it on the table with his hand casually over the top. She rolled her eyes, careful to keep them averted from his sharp gaze and picked up her own cup of coffee to take a sip as Reyes snarled, "Didn't ask you the question, now did I?"

The doctor opened his mouth to respond, then closed it, his eyes glued to the gun. Then thought about it and opened his mouth again, clearly very unsure of what to do. Once again, as he frequently was in Reyes presence, Miguel was utterly terrified that he was about to be executed. Casey sighed and reached over her head to pet Reyes on the shoulder in an attempt to sooth her beast once more. She turned her face to his and gave him a sunny smile.

"We'll be fine, darling," she murmured, rubbing her lips whisper soft against his unshaven cheek.

She felt the instant easing in his muscles and marveled once more at how quickly this hard, intense man had fallen under her spell. God, he knew how to make a woman feel special, as though she were the only person that existed in his world. He absolutely adored it when she touched him, stroked him, smiled at him and called him endearments. At one time in her life she would have shrugged off such things as manipulations. But over her weeks spent with this man she was seeing these things as just... feeling good. Necessary to existing.

When Reyes didn't move to put his gun away she turned in her seat, took his jaw in both of her hands and turned his face to hers. He allowed her presumption. She leaned in and pressed her lips against his, darting her tongue against the seam until he allowed her entrance. She gave him a quick heated kiss, drawing his attention away from the doctor, allowing the other man a hasty escape from the room. Which, of course, a man with multiple medical degrees was smart enough to take advantage of.

By the time Reyes looked up, he realized he'd been duped by his sexy but conniving woman. He grunted, took her blond braid in his fist, jerked her head back, careful not to strain her neck, and gave her a long, stinging kiss as punishment until she was moaning and begging for release. She touched her swollen lips with trembling fingers, her breath coming out in short, panting bursts while he looked down at her with dark satisfaction. When he finally allowed her up, she clutched the edge of the table for support and glared at him, "You're such a barbarian!"

"Finish your breakfast," he told her as he picked up his gun and turned to leave. "You may have Dr. Garrido and you may have your privacy to speak with the man. Keep to the mansion and the immediate grounds around the house."

She nodded and smiled, her fingers still lingering on her

lips. Now that the pain was receding, pleasure was beginning to blossom. She licked the taste of him from her skin, enjoying the way his velvet eyes darkened as he followed the movement. "Thank you, Reyes," she purred huskily.

He froze in the process of moving away from her. Then he groaned and lunged for her, tearing her out of her chair by an arm and slamming her ass back against the table. "Then thank me," he growled, his lips hovering over hers.

Her eyes lit with excitement. The enduring embers that constantly simmered within her flamed instantly to life flooding her pussy with slick heat. She moaned against his mouth and bared her teeth at him, sucking his bottom lip into her mouth, calling to the savage, begging him to come out and play with her. She knew what she was doing, knew it wouldn't take long to snap his control. In fact, she'd spent the past weeks learning him. Learning exactly what it would take to force her dark, exquisite lover. Right. Over. The. Edge.

He tore his face to one side, away from her nipping teeth, gripped her by the throat and pushed her down on the table. "You want to play, nena?" he growled down at her, his eyes glowing molten fire at her.

She licked her lips and nodded, peeking up at him from beneath her lashes. Slowly she spread her legs against the edge of the table, wiggling them past his thighs until she could inch her knees up his hips and grip his waist. Her skirt fell back, revealing a tiny thong. She knew what he saw when his eyes moved from her face to her pussy. She was very wet for him and her panties would be soaked through. She moaned and reached a hand down her body, drifting first between her breasts, fuller now from his care and attention, over her belly and across her hip.

She touched the pads of her fingertips lightly against her panties. His own hand tightened on her throat, his fingers biting into her skin. She choked a little, though she doubted he even knew he was gripping her so tight, he was so focused on what she was doing to herself. She didn't care. She loved the things he did to her body; the way he ruthlessly brought her alive before sending her tumbling into the dark abyss of searing surrender. She slid her forefinger along the edge of her thong and then dipped it inside the sticky fabric. She smiled slightly when he frowned because the cotton crotch of her panties obscured his view.

Casey slid her finger further along the folds of her slit until she reached the entrance of her dripping vagina. Her eyes rolled back at the look of utter, ferocious worship on his face as he watched every, minute movement she made with barely leashed restraint. He was so beautiful, so perfect. His face, so savage, each scar taut as he strained with the effort it took to wait and see what she would do next.

She maneuvered another finger inside the thong, careful not to disturb the fabric, rather enjoying the control she had over him. She liked to tease her dark captor until he finally broke. She slid her fingers up and down her labia, rubbing the pads in circles along her clit whenever she reached the top, sparking waves of heat and pleasure through her quivering body. His burning eyes only made the sensation more intense as her orgasm built.

Just as Casey was about to tumble over the abyss and into the glorious arms of her orgasm, Reyes gripped her wrist and slammed her hand against the table. Her eyes flew open and she uttered a gasp of dismay. He stared down at her with a combination of fierce hunger and, now unrestrained, furious lust.

"You think to play games with me, *cariña?*" he growled. He pulled her fingers up to his lips and sucked them into his mouth, licking the juices from her before releasing her wrist. Then he reached between them and tore her underwear away. She cried out as stinging heat slashed across her thigh where the fabric futilely resisted his strength. "You will take your orgasms from me only if you want to play naughty games."

He unbuckled and unzipped his pants. She felt him shift and tried to see, but he still had her pinned to the table by her throat. He shoved his cock past the barrier of his underwear, yanked her closer to the edge of the table until her thighs were forced wide against his hips. She squirmed against him. She was dripping wet for him and they'd engaged in non-stop sex for almost four weeks, but when he was like this his entry was always rough. She knew she would be sore after.

Casey cried out as he slammed full length into her, arching her chest upward as much as she could while still being held down against the hard, unyielding table. Reyes grunted as pleasure coursed through him. He leaned over her, placing a hand next to her waist and began thrusting, using her aggressively while she writhed on the table, both seeking relief from the invasion and reaching for her own building orgasm.

Reyes never failed to fulfill Casey when they came together. She didn't know how he managed to make her come as often and as hard as he did, but she'd become greedy for everything he could provide. Soon she was begging for it, gripping the arm that still pinned her by the throat, using it for an anchor and lifting her hips to meet his thrusts as he slammed into her. She felt him approach orgasm, felt the tightening of his fingers around her throat as her pussy tightened around his body, gripping him hard. Streaks shot through her head and she chased after them, her hips lifting slightly, only to get slammed against the table with each snap of his own. She wondered if the sparks in her vision had colour or if it was her imagination.

"Ahhhh god, Reyes!" she whimpered as she exploded, digging her nails into his arm.

He grunted, his body stiffening over hers, his fingers flexing against her neck, but not tightening enough to actually cause damage, proving to her that he knew exactly what he was doing all along. He cared too much about his precious queen to ever cause harm. Tears flooded her eyes as that thought filtered through her head while she floated down and the hot gush of semen bathed her cervix. She blinked the tears back so he wouldn't see them and think he'd hurt her. He must never think that.

Reyes carefully released her throat, trailing his knuckles across the delicate skin and over her breasts through the fabric of her shirt as he moved away, pulling out of her. She felt a trail of cooling semen on her thigh and, glancing around at the scattered dishes, giggled at their desecration of the breakfast table. She decided it was probably for the best that Miguel had taken a walk. Casey wasn't entirely certain Reyes wouldn't fuck her in front of an audience. He was definitely enough of a caveman to stake his claim in front of other men and then murder any witnesses.

Reyes backed away, rebuckling his belt and admiring the sprawl of his woman over the breakfast table with warm smugness. As he turned to stride from the room he said over his shoulder, "If the doctor touches you, he dies. If he leaves you to suffer in any way without immediate relief, he will wish for death long before he dies."

"These death threats are getting old, Reyes!" she called after him, shoving herself up on an elbow and reaching for another piece of melon.

Once he left, she hastily scrambled off the table and rearranged her outfit before going to her bedroom for another pair of panties and then searching out the doctor. She was a bit worried he might be looking for an escape route off their extremely fortified mountain.

She found him a few minutes later, but felt it wiser to

keep Reyes' stipulations for their forthcoming private meetings to herself. She did, however, outline where they were to
walk and tentatively discuss which medications she should be
taking and how she should get hold of the doctor when they
weren't together and she needed him.

Miguel was surprisingly at ease in her presence and they
became fast friends over the following weeks. He even agreed
to accompany them to Casey's appointment in Brazil, at
Casey's begging and with multiple promises that Reyes would
be on his best behaviour.

"I'm just going to be so much more comfortable with you
there," Casey enthused, her arm looped through Miguel's as
they boarded Reyes private plane in La Paz. "I want you to be
able to give your professional opinion every step of the way. I
trust you completely."

Reyes snorted from behind them. Casey tossed him a
scathing look over her shoulder and lifted the frozen drink
he'd bought for her to her lips. She'd craved a Slurpee since
leaving America and bugged Reyes pretty constantly about it
every time he said something extra awful to her new best
friend as a form of revenge. He'd finally broken down and
found her one on the way to the airport. His eyes went
rapidly from annoyance over her grip on Miguel's arm to
blazing lust as her lips, now stained bright pink from the
cherry-flavoured Slurpee, wrapped around the straw and
sucked eagerly at the sweet treat.

"Fuck," he growled and reached for her other arm,
yanking her back against his chest and away from Miguel's
touch. "You like to tease me and play with another man's life,
nena?"

She giggled while the doctor pretended not to hear the
exchange. Once they boarded, Casey made a point of sitting
next to her doctor friend while Reyes sat with his men. The
space was small enough that his razor-sharp gaze could watch

his woman at all times. He was not remotely worried about her interactions with the relatively youthful neurologist, but he didn't particularly like anyone near her for any length of time.

As with their last flight, Casey watched everything about the takeoff with fascinated enthusiasm while Reyes watched his woman, his face impassive, his gaze hungry as always. After the plane lifted above the clouds and the beautiful mountain scenery no longer captured her attention, she turned to the doctor and asked the question that wouldn't stop gnawing at her. Her anxiety increasing the closer they got to Brazil.

"What if they find something in my head?" Casey whispered, her worried eyes on Miguel's face.

"You mean like a tumor?" he asked bluntly, addressing her worst fear. How could a person have such debilitating migraines and not have something seriously wrong with them? Yet he'd reassured her over and over that the likelihood of tumor was astronomically slim.

She nodded her head, but his words did assuage her fears; she knew it showed on her face so once more Miguel went over the facts with her.

"We've been over this many times, Casey. If you had a mass in your brain, there would be many more signs and your headaches would have gotten progressively worse over the years. But your coordination and motor skills are fine. Your vision is fine, except for the colour-blindness, which you've had since birth. You do admit to some memory loss, but this seems to be a by-product of your accident." He covered her hand in his and squeezed. "Be brave, Casey. This is one of the best neuro-clinics in the world. The scans and the x-rays will only help to reassure you. Don't fear what they'll tell you. They'll give us better ways to cope with the headaches."

Casey liked the way he said 'us'. Ignoring Reyes' typical

murderous glare, she looped her arm through Miguel's and held on to him for a while, needing his steady, calming reassurance. She'd gone from a complete lack of touch in her life to now basking in the glorious caresses of her lover and the completely plutonic, but nonetheless reassuring presence of her doctor. If Reyes didn't like that she was giving her attention to both men, he could jump off an airplane. He'd gotten her a doctor for her safety and sanity and she was finding comfort in his gift.

She snuggled back in her seat with a sigh and closed her eyes. She tilted her head slightly toward Miguel, though not completely leaning on his shoulder. After all, she wasn't totally trying to get the man killed. She would accept his reassurances along with the solid, protective strength that Reyes surrounded her with and be brave for her upcoming ordeal.

CHAPTER TWENTY-SIX

Casey wasn't happy. And when Casey wasn't happy, Reyes wasn't happy. She was sitting in a private room at the Brazilian clinic with her lover pacing close by and his men standing off to the side, watching over their charges. All these big men in the small room absolutely dwarfed the space, until Reyes finally growled at two of them to take a walk, leaving only Reyes, Alejandro and Casey behind.

Casey gripped the edge of the uncomfortable plastic chair until her knuckles were white. She rocked back and forth, back and forth. Her ankles were crossed and tucked under the chair. She wondered why a clinic as expensive as this place didn't invest in better chairs. Maybe they didn't know. Maybe someone should tell them. Maybe they had a comment box. Maybe they spent too much money on their high-end lab equipment and couldn't afford decent chairs. Perhaps she would get Reyes to donate better chairs once they flew back to La Paz and she was safely away from this place. Unless she actually did have a tumor. Then she was going to sue them; because she was vindictive that way, not because it was actually their fault she had a tumor.

Casey sighed and reached for the end of the string on the neck of her hoodie and put it in her mouth to chew on nervously. She wasn't actually going to sue the clinic or let Reyes do anything evil to the doctors. She wasn't truly vindictive. She was just scared. She shifted in her seat again and pulled her long legs up to sit cross-legged, glad she'd chosen comfort over sophistication when she dressed this morning.

They'd arrived last night in Rio de Janeiro and stayed in a luxury hotel. This morning she'd chosen a pair of leggings, a black hoodie with a rose dipped in blood on the front and a pair of Sketchers. She'd piled her hair on top of her head in a knot, which had long since come loose to tumble in waves down her back. She wasn't sure where the elastic had gone and the loss was really bothering her. Was the hair elastic still in the break room? Or maybe it had fallen in the MRI machine?

Most of her time at the clinic had been spent waiting to be called in between tests. Casey personally thought Reyes did a remarkable job of not freaking out with how long everything was taking and how many people touched her, though Casey was certain the doctors thought otherwise. His vicious caveman was firmly in place the entire time. He particularly hadn't liked the MRI machine, nor anything that required her having to get undressed. He'd stood beside her for each procedure, his bulging arms crossed, his death glare firmly in place. When he was forced to leave her side, the poor doctor asked Alejandro to explain the procedure and then took off in case Reyes objected. Each needle, each test had to be fully and completely explained before anything was allowed to touch her and even then, it usually took Casey herself arguing him into compliance. She began to wonder how they weren't kicked out of the clinic and asked never to return.

Money and power.

Casey lifted her eyes and watched the men in the room. A

soft bubble of laugher erupted from her. Alejandro and Reyes looked as nervous as she felt, which, oddly, settled the butterflies in her stomach. Reyes, of course, looked fiercely protective as he paced from the window back to the chair where she sat, absently brushing his large, rough fingers across the fine strands of her hair as he passed.

Alejandro had taken up a post by the window where he squinted with deadly concentration out into the parking lot two stories down, the set of his shoulders filled with tension. Casey could only surmise that her current situation was causing him worry since she didn't think there was any worry of an imminent attack. She watched him with affection. The off-putting Bolivian seemed to soften towards her over the past several weeks. It was clear that he found her absurd statements hilarious and would erupt in a full-bodied laugh whenever she said or did anything that set the boss off. He'd even taken it upon himself a few times to poke the beast just to get Casey going. She'd known what he was up to and thought it was pretty funny.

Miguel was with the other neurologists reviewing the test results. The clinic doctors had been kind enough to invite him as a professional courtesy to consult with them knowing that he would be treating Casey in the foreseeable future. Casey was extremely grateful. She's grown to trust Miguel implicitly.

Finally, after what felt like a decade had passed in that small, airless room, the door opened and Miguel entered with two of the clinic doctors. *Just in time,* she thought. She was positive that Reyes was about to start tearing heads off and demanding answers.

The breath rushed from her lungs and Casey felt faint. She could tell immediately from the look on Miguel's face that something was gravely wrong. His olive skin had an ashen tone and he refused to meet her eyes. Tears filled her eyes and she dug her fingers into her knees, attempting to pinch her skin hard enough to infuse some courage into her body. She wanted to open her mouth, to say the words and confront the truth. To be the first one to fill the silence. But the truth was, Casey was a coward. Her time with Reyes helped her to realize that she'd never been able to face the truth of a situation. She had avoided reality because it was too scary for her.

Finally, she managed to square her shoulders and look up, her face hard. Reyes and Alejandro came to stand on either side of her, like sentinels. It was almost laughable how much support she had in these big, strong immovable men with a wealth of power behind them compared to before with Ignacio. Reyes would move mountains, burn cities and search relentlessly for answers if it meant helping her.

Reyes placed his hand on her shoulder and without looking at her, demanded, "Tell us what you found."

"Señor..." the head neurologist spoke hesitantly. Casey began to feel faint. Did she actually have a tumor? Had the impossible really become possible after all? "Perhaps you would like to speak with us in the hallway first."

The panic rose up through her and waves of dizziness washed over her. But she desperately fought against fainting, she needed to know her fate. She carefully inched her hand up toward Reyes until she was clasping his hand where it rested on her shoulder. He still refused to look at her, but she could tell from the tension in his body that he was desperately worried. His body vibrated with the telltale signs of growing rage that threatened to erupt in violence.

His voice betrayed none of this when he spoke with chilly precision, "Speak. My wife is a strong woman. She can handle whatever you have to say."

Casey closed her eyes, took a deep breath and slowly stiffened her spine, stacking it until she was sitting as straight as she possibly could. When she opened her eyes, she fixed them on the wall between Miguel, who stared at the floor between his feet in utter dejection, and the other doctor. She wondered if Miguel was regretting his decision to hang with the other doctors. His intentions had been good. He'd get to learn some new techniques, share some professional expertise and help in the decision-making process when it ultimately came to the best interests of his patient. Now he didn't seem so keen on the idea. He looked ready to bolt.

They all looked ready to bolt.

"Please," Casey said in the same tone of voice Reyes had used. Chilly and commanding. "Tell us what you found."

The doctor gave her a clipped nod and pulled up one the plastic chairs so he was sitting opposite of her when he spoke. Casey respected him a little more when he pulled that move, considering her sentinels both stiffened and looked utterly unimpressed with the man's proximity to his patient. Apparently, Reyes was finished with having these people anywhere near his woman. She squeezed his hand so he wouldn't attack the man before she got her much needed information.

The doctor addressed only her, plunging directly into his findings with no preliminaries. "Your initial bloodwork findings have come back normal, there doesn't seem to be any hormonal issues that are causing your migraines, though we'll send it away for further checks. And of course, as we explained earlier, research in this field is always developing."

Casey tried hard not to roll her eyes and waved her hand impatiently at him. He'd gone over most of this already. She'd been pretty positive her migraines weren't hormone related. Obviously, he was stalling as he built toward what was actually wrong with her.

He leaned forward, shifting in the chair. She thought she detected a slight wince. *See, the chairs are horrible! You monsters torture us with the chairs and the MRI machines!* she wanted to shout at him, but dug her fingers into the back of Reyes' hand instead. He didn't even twitch as she sank her nails into his flesh, knowing the pasty doctor was working his way toward a truth that would shatter her. She wondered where he was from. He really was quite pale, and to a woman with colour-blindness a person almost had to glow for that to become apparent. His accent seemed European or something. And his name... what was his name again? She frowned. Oh, his lips were moving again. Time to tune back in.

"... Your MRI came back completely normal."

Casey frowned when he stopped talking and simply looked at her. She waited for him to go on with more of an explanation. There had to be something. Something to explain the migraines, the memory loss, the weird personality ticks, the drifts she took. It couldn't all be the trauma of a failed marriage. It had to be physical. Or... or she was weak; too weak to run an empire with Reyes.

When the doctor didn't give her any further explanation, she said in a voice dripping with ice, "Then explain the memory loss."

The doctor's face softened with sympathy and he reached out to take the hand that had clenched tightly in her lap. Reyes reacted immediately, snarling in response, "You've touched her enough for one day. Touch again without permission and lose a hand. Get on with your findings and move on to the next patient."

The doctor's face blanched and his head snapped up. He gaped at Reyes for a solid ten seconds before he remembered what he was supposed to be doing. Casey would have felt bad for him if her butt wasn't so numb. A private clinic really ought to afford better furniture!

"Right!" The doctor hurried to open the file he'd been clutching between his legs. Casey glanced back sharply at Miguel who'd shifted uncomfortably and looked even more upset than before. Really, the man looked as though he was going to cry! They must now be approaching the upsetting news.

"It's a tumor, isn't it?" Casey blurted out tearfully.

"Of course not, Mrs. Reyes," the other doctor that had remained silent throughout the entire procedure, and, in fact, most of the day, murmured soothingly. "You're clear on any form of mass. Benign or otherwise." She smiled kindly.

Casey smiled back tremulously, grateful for the straight answer. Jesus, she'd wished that particular doctor had been the one giving her the news. She seemed to have a better bedside manner than all the men put together. And Casey would bet money that she'd pick better chairs too.

"Then what the fuck is wrong with my wife?" Reyes snapped, finally losing patience and giving the room his favourite 'I'm about to fuck shit up until I get all the answers' glare. Casey giggled, despite her tension. She loved when he got all protective and angry. It made her feel warm and fuzzy.

The doctor cleared his throat and leaned back in his chair, putting some distance between himself, the mafioso couple and their equally terrifying second-in-command. He spoke quickly and directly, "While Casey's bloodwork and MRI are normal, her x-ray has shown anomalies. The fracture lines in her skull are not consistent with an impact from a car crash."

Reyes' fingers bit deep into Casey's shoulder causing her to squirm. She expected him to say something, to rage and demand answers. In fact, she waited breathlessly for him to do just that. When he remained silent at her side, continuing to bruise the tender flesh of her shoulder, she tilted her head back, her hair shifting against the hood of her sweater and gave him a questioning look. He looked back down at her, his own expression completely blank.

Her lips parted and her eyes widened in accusation. "Y-you knew?" she whispered.

She didn't need an answer. His lack of reaction told her everything. She tried to force her frozen brain to work, tried to understand what was happening in the room around her. The subtle shifting of the bodies. The painful bite of Reyes fingers. She reached up and pried his fingers away. He allowed it. She was under no illusion that she could have removed his hand if he wanted to keep it there. No, he was giving her the distance she craved in that moment.

He knew. *He fucking knew*. Which meant they'd come to Brazil not to find answers, but to find confirmation of some kind.

She lifted accusatory eyes to his and said coldly, "Ignacio told you something, didn't he? Before he died."

Still his face remained flat. She uncurled her fingers and tensed, preparing to fly at him, rake her fingers down his impassive, scarred face until he told her the truth, told her what her late husband had told him before Reyes killed him. How had she ever trusted this man? A heavy hand landed on Casey's other shoulder, pinning her to the chair. She jumped, her head snapping around to confront the one that dared touch her while her heart was in the process of shattering.

Alejandro gave her a slight shake of the head. He'd read her mind and was telling her not to attack Reyes. She took a deep breath and ruthlessly brought herself under control. He was right. She'd grown comfortable with Reyes as her lover, her confidant and even, sometimes, her friend. But he was still the Bolivian boss. If she attacked him in a room full of people, he would have to retaliate; to brutally, ruthlessly shut her down. He could not afford to show weakness. Not with her, not with anyone.

With Alejandro's warm, comforting touch and Reyes dark presence at her side she turned to the doctor and demanded, her voice imperious, "Tell me the rest."

He nodded, his eyes on hers, a mixture of awe and pity.

He opened the file and removed the x-ray, holding it out for her to see. "It's remarkable really, how well your brain has healed from the type of injury we're seeing here. Your description of multiple surgeries and a five-week medically induced coma are consistent with this type of trauma. I believe that the migraines are probably a result of the original trauma that occurred when you were eighteen though we aren't able to absolutely confirm this diagnosis. We can, however, give you better medications to help manage the symptoms."

She brushed off his reassurances and focused on the one important word he kept saying over and over again. "What trauma?"

He dropped his eyes, finally refusing to look her in the face. The room seemed to go completely still and she realized every single person in the room knew the truth of what was on the x-ray except for her. She stared at it, forcing her brain to acknowledge what everyone else could see, but she was somehow missing.

The doctor touched the photo and traced the tip of his fingernail along something she still couldn't understand. A delicate pattern of some kind radiating out from a dark spot. Without looking up, he said softly, "Gunshot wound to the head."

CHAPTER TWENTY-SEVEN

"Impossible!" Casey snapped after a moment of silence. "I was in a car wreck. It killed my entire family!"

No one moved. No one said anything. They simply waited, statues in a still room as denial crashed over her. She felt hot. Prickles of heat penetrating all down her skin as some kind of truth tried to sweep over her. She shook her head and then she pushed her shoulders up, shrugging Alejandro's hand away. He knew. He knew just as much as Reyes had known. They'd all known.

But they were wrong.

Her family had died on a highway. She slammed her eyes shut and buried her hands in her hair, gripping the pale blond strands in tight fists as she forced herself to conjure a memory that wouldn't come. Had never come. A memory of a happy family driving, screeching brakes, twisting metal, the smell of fire, people screaming, ambulance sirens. Nothing. There was nothing. There had never been any memories of the accident.

Ignacio and his doctor had assured her the trauma was too great and that she would probably never remember. A sob escaped her lips. She opened her hand and smacked herself in the side of the head. Something was trying to surface. Another memory, something powerful was rising up. Dark and swirling, images flashing like a movie in fast forward. Glimpses of something she couldn't hold on to.

"Leave."

Casey barely registered his voice as Reyes ordered everyone out of the room. She wanted him to go too. Wanted him to leave her alone while she floundered in the murky blackness of her own brain. But she knew he wouldn't. He would relentlessly watch over her. Whether she wanted it or not.

She felt the heat of Alejandro leave her side. Felt the coolness down her side and registered the closing of the door as they were left alone together. Deciding her ass had been numb for long enough she tried pushing herself off the chair, but her body had other ideas and she slid to the floor instead, landing with a thump on her knees on the cheap linoleum. Reyes tried reaching for her, but Casey snarled and slashed her hand at him.

"Don't touch me!" she yelled, her voice echoing in the room.

She felt the instant tension snap through his body, knew he wouldn't allow this kind of insult pass from anyone else, no matter what kind of day they were having. She waited for retaliation, waited for him to haul her to her feet and force her compliance. She was weakening before his eyes. She wasn't the woman he'd been spending weeks loving and building up, preparing for a position at his side. She was the pathetic creature he'd found in Miami.

He didn't say a word though. He just stared down at her as she continued to sink into the pit of swirling dizziness capturing her mind and sweeping her along on a tidal wave of madness. *Shot in the head*. She'd been shot in the head. She should be dead... but she wasn't. Her family was though. She lifted accusing eyes to the man that could give her the answers.

Her voice was hoarse but strong when she spoke. "They were shot too, weren't they?" she demanded. "There was never any car wreck. All of them were shot. My mom, my dad, my brother and sisters. All murdered."

He didn't even hesitate. "Yes."

She screamed, the sound tearing from her throat as rage and sorrow crashed through her chest and erupted out of her mouth. It echoed through the room. She rocked back on her heels and screamed until she couldn't anymore, until her voice died away into soft cries. Reyes didn't try to touch her this time though. She saw him flinch for just a second and something like anguish cross his features before he reverted to his impassive expression. He felt her pain as it rippled through her body. As denial fell away and reality settled on her shoulders like a bleak, shadowy cloak. She pictured the horrific way in which her family had died. Had they died one at a time, execution-style or had they been slaughtered like animals as they'd tried to run?

"But I survived," she said, drawing herself up on her knees. Awe, terror and despair mixed in her voice as she processed the magnitude of her new truth. "I survived getting shot in the fucking head."

He nodded, his eyes meeting hers. He allowed her to see his vulnerability, the sheer relief he felt that she'd survived. He wasn't even going to pretend that he was detached about the possibility of her having died. They'd gone past that point in their relationship. Too much had happened to them.

Casey struggled to her feet. Reyes reached out to help her but she slapped his arm away and then gave him a hard shove for good measure. She could feel the tightening of his body, the need for him to grab her, to take what he wanted regardless of her feelings. She saw the powerful ripple of muscle down his arms and the tendons in his neck stand out as he gritted his teeth and glared at her.

She stood her ground though, fists clenched and hissed at him, "You knew and you brought me here!"

He nodded in confirmation, but said, "Choose your words carefully, *nena*. I know you're hurting, but I am still your master, your king."

She bared her teeth at him. "What are you going to do, Reyes, finish the job?" she snarled, pointing a finger at his chest.

He grabbed her wrist so swiftly she barely had a chance to back up before he was slamming her into the wall behind them. "Is that what you want, Casey?" he growled into her face, reaching for her other wrist and dragging her arms over her head. "You want me to finish the job? Because I won't allow this. *Mi reina* will stand strong or she will die. You decide."

She thrust her chin out at him, growling back in defiance, tempted to tell him that he was welcome to finish the job, but then something pushed at the edge of her consciousness; a memory that was waking up slowly, stalking forward. She gasped, her vision flooding with something. A horrible, terrible colour. Red maybe... yes it must be red, this terrible thing that washed over everything. Then the memory flooded in as though it had been waiting for this moment, whispering in the wings of her subconscious, fluttering until she was either strong enough to handle it or weak enough that she could no longer deny it.

She saw them all. Lined up on their knees, begging for their lives. Her parents begging for the lives of their children as they were shot one at a time execution-style by a group of men. Then she saw... she saw... Ignacio... standing over her, a look of almost longing or maybe loss on his face as he turned away and pulled the trigger. Then she fell. But she was still conscious as she lay on the floor, blood seeping from her head, across her face, dripping from her chin as she watched her family die. She blinked. Mother down. Blink. Sister down. Blink. All down.

Red. Is that what this colour is? This shadowy thing spreading out across the floor from her face as Ignacio and his men walked away from her.

Blink. Inky, cold blackness.

"Casey?" Reyes' voice pulled her back, his hands tightened on her wrists reminding her that she had always been his pawn.

"You brought me here, to the clinic, to find out for sure. Didn't you?" she whispered.

He didn't lie to her. That was one thing she admired about Reyes, even while he gripped something inside of her and crushed it. "Yes, *nena*, I needed to know if Ignacio was confessing the truth. Not all men are honest under torture," he told her brutally. "But I also wanted to know if they could help you here. Give you something to ease your headaches."

She stared up at him with something approaching hatred. "Take your hands off me! Leave me alone!" she snarled.

"Never!" he thundered back at her, finally snapping under the pressure of seeing his woman take constant hits and being unable to do anything about it. "I will never leave you alone, Casey Reyes."

"Reyes is not my name," she said scathingly, fury vibrating through every word. "I am *not* your wife. The name I carry is tainted with the blood of my family."

"You will marry me, *nena*, and you will take my name," he snarled, lowering his mouth to hers and pressing it gently against the curve of her trembling lips despite the violence swirling around them. "Nothing less is acceptable. You have belonged to me from the moment I set eyes on you. From your fucked-up eyes, the grey world you live in, the pain in your head to the mark on your hand. It all belongs to me. It's mine, Casey, you understand?"

Her heart pounded at the intensity of his words while tears seeped from her eyes as visions of her dead family continued to flash through her brain, tormenting her in a vivid re-play like it had happened only yesterday instead of a decade ago. He continued to brush his lips against hers, soothingly, possessively.

"You want to marry me, Reyes?" she whispered, her breath shuddering against him as his tongue dipped out to taste the edge of her mouth. "You want to keep me forever? Willing and heart whole?"

He opened his eyes and looked into hers. Burning heat from that dark, possessive gaze. She knew what he was telling her. He could take her and keep her without her permission. He'd already done it. But she also sensed the longing within him. The longing for his queen; the woman that could willingly stand strong and reign by his side.

"What will it take?" he asked.

She smiled without warmth, her lips curving against his. "I want everyone involved in the death of my family. The person that gave the order, the people that covered it up, the men that pulled the triggers. Everyone. I want to kill them all, Reyes."

She felt the catch in his breath. His fingers bit into the flesh of her hip and he slammed her against the wall, pressing his hard erection against the cradle of her thighs. Her blood-thirsty declaration had turned him on. "You have my word, *mi reina*," he growled against her mouth before slanting his lips over hers. Casey tugged her wrists from his restraining hold, buried her hands in his hair and kissed him back.

I want to see red, she thought, *I won't rest until I see red again,* as she drifted in a haze of hate and desire.

CHAPTER TWENTY-EIGHT

"Casey, *ven aqui ahora*!"

The thunder in Reyes' voice was enough to send the birds in the bushes fleeing for the skies. Casey stiffened but didn't turn to look at the man emerging from the house to shout at her back. When she didn't immediately respond to his demand, she felt the snapping anger in his demeanor reach out for her across the expansive yard. Then she heard him stalk toward her as he moved with the lethal grace of a jungle cat. She could tell from the edginess of the nearby guards that he was making his way toward her. She stiffened her posture, but maintained her position next to the fountain at the back of their colossal mansion.

She'd been avoiding him for more than a week, since their arrival back from Brazil. She had murmured that she'd needed space and even lied to him, telling him she'd had a vicious headache. When he'd questioned her, she'd assured him it wasn't a full-blown migraine, but that it was bad enough for her to require her own room so she couldn't be disturbed. He had been annoyed and flat out refused, but her arguments had won him over. What if he disturbed her in her sleep, jostled her head? She had assured him it would only be temporary. But she knew he was losing patience. And, apparently, it was now gone.

Casey wanted to feel bad for lying. For being disloyal to the man that was tirelessly searching for her family's killers so he could present their heads on a platter to his chosen queen. But she couldn't bring herself to feel guilty for misleading the person who had known all along and never said a word. It should have been him to tell her about her family. About the hole in her head; the damage to her brain. In her heart, she felt like he'd built her up only to cut her adrift when she needed him most.

He seized her from behind and flung her around to face him. She was wearing heels so she was face to face with him when she turned. Perhaps she'd sensed this confrontation coming. Knew that he'd had enough of her illusiveness.

"I told you to come to me," he snarled, his dark eyes livid with warning. "You do as I tell you, every time I tell you, when I tell you to do it, Casey."

Casey knew she was skating the dangerous edge of his patience, but she couldn't bring herself to care. She tugged her arm, trying to pull it from his grip. His fingers dug into her flesh, refusing to give up his hold. She pressed her lips together and said, "I'm not your dog, Reyes. I don't have to come when I'm called."

His nostrils flared in reaction and she winced at the brutal tightening of his hand. There would definitely be bruises later. "And this is how you want to play it with me, *nena*?" he asked, his voice surprisingly quiet considering the waves of anger pouring from his body. "After I have allowed you a week of space. Allowed you to lie to me, to go to another room and withhold your body from me? I have given you all the tenderness and understanding a man in my position is capable of." He stared hard at her, allowing his heated gaze to linger on her lips before moving back to her eyes so she could see the determination there. Her grace period was definitely over. "You want to be very careful in your next words, *mi amor.*"

Her eyes traced over the scars on his face; the scars that declared him king. The deep, pitted lines that marked his battles and made him the hardened leader that he was. He was tough and commanding, everything that she was not and never could be. She didn't understand why he wanted her. She was nothing to a man like him. She should have died on that floor with the rest of her family. She was a fake survivor. A ghost living in the shell of a broken woman. She was a false queen.

She turned her head to look away from him toward the mountains across from their hidden valley. Their home was really spectacularly beautiful and if she was being honest with herself, truly honest, if she could have chosen to live anywhere in the world, despite having been essentially brought here against her will, she would have chosen this place anyway. It was breathtaking.

"Just go away and leave me alone, Reyes," she murmured absently, her eyes taking on an unfocused faraway look as she continued to gaze into the distance.

She felt the heat of his rising anger wash over her as he clasped his hand over her other arm and shook her until her head snapped up. "Look at me, damn you," he gritted from between clenched teeth. When she finally did, forcing herself to focus on his blazingly angry, dark face, he spoke again, his voice throbbing with quiet authority. "Last chance, Casey. It's time for you to stop drifting and come back to me now. Let's do this the easy way, *cariña.*"

She studied him for a moment, tempted to give in. Tempted to recapture the weeks before she remembered what happened to her family, before she found out what had happened to her, but she couldn't. She couldn't trust him.

And worse, she couldn't trust herself. She wasn't brave, she wasn't strong, she was just… numb to everything. She was the pale imitation of a woman who should've died ten years ago.

"Fuck you, Reyes!" she spat, smacking his chest with her open palm. "You don't get a say in what I do. You withheld the truth from me. You broke me just as much as Ignacio ever did, maybe worse. If this is how I choose to deal, then you get no say in the matter."

A part of her knew she was being too hard on him, that he'd had her best interests at heart. That he could have kept the truth from her indefinitely if he'd chosen. But she was so damn angry and in so much pain over the fresh feelings of loss that she couldn't seem to control herself and Reyes was the only one she could strike out at. So rather than heed the inner voice telling her to step carefully with the vicious mob boss, she struck out at him.

"You dare to say his name to me?" Reyes growled dangerously, "You dare to compare me to that weak-willed excuse for a man?" His voice rose in a snarl as he said, "His name does not pass your lips again, understand?"

"What are you going to do about it?" she charged back at him.

"I'm going to wake you the fuck up," he snarled and turned, hauling her with him, heading toward the house.

Casey thought he meant to drag her inside the house and up to their bedroom, but he didn't. Instead he skirted the house and strode toward a side of the compound she had never been to before. She could barely keep up to him in her high heels and with his long, agitated strides. She had to run and was sadly out of breath when they arrived at a nondescript concrete building. It's very blandness was utterly terrifying.

"Wh-where are we?" she asked hesitantly, clutching at a stitch in her side and trying to hide her panic.

He ignored her question, instead nodding sharply at a guard stationed by the door. The guard opened the door for them and stood aside to let them pass. Reyes readjusted his grip on her elbow when she tried digging her heels in and dragged her through the doorway and into a dimly lit hallway that screamed 'once you enter this passageway, you will never exit.' Casey walk-stumbled after Reyes as he pulled her impatiently down one long corridor after another.

"I-is this some kind of prison?" Casey asked timidly.

"Yes." His answer was immediate and clipped, not inviting further commentary, but the sheer size of the building prompted her to speak up.

"How many people do you keep in here?" she asked incredulously.

He didn't answer, instead, stopping so abruptly that she nearly ran into his back. He punched a code into the panel next to a thick, metal door, pushing it open when a little light flashed. He dragged her through the door and gave her a shove into a small, airless room; finally releasing her. Casey rubbed her arm and looked around her in utter dismay, terror swirling around the pit of her stomach and crawling up her throat. She was in some kind of prison cell. The door slammed shut, echoing ominously in the horrible room. She swung around, her arms wrapped protectively around herself.

Reyes stood facing her, locked in with her. She shivered, apprehension crawling up and down her spine. She almost wished he'd locked her in and left. Nothing good could come of the dead-eyed look he was giving her. She was positive it was the same look he gave the people he tortured horribly for whatever information he needed from them right before he sent them to a grisly, bloody death. The same look he'd given Ignacio.

"Please..." she whispered, backing away from him.

"You had your chance, *nena*. I believe you told me to fuck

off, that I had no say in how you dealt with your grief," he told her coldly, stalking toward her. He tugged at the hem of his shirt and then pulled it over his head. She watched in horrified fascination as he revealed his beautiful tanned torso, littered with scars. He let his shirt drop to the floor and snaked an arm out for her. Casey threw her hand up to block him, but he grabbed her wrist and dragged her toward him, pulling her against his chest and snarling in her face, icy disdain giving way to heated rage.

"And I'm telling you," he growled into her face. "Every fucking thing about you is my business. Your happiness, your sadness, your grief, your *very* life. Your everything. You're about to learn how much you belong to me, Casey."

She whimpered, terror streaking through her veins with each word. She began fighting him as he started removing her clothes with ruthless efficiency, ignoring her cries of fright. He stripped off each article of clothing until she stood naked and shivering in front of him. She wasn't shaking from cold, but from the humiliation of being dragged from the yard into a prison and stripped bare. She was shaking from fear of the unknown and from fear of the look in his eyes. Reyes was looking at her without pity and without mercy. She knew her pleas would fall on deaf ears. He was going to do whatever he'd planned on doing. She'd had her chance to give him what he wanted and she threw it in his face without grace or the gratefulness a man in his position expected. Now she would pay.

Casey frantically searched the space around her, looking for anything that might help her. A way out, a way to fight him off... anything. Then her panicked eyes landed on something that nearly sent her spiraling into the dark places in her head. Chains. He had chains in his dungeon. Because now there was nothing else she could call this place he'd dragged her into. Her frantic search also yielded a long steel bench and a floor drain. Oh god. This was some catastrophic shit.

Was he finally done with her? Was this it? Had he brought her to this awful place to kill her?

Without any sort of preliminaries, Reyes flung her around so she was facing away from him and dragged her toward the metal bench. Casey fought him with everything she had, but her strength was absolutely nothing compared his, nothing! He looped an arm across her slim waist and lifted her off the floor.

"No, no, no!" she screamed, kicking her feet into the air and trying to pry his arm from her, expecting at any moment to feel the cold caress of a blade at her throat.

The most terrifying part was his lack of words. He said nothing to her as she screamed and cursed at him and then calmed enough to beg him to stop whatever he was doing. He simply held her off the floor, pinned against the warmth of his hard chest and waited her out until she tired and lay whimpering against him. Then he shoved her abruptly forward, facedown over the metal bench.

Casey surged up with a hoarse scream, throwing her head back, hoping to crack her skull into his nose. He was a trained combatant though and easily ducked her inexperienced hit. He held her down with a knee in the middle of her back and placed a broad palm over her head, holding her cheek against the cold metal. He reached over her and yanked one of the chains down from the wall, pulling it toward her pinned body.

"Oh god, please stop," she begged. "Please don't, Reyes! I'm sorry, I'll come back to your bed!"

He continued to ignore her as he clasped the metal around her wrist and adjusted the size to fit her slim wrist with such easy precision that she realized he'd had plenty of practice. A shiver of fear wracked her naked body. He reached over her head, the heat from his naked chest warming her back and pulled the chain on the other side down. Casey tried to pull her hand underneath her body in a desperate attempt to hide it from him, but he pried it out and snapped the cuff over her other wrist.

Once she was secure, he backed away from her, trailing his fingers from her head down her back, across her spine and ending in a hard slap across her ass. Casey yelped and jerked. The chains were loose enough that she could rear back. Reyes immediately remedied that. He slid something along the wall, which adjusted the chains until she was forced to lay with her torso flat against the cold bench, her knees on the floor her arms spread wide.

A sacrifice.

CHAPTER TWENTY-NINE

Casey shivered helplessly, whimpers of fear erupting from her throat. She managed to bring herself under control enough to ask, "A-are you going to k-kill me?" her voice sounded unnaturally high-pitched as it echoed through the room.

She tried to crane her head back to she could see him where he stood behind her, but it put too much strain on her shoulders and she was forced to lay with her cheek against the cool metal staring at her right wrist chained above the bench. She jumped and cried out as his palm landed harshly across first one of her ass cheeks and then the other.

"Now why, after I have gone through all this trouble to acquire you and assure your health, would I simply dispose of you, *nena*?" he asked, his voice cool and dark.

He was right. She'd asked a stupid question. Of course, he wasn't going to kill her. He'd waited months to get his hands on her. He'd killed and tortured for her. He'd provided for her, flown a doctor in for her and taken her to one of the best clinics in the world. But Casey had never been one to think logically when she was threatened. She still couldn't work out what he meant to do to her, though her lack of clothing was a concerning development.

"A-are you going to hurt me?" she asked, her voice cracking.

She flinched and wiggled her ass, expecting another hit to that already tender flesh, but none came. He chuckled darkly, "Most assuredly, *mi amor*. If this doesn't wake you the fuck up, then nothing will."

"What?" she asked sharply. "What'll wake me up?"

Her head snapped to the side and up as he pulled her hair back and kissed her hard while running his hand roughly down the arch of her back. He sank his fingers into the flesh of her ass cheek and squeezed until it hurt. She whimpered into his mouth. He was being careful not to wrench her neck, but she was desperately frightened. She knew he intended to have sex with her, but she wasn't wet at all. It was going to hurt if he tried to fuck her while she was on her knees and chained to a bench in his torture dungeon.

He must have realized that she was too scared to be turned on because he began alternating harsh touches with gentle sweeps of his fingers across her body, as though petting and coaxing her flesh with pleasure before punishing through with pain. The combination started to work as it distracted her terrified brain from worrying about his intentions and focused it on the magic of his flesh against hers. The heat of each strike as he hit her, the burn as it spread across her nerve endings and then the soothing, caressing stroke that would follow.

Reyes shifted to the side of her, the rough fabric of his pants sliding between her legs as he forced his thigh across her labia. She cried out and started to arch into him before she caught herself. He'd spent weeks conditioning her to this kind of delicious torture. Now, he'd chained her down and was giving her a taste of how much darker he could take things if she didn't give him what he wanted, bent to his will, became his queen on demand.

"Reyes!" she cried out when he reached down, wrapped his hand around her leg above the knee and jerked her legs wide apart. Her knee scraped painfully across the concrete floor.

She wasn't expecting a hit directly to her tender pussy and screamed in shock when he slapped her there, his fingers smacking against the tender lips of her labia. She jerked hard against the bench, a jolt of pleasure and pain shooting right through her pelvis and up into her torso. Heat flooded her veins and moisture gathered in her core. Before her brain had a chance to process what he'd done to her he slapped her again and again, until the sound of the strikes was undeniably the sound of a hand hitting wet flesh.

"Like that, do you, *nena?*" he growled, pride throbbing in his deep voice.

He began alternating between slapping her ass in hard strikes and her pussy as she squirmed against the bench, begging him. She was no longer begging him to let her go. Now she was begging for another kind of release. She'd widened her legs even more, uncaring of the scrape against her knees. She could feel the gathering wetness of her pussy beginning to drip down her thighs.

"Oh god, Reyes," she yelled, her head still twisted so she couldn't see him. "Please just fuck me now!"

She was so ready to explode into orgasm from the stimulation of his strikes that she was now rocking her hips back into each blow and twisting her shoulders as much as she could to give her even more thrust. She just needed him to let the tip of his finger linger a little longer against her hard, throbbing clit and she would go right over the edge, but it was like he knew! He snatched his hand back the second he sensed he was about to rock her orgasm until she was ready to start screaming in frustration.

"You aren't ready to be fucked yet, *cariña*," he growled from behind her.

"What the fuck do you mean?" she yelled incredulously. "I couldn't get any wetter if you dumped me in a lake. Fuck me now or die you monster!" she demanded, her voice starting to waver from too much screaming. "I'll murder you if this is your plan. To make me all horny and then leave me."

He chuckled. "Not to worry, *nena*, it's not my plan to leave you high and... wet," he chuckled, then he ran his fingers through her sopping pussy and slid two of them deep into vaginal passage, stretching her until she was moaning and squirming. Then he ran them up to the tiny, puckered hole of her ass and spread the wetness there. He said, "It's not my intention to fuck this pussy at all."

She froze as he used her natural lubrication to work his fingertip into her ass and begin to stretch her. It took a minute for her brain to catch up to his words and actions. During that time, he managed to work his finger into her incredibly tight ass, wiggling it in until he bottomed out. She cried out and arched her back down toward the bench, wrenching her arms hard against the cuffs.

"Shh, *nena*," he urged, leaning across her, his finger still buried in her ass. He ran his other hand up her side soothingly as he whispered in her ear, "You need to calm down or this is going to hurt."

"Fuck you, *culero*! This is going to hurt a motherfucking lot no matter what you do," she screeched at him, tears gathering in her eyes. "First time anal sucks!"

He froze and then she felt vibrations against her back as he started to chuckle. "How would you know it, ah, sucks if it's your first time, eh, *nena*?" he asked in a perfectly reasonable voice that made her want to stab his eyes out. How dare he laugh at her while she was terrified he was going to tear her ass wide open with his monster dick. Tears began trickling from her eyes across her nose and down her cheek to pool on the metal beneath her face.

"*Culero*," she muttered.

He stopped chuckling. He shoved a second finger into her ass drawing a scream of pain from her and reached to grip her face with his free hand, gripping her cheeks hard. "You call me an asshole again, Casey, and I will make sure it hurts as much as you expect it to, understand? Swallow the disrespect."

She nodded as much as she could. He released her face and she put her head down, face down on the bench, pressing her forehead against the metal. She was done trying to see him, trying to see what he was doing to her. He got what he wanted. He got her to respond to a monster, the Bolivian mafia boss. Now the boss was going to show her exactly who owned her, every inch of her. And she would never cross him again.

She tensed as he stood behind her. Was he going to fuck her standing up? She frowned when she heard him walk away from her, then shuffling as though a drawer was being opened and closed. Strange, she hadn't seen any shelves or anything. Not that she'd looked at the room very closely.

She lay chained down, waiting with tense expectation as he approached her again. Something small and plastic hit the floor and bounced next to her causing her to jump. She frowned and whimpered. What the fuck was he doing? Then she gasped and jumped again, straining against the chains, rattling them against the wall when she felt something cool and gel-like hit her ass crack and slide into her heated anus.

"Motherfucker!" she yelled.

He slapped her ass again, much harder than he had hit her yet. "*Silencio!*" he snarled. "You are lucky I am in the mood to make this easier for you, woman. One more word and I will beat you into submission before fucking this ass with the brutality it deserves. Remember who I am." The last sentence was gritted with such intensity that she slammed her lips shut on a whimper and tilted her forehead, pressing it hard into the cold metal.

He slapped her ass again then slapped her pussy before moving his fingers to her ass and sliding them deep into the forbidden hole. Her moan turned into a scream as the pressure increased. She continued to squirm, moan and cry out hoarsely, her voice cracking as her raw throat gave out while he pumped his fingers in and out of her, preparing her ass to take his cock. He massaged and stretched her, forcing her body to take the width of first two fingers and then three until the painful burn of invasion began to give way to a gradual tingle of pleasure. Unwillingly she started to move her hips in a way that increased that pleasure until she was asking for more.

Finally, after several minutes of preparation and more lubrication he removed his fingers. Casey cried out hoarsely in disappointment and tried seeking his leg out with hers. Then she heard the jingle of his belt and the tell-tale *thunk* of his pants hitting the floor. She froze, knowing what was coming and huddled her hips as much as she could against the bench. Her breathing grew ragged as he gripped her hips and dragged them back toward him stretching her arms until they wouldn't go back anymore. The chains rattled.

"I fucking love that sound, *nena*. Especially when it's you under my hands, in my dungeon," he growled from behind her.

His fingers dug into her hips, flexing them deep into the flesh of her hips for a moment before he moved one of them over to the small over back and then across her ass and into the dip. She whimpered as he ran the velvety tip of his penis through the lubrication and up the crack of her ass. It felt so good she couldn't help but twitch her hips back into him and moan her pleasure, even knowing the pain that was about to come. Then she felt him place the tip against her anus and start pushing.

She breathed hard and arched her back trying to push back against the overwhelming fullness. Reyes pressed his hand into the middle of her back and pushed her down, pinning her ruthlessly to the bench until she had no room to move at all, then began sliding his thick cock into her anal passage. She tried to push back against his ruthless entry but, if anything, she made it easier for him to slide further in. She screamed and thrashed, throwing her head back until he finally stopped, having thrust his entire length into the depths of her heated passage.

"Fuck, *mia nena*," he gritted savagely from behind her. "So fucking tight, so good."

She gritted her own teeth against the pain, glad that he wasn't moving, positive he would tear her apart if he so much as twitched inside her. She flinched when he shifted slightly to reach underneath her, but he only reached for her clit, running his fingers over the slippery nub, drawing sparks of pleasure to override the pain. She cried out and rocked into it, sliding herself up and down his cock a tiny bit and sending new sensations throughout the tiny nerve endings in her ass. She gasped and began rocking harder, seeking more of the pleasure that was suddenly building.

"*Si* Casey, *si nena*, just like that!" he snarled from behind her, gripped her hip hard and pushed further into her, easing his length in and out of her in gentle strokes while massaging her clit with his other hand until she was writhing under him, begging for release.

Casey spared a few precious seconds to realize the care he was taking to make sure her first-time anal didn't suck. That she was indeed building toward release and not being torn in two from a cock that could do real damage to her pussy let alone her virgin ass. She could tell from the tension in his body that he was having trouble holding himself back from just slamming into her; gripping her hips in both hands and pounding her hard.

"Come for me, *cariña*," he growled. "You need to come for me now."

She could feel the flaring of his dick as it grew impossibly harder and longer, his strokes growing rougher. She cried out as he slammed himself into her tender ass, pain and pleasure flaring and radiating throughout her body. He pinched and flicked her clit until she was lost in a messy world of swirling spinning dizziness.

"Come!" he shouted.

His thrusts grew progressively rougher and more painful. Tears gathered in her eyes. He rubbed her clit harder, forcing her higher and higher. She threw her head back with a savage scream of her own. She'd intended to scream at him to stop. Stop the torture, stop forcing her to feel these vastly different things. But it hurt so fucking good that she never wanted it to stop. Instead she did as he demanded and came for him in an explosion of white sparks that dimmed her vision for a few seconds.

She slammed her eyes shut so she wouldn't pass out, wrapped her fingers around the chains as best she could and held on for dear life as he continued fucking her ass for several more strokes before finishing. She felt the hot rush of semen as he filled her anal passage. It felt different than when he filled her pussy. He pulled out and finished across her ass cheek and thigh, marking her.

The possessive culero, she thought weakly, slumping against the chains and resting her cheek against the cold metal of the bench.

Reyes reached over her head, a bead of sweat dripping from his wide chest and landing on her shoulder blade, and uncuffed first one wrist and then the other. Casey moaned at the painful rush of blood through her veins and the pull of tender flesh. She curled her wrists underneath her torso against her breasts and huddled against the bench hoping like hell he was done with the torture. She ached *everywhere*.

He sat her on his lap and curled her up, tucking her head beneath his chin, then settled with his back against the bench. Neither of them were comfortable. Reyes was sitting with a metal bench digging into his back, though Casey was having trouble truly caring about his comfort given what he'd just done to her. And she was leaning against his sticky, sweaty bare chest and sitting on his still semi-hard dick with the zip of his pants digging into her tender ass. She glanced down at her bare thigh where her leg was curled up. There was a streak of something sticky. She realized it must be semen mixed with blood. If she didn't badly need the comfort of his arms at the moment she would probably haul off and punch him.

After sitting in silence for several moments while their racing hearts calmed and she wondered if she would ever sit again, he finally spoke.

"Come back to me, *nena*," he whispered against the top of her head, kissing her hair.

Tears filled her eyes and she took several shuddering breaths before answering. "It hurts too much, Reyes. The numbness feels so much better. I can cope with that. When there aren't any feelings. I... I just don't think I can survive the memories when they keep rushing at me every time I close my eyes. And your love... it makes me feel too much, hurts too damn much. I should've died with them." Her voice broke on the last word and she ended on a sob.

His arms tightened around her and squeezed until she

almost couldn't breathe, but it was a good kind of hurt. It reminded her that she was still alive and that he wasn't going to let her slip away to die in a pool of her own blood with a bullet in her brain. The tears came faster and harder. He let her cry until there were no more tears.

He took a fistful of her hair and forced her head back until it rested on his bicep. He looked into her swollen, tear-stained eyes and said, "You are alive, *mi amor, mi reina*, don't waste this gift. Time to wake up, understand?"

She took a deep breath in and then let it shudder out from her. "Okay, Reyes," she whispered, tilting her head to the side and pressing a kiss against his stubbled jaw. "Time to wake up."

The edge of his lips curved a little, softening his profile a little. Then he said, "Good, *nena*, because I have some information on the motherfuckers that took your family. We fly to Venezuela tomorrow."

CHAPTER THIRTY

The man looked as though he'd seen a ghost, yet Casey was positive she'd never seen him before. He stared and stared at her as though unable to drag his eyes away from her. She knew she was a good-looking woman. She knew her beauty lured men to her, powerful men like Ignacio and Reyes. But, somehow, she didn't think it was her uncanny resemblance to Marilyn Monroe that was making Sotza, the Venezuelan boss, look at her like she had two heads.

She was about to ask if they had met before when he abruptly turned to Reyes and snapped in a clipped British accent, "Who is this? I refuse to negotiate business in front of a newcomer. Send your little girlfriend away if you expect to talk."

Casey felt the thick, palpable tension in the air, winding like a serpent, getting ready to strike for daring to insult the Bolivian's woman. Casey side-eyed Reyes. Yup. Though he looked at ease, standing in his superbly cut dark suit, his arms crossed over his broad chest, waves of fury were rolling off of him. Alejandro and the rest of their men were looking just as menacing.

Casey glanced back at Sotza with a raised eyebrow. From the look on his face, she could tell he was regretting his words. The imp in her really wanted him to eat them, but she knew she needed to play nice to get to the goods. She smiled pleasantly and was about to speak when Reyes interrupted with a growl, "She is my wife, *not* my little girlfriend. You will be respectful and civil when speaking to her." Apparently, despite his assurances that this meeting was in her hands, he couldn't help but defend her honour. Sweet.

She didn't bother correcting Reyes' continued insistence on calling her his wife when she was not. Instead she looked intently at Sotza and then nodded toward a beautifully tiled walkway. "Walk with me, señor," she said pleasantly. "Tell me why you looked at me the way you did."

Sotza appeared somewhat relieved that she was calling her guard dog to heel and taking the reins. Clearly, he didn't want a bloodbath on his home front. Casey indicated that they should walk together side by side, turning their backs on the veritable army and moving with the Venezuelan arms dealer toward the path. He hesitated only a moment and then allowed her to lead him, perhaps a mixture of curiosity and fear of retaliation from Reyes guiding his decision.

"Was it because I look so very much like my mother?" she murmured when they were out of ear shot of anyone else.

Tensions visibly vibrated through him for a moment and then he relaxed. They strolled leisurely down the path. Reyes remained close by, monitoring Casey's body language, but ultimately trusting her with this exchange. They'd talked in depth about what to expect and how the interaction should go down. He had convinced her that since it was her family and her ultimate happiness at stake that she should be the one to direct the discussion with Sotza while her king protected her back. She could tell though that Reyes was nervous on her behalf. He didn't know what to expect. She was always his wild card.

Finally, after they'd walked the path for several minutes, leaving armed bodyguards behind and entering into a peaceful garden along the Eastern wall of Sotza's property, he began to speak, gifting her with the truth. "Your mother was a stunningly beautiful woman, with white gold hair and bright green eyes. She could bring a man to his knees with a single look. Her grace and beauty were renowned in our circles. Your father was the envy of many... myself included."

Casey felt a rush of gratitude. These were the first kind words she'd heard about her parents in a decade and they felt oddly comforting. They wrapped themselves around her heart and helped to replace the awful images of execution that had been playing like a clip show on repeat through her brain since her memory had returned.

"Thank you," she said huskily.

Sotza nodded and waved her toward a stone bench, urging her to sit next to him. She glanced toward Reyes, whose expression was unreadable behind dark sunglasses. He stood to the side, arms crossed in front of him, not even bothering to pretend that he wasn't staring intently her way. Casey gave him a half smile and sat with Sotza, turning to give her attention to the half Venezuelan, half British man. He was really very handsome in a Brioni suit, tailored to perfection along his sculpted frame. Tall and slender, regal almost, he was probably about twenty years older than her.

His skin was perfectly tanned, his dark hair, grey at the temples, was brushed back and at the sides. He was the picture of cool, sophistication with an exotic twist. He was a difficult man to get any kind of read on, except when he gazed at Casey for too long, then she saw small sparks of emotion. As though he were struggling with his own long-buried memories. So, she looked at him, really looked at him and tried to see the truth.

She tilted her head to the side, her white blond hair sliding over her shoulder and swinging toward him. She saw his gaze shift along her body, saw the flash of intense longing before he shut it down.

"You knew my mother better than you're saying," she said bluntly. He turned his head toward her, the look in his eyes at first cool and chastising. "Please tell me," she urged him. "Everyone I used to love has fallen. Murdered in our home by execution, one at a time. I watched as my mother was forced to her knees. Watched as she begged for the lives of her children, right before they put a bullet in her head."

He flinched, a ripple running through his frame. Terrible fury, similar to what she'd seen in Reyes eyes flashed through Sotza before he blanked his expression once more. The dead eyes. Yes, this she knew well and could deal with. It was that momentary flash though, that she intended to take advantage of. She knew she had him. She reached out and placed her hand over his. He allowed the familiarity.

"Please help me Señor Sotza," she whispered, squeezing his hand. "My blood was stolen from me, I was harmed beyond repair and then I was taken as some kind of prize by the man that shot me in the head. Their deaths rocked our world, yet no one lifted a finger for me."

His hand jerked underneath hers, but she refused to let him go. She studied him as he processed her words and, for a split second, seemed to crumple. As if in slow motion, his other hand moved over to cover hers. She saw Reyes jerk out of the corner of her eye, his arms loosening to fist at his sides. He did not enjoy the hold Sotza had on her; that the Venezuelan could possibly hurt her before Reyes could physically get to her. Though she didn't look toward her protective lover, she shook her head slightly to keep him at bay.

Sotza looked at her then, allowing her to see the pain and fury in his dark eyes, though his face was carefully blank. He spoke in low, measured tones, "Yes, I knew her well. She was supposed to have been mine. I saw her and loved her first. I courted her slowly, gently... we were both young. Our fathers worked together. But then she met your father, a young *capo* in the *familia* organization."

"My family?" she asked softly.

"Yes," he agreed. "Your father... he was exciting for her, fun and he made her laugh. He took her dancing and swimming. Things I couldn't do for her while I was here, helping my family run our own organization. And my own humour is... sadly lacking."

She smiled at him sympathetically. "I understand, this business is murder on a sense of humour, señor."

He laughed sharply. "I see you are also like your father. I didn't stand a chance against a man like that. I must admit, I had thought about taking out the competition." He glanced toward Reyes. "But then I met him and saw why she loved him. He complemented her in every way that I couldn't. While I was darkness to her light, he was light to her light. They were an extraordinary couple, full of energy and bold *joie de vivre*, if you will pardon the expression. I couldn't bring myself to take away something that she loved with such passion... and then she fell pregnant with you and I was forced to let her go."

Her throat felt suddenly dry and painful with the need to cry. She pressed the heel of her free hand against her eye for a moment. Then she blinked back the tears and swallowed past the lump. "M-my memories of them are fuzzy. It's like when I was shot in the head and then went into a coma after, my childhood memories were scooped out. But they are slowly returning. It... helps to hear you speak of them fondly. Or almost fondly in my dad's case."

He chuckled. "I grew to enjoy his company. It gutted me when your family was taken."

"Then why did you allow Ignacio to take me? To keep the only surviving member of my mother's family?" she asked, turning to him, anguish bright in her eyes.

He took both of her hands in his and spoke earnestly. "Child, I... or rather I should say, we, all of us in the underworld circles thought you were dead. I admit there were rumours of a beautiful woman with white blond hair decorating the arm of Hernandez in Miami, but none of us thought it could be you. Not after what had happened. There is a grave with your name on it right alongside theirs. I personally attended your funeral."

Her mouth fell open in shock. She hadn't known that. Ignacio had never allowed her to visit the graves, assuring her it would be too traumatizing, bring back memories of the accident. Instead, he hadn't wanted her in that graveyard because she would have seen her own grave, started to question him about the accident and unravel the truth.

Sotza shook his head and continued, "Of course, this was a weak excuse. I should have looked further into the rumours. It was too convenient that Hernandez had married a woman that looked so much like you, had the same name and was the correct age. I should have flown back to Miami myself and looked you in the eye. I should have done it for Sandra. But I was too damn grief-stricken. I didn't want to believe it could be true."

She nodded her head, still stunned by everything he was revealing to her.

"I'm sorry, Casey," he told her quietly. "So very sorry."

She lifted her head and pierced him with eyes shimmering with determination and emotion. "Then help me Señor Sotza," she said grimly. "I want revenge on the people that did this to my family; the ones that planned this and the ones that pulled the trigger. I won't rest until they're all dead. Give me this and I will forgive you, both for myself and my mother."

He stared back at her, unable to smother the emotion in his dark eyes. She saw the sadness and his own need for vengeance reflecting back at her. A cool smile played around his thin lips as he masked every trace of feeling. "Of course I will help, child. As it happens I have been doing some digging over the years, attempting to find the source of the hit. There were many rumours floating around at the time, but as more time passed they died away. Still, one in particular persisted. This one I looked into and found some truth."

Casey's heart started pounding in anticipation. She had to remember to school her features. "And?" she asked.

"Though I wish to lay all of my cards at your very lovely feet, my dear, I am still a businessman. I find myself reluctant to give you this information and watch a cherished link to my past walk out of my life, possibly never to return," he said, a twinkle in his eye.

Casey laughed, knowing exactly where he was leading her. "I see," she replied and tapped a fingernail against her lip. "And how exactly would you propose to remedy this dilemma?"

"A trade negotiation with new routes into the United States," he said without pause. "With you as my main point of contact and twice-yearly meetings."

Casey nodded her head and smiled. "I think this can be arranged," she told him and then removed her hand from his, deciding Reyes was probably reaching his limit of her touching another man, even if it was in pursuit of information. "Come let's walk and discuss details, you can show me the rest of this magnificent garden."

Sotza stood, nodded toward Reyes and led her down

another path. He turned to her and said enigmatically, "I have another gift for you, my dear, one that I will give for free." His face softened as he spoke. "I found this particular treasure when I was digging for information on your family."

CHAPTER THIRTY-ONE

C asey was starting to panic. This was *not* good.

"Get the men off my fucking plane," Reyes snapped at Alejandro, his hand tight on hers as he dragged Casey across the tarmac toward the private jet. She nearly had to run to keep up with his rapid strides despite her long legs. She was cursing her choice of spiked high heels. Had she known she would be marathon walking she'd have chosen flats.

"What about the pilot?" Alejandro asked, confused.

Reyes didn't bother to respond, just walked faster until Casey was actually running to keep up.

"Right," Alejandro said. He shot Casey a pitying look and jogged toward the plane to empty it before Reyes and Casey arrived.

Reyes hadn't said a single word almost the entire time they were at Sotza's. He'd watched her interactions intently and listened as she'd negotiated each minute detail with the tough Venezuelan businessman, but he'd never once stepped in. Had she overstepped? Promised too much in her quest for vengeance? Had she given away too many of Reyes' resources?

They'd discussed what she should and shouldn't say, but Casey had definitely branched out on her own, instinctively knowing when to push Sotza and when to back off. He was not a man to take bullshit lightly, despite the soft spot he clearly held for Sandra's daughter. Casey had felt as though she'd needed to pull out all the stops when maneuvering the older man into a position that was advantageous to her and the Bolivians. But one look at Reyes' face now and she was positive she'd done something wrong.

His men left the plane quickly, not looking at her as they passed, though she could feel their tension.

"*Vete*," he barked, pointing toward a distant hangar.

Casey wanted to beg him to let her go with them. What had she done to deserve his fury? He could have stepped in at any time and taken over if he thought she was doing it wrong. Was he going to punish her for fucking up her very first negotiation? Remembering her time in the dungeon back home she shivered. He pulled her behind him as he marched up the stairs and onto the plane.

Reyes dropped her arm and turned to her, his eyes glowing with an intense dark fire that seemed to reach out and lick every part of her. She backed up a couple of quick steps and held her hand out to him.

"Please, Reyes," she begged, breathlessly. "I don't know what I've done..."

He reached out, snatched her wrist with a groan and dragged her into his body. She shrieked in surprise and grabbed for his biceps, clinging to him with wide, worried eyes. He claimed her lips in a fierce kiss. It was hard and somewhat brutal, as though he couldn't get enough of her fast enough. He held her tightly against his body, his embrace one of passion, not punishment as she had been expecting. When he finally let her breathe, she gaped at him.

Finally, he spoke, laying her fears that he was angry to

rest. "Where the fuck did you learn to negotiate like that, woman?" he demanded, punctuating his words with hard, stinging kisses. "Was so fucking *caliente*, I couldn't wait to get you back here so I could fuck you properly. It was everything I could do not to strip you in the car and take you in the back seat."

"Oh!" Casey gasped. So *that* was what had been wrong with him. If she weren't so damn happy he wasn't angry with her she would berate him for being such an intense jerk and scaring her.

"Would've had to take out my own guys for witnessing you having an orgasm," he grunted and then backed them up until he was sitting on one of the benches. He pulled her down on top of him until she was straddling him with her skirt pushed up her thighs.

He tore at her clothes, uncaring that the seams of the delicate fabric were giving way beneath his hard, demanding fingers. Within seconds her demure blouse lay in shreds on the floor. She clung to his shoulders attempting to return his kisses, her own passion rising equally with his. She flung her head back, giving him access to her throat.

"I know lot's about negotiating," she panted. "I paid attention when I was a kid. I was the oldest child in my family and my daddy let me listen in on his meetings sometimes. He didn't care that I was a girl... I guess he knew I'd be a mafia wife one day and wanted me to be as prepared as I could be. As for Ignacio... well he and his guys thought I was just some stupid, pretty girl so they weren't shy about talking in front of me. Oh, fuck!" she moaned when he bit down on the flesh of her shoulder, marking her. Her pussy flooded with heat for him, impatient for the man that had taken over her life and brought her more pleasure than she could ever imagine. "I guess they never imagined what this cracked brain was capable of retaining," she mumbled, clinging to his shoulder with one hand and his hair with the other.

Reyes growled angrily, gripped her by the back of the head and swung her forward until she was face to face, nose to nose with him. Recognizing the thunder in his eyes she tried to shrink back, but he forced her to continue straddling him. "You will never disparage yourself again, Casey. Understand?"

She nodded, her eyes filling with tears.

"Say it!" he snapped.

"Never again," she whispered leaning her forehead against his. God, she was falling hard for this man.

"*Mi Reina* is not fucking cracked," he growled, "*Mi reina es perfecta.*"

A tear slid down her cheek and she cupped his face in her hands and said with all the conviction in her heart, "*Mi rey es perfecto.*"

He slid his hand down her front, between her bare breasts and over her bunched skirt into her panties. She squirmed when he slid his fingers along her aching clit and then down further into her dripping pussy. Her legs tried to automatically close in reaction to the rough touch of his thick fingers against her soft pussy, but he forced her wider by spreading his knees and tipping her backwards on his arm.

Her cries filled the airplane as he pressed two thick fingers inside her and hooked them against the front wall of her vagina, massaging her. It was too much! Too many sensations flooding her at once. She squirmed on top of him, trying to get closer to the intense feeling building inside her while also trying to twist and crawl away from him. He held her tight, his arm wrapped securely around her waist, anchoring her against him.

Casey would have marvelled at the incredible strength it must have taken for him to hold her up except she was too preoccupied with what was happening to her body. She brought her legs up on either side of him, her knees quaking as building pleasure streaked through her. He flicked his thumb over her clit and sent her spinning over the pinnacle of some kind of super orgasm.

She shrieked and reached out blindly to clutch him, gripping his neck and dragging herself foreword, rocking her pussy up against him and grinding into whatever friction she could find to prolong the blissful aftershocks. She vaguely heard him groan and felt him pull his fingers from her sopping wet passage. She moaned in protest, tilting her hips against his stomach and trying to ride him. She so wasn't done coming yet.

He reached in between them, tore at his belt and unzipped his pants. He hastily shifted them until he was able to pull his hard, thick cock up between them. Casey panted, lifted herself slightly and allowed him to guide her down. She moaned, her head falling back as he began to fill her inch by slow inch. She wiggled a little when it became too much, the sensations overwhelmingly full.

"You can do it, *nena*," he groaned, nipping and licking at her exposed throat and breasts. "You can take me."

He took her hips in his broad hands and pulled her all the way down until he was impaled deep inside. She moaned and squirmed, tilting her hips forward and back as much as he would allow, rubbing her clit against him until she was seconds away from coming again. He took her nipple between his teeth and teased, increasing the pressure until she was ready to explode.

"Come for me again," he grunted against her, his voice a guttural groan.

Casey dropped her hand from his neck, running it down the chiselled muscles of his chest to his stomach and then curling her fingers toward her own clit. He leaned back and dropped his head so he could watch as she worked her fingers in between them, using the pads of her fingertips to draw herself closer and closer while her knuckles brushed softly against him, driving him crazy.

"Harder, Casey," he demanded. "Touch harder. Come now."

As though her fingers were somehow connected to him, she did exactly as he commanded, pressing harder against her own slippery flesh while he fucked up into her, filling her channel with his hot, hard flesh until she was once more flying into the embrace of another magical orgasm.

"Yes!" she screamed happily, flinging her arms back so suddenly he had to grip her tighter so she wouldn't fall off his lap. She rocked on top of him, riding him harder, drawing out her orgasm as her pussy spasmed around him.

"Fuck!" he snarled, gripping her waist tight and slamming her down on his cock repeatedly until she felt him grow inside her. She squirmed at the sudden discomfort and gripped his shoulders, hanging on as he forced her to ride him savagely until he was spurting his semen up into her.

He slammed her down once more on his cock and stopped moving, holding her tight on his lap. Casey collapsed against him, resting her head against his shoulder. She breathed heavily, eyes closed, totally blissed out.

After a few minutes, she managed to pull herself together enough to push back from his shoulder and look at him properly. She pressed her forehead against his and sifted her fingers through his thick hair. "Let's go to Mexico," she whispered.

His dark eyes heated with fire and she felt his cock stir inside her again. "*Si, nena*. We will go to Mexico next."

CHAPTER THIRTY-TWO

Reyes picked up her hand, brought it to his mouth and kissed the fingertips, all while looking at his host, Benito Alvarez, Mexican cartel boss. Benito sat at the head of a massive table, surrounded by his men, while Reyes sat a few seats down the left side. He listened with barely concealed patience to Benito's words of long-winded congratulations toward his Bolivian counterpart, mixed with liberal amounts of self-praise. Reyes forced himself to maintain his hold on the cool, pale blonde's hand, though he didn't so much as glance at her as she played her part to perfection. He felt her shift slightly in her seat as she reached for her wine goblet and took a small swallow of the rich, red wine, the sleeve of her burgundy dress falling away from her arm. He should have warned her not to wear that colour.

"I must admit, Señor Reyes, I had expected your... companion to be somewhat different," Benito said with a disappointed sigh.

Reyes felt her stiffen next to him, but, as discussed, she kept her lips closed and allowed the men's discussion to flow around her without comment or complaint. He knew it wasn't easy. They had arrived at the Alvarez compound three days earlier for their negotiations and her presence had been the cause for several comments. Benito and his men baited her with several comments about her American origins and her place in Reyes' bed. They had agreed to allow any insults to pass freely since they were bent on keeping the negotiations peaceful.

Reyes stroked a finger over the back of her hand. He knew how much she despised listening to Benito spew his garbage around a table filled with his own men, men loyal to the Alvarez cartel. Reyes felt her relax under his gentle guidance. She picked her wine up and continued sipping while picking at the cheese plate in front of them. He had to give Benito props, though his manners were disgusting, he set a decent table. They were surrounded by treasures of immense wealth as well, gifts from the Mexican cartel to the Bolivians in appreciation for bringing forth new business, new trade routes and a new partnership. Among the gifts were weapons, jewels and money. But the most breathtaking and, perhaps, telling of Benito's penchant for drama was a human skull, now sitting in the middle of the table directly across from Reyes, adorned in coins and jewels. Its eyes glowed with a particularly sinister beauty, having been set with two exquisitely cut emeralds.

"And what exactly do you mean by that, *amigo?*" Reyes drawled lazily, declining his own wine in favour of water.

"I was told she was unusually stunning," Benito said bluntly, his sharp eyes on the woman at Reyes' side.

Reyes placed her delicate hand on her own leg and stretched his arm around the back of her chair, wrapping his fingers around the back of her neck through the blond strands of her hair. It was a move meant to show possessiveness and shut down this line of discussion. He felt the tension thrumming through her body as he touched her, as the air in the room thickened while Benito played with his guests. After three solid days of Benito's abrasive personality, Reyes was more than ready to take his woman and quit the Alvarez cartel. Permanently.

"And is she not stunning?" he asked through gritted teeth, knowing he should just accept the insult and move on, but feeling sufficiently slighted on her behalf to engage with the pig-like Mexican. Tension filled the room, making the men around the table shift uncomfortably and look to Benito for his reaction.

"Of course, my friend!" Benito was quick to reassure Reyes. "She is a beautiful woman, there is no denying this." Benito's eyes flowed liberally over her petite frame, pausing on her full chest before paying particular attention to her face. Then his voice became more serious. "But not unusual. Now, I have heard rumours of your woman..."

"What rumours?" Reyes asked sharply.

Benito flicked a look at the Bolivian boss that suggested a conspiracy, but Reyes sensed a smugness in his attitude. As though he knew a secret that only he could share. "I had heard that you might have picked your woman up from the late Ignacio Hernandez, recently of Miami." When Reyes said nothing, merely remained in his seat, posture relaxed, Benito continued. "But that would be impossible since I recently gave the order for Hernandez to dispose of his little bitch. Especially if he thought there were any threats to Miami."

Though he wanted nothing more to rip the man's still beating heart out of his chest and shove it down his throat, Reyes remained seated and merely raised an eyebrow as though he were listening to an interesting story.

Clearly annoyed that he was getting no reaction Benito's

words became more clipped. "Ignacio's second, Diego, has reported her death to me... but the rumours..."

"And why exactly would rumours bother you?" Reyes asked negligently. "Indeed, why order her death at all? A woman of her standing? She was nothing to you, just the wife of a pig."

Benito chuckled and nodded his head. This was the kind of language he understood. His lack of respect for women was renowned. He had no wives himself and simply fathered children illegitimately, building his cartel with as much of his own blood as he could. "I couldn't have anyone discover the truth of his pet."

Reyes picked his glass up on the pretext of having a drink, but used it to hide the shaking of his hand as rage throbbed through his veins, threatening to erupt and fuck all of their fine plans. As he lowered the glass, her hand wrapped around his and steadied him. Their eyes met and her steady green gaze told him to hold it together, grounding him in that moment. He'd gotten to know facets of this woman over the past three days. She was kind, steady and determined. She was willing to sacrifice much for her family. She helped calm the rage and reminded him of his duty.

Reyes turned to their host once more and asked in a careless voice, "I am curious. Do please tell me why you are so interested in Hernandez's pet and why my woman's resemblance to her or lack thereof should matter so much to you?"

Benito stared in utter consternation as though he'd expected fireworks and gotten a wet fizzle instead. Then he laughed, shrugged his shoulders and leaned back in his seat with hands folded over his belly. "Ah, the rumours must have been wrong then. My mistake, *amigo*," he announced and took a bite of cheese. "You see, this Casey, she has been a thorn in my side for years. She should have died many years ago when I ordered her parents taken out."

"Interesting," Reyes said. "Well I can assure you that this woman is not now, nor was she ever, Casey Hernandez. But out of curiosity, why did you have this family killed... the ah, Hernandez woman's family?"

"Business," Benito replied with a shrug. "Her father ran the mafia up in Florida for many years. Ignacio had his small piece but wasn't satisfied. He came to me with a plan to take the boss out and take his business, provide me with cheaper trade routes, easier, less dangerous ways into the US. All I needed to do in return was provide some firepower for the hit. He was a little squeamish about taking out the whole family, apparently had a thing for the girl. Was even set to marry her, but that isn't our way."

Reyes breathed hard through his nose and forced himself to release the muscles in his shoulders before Benito noticed anything unusual. He curled his lips back in a semi-smile, hoping it didn't look too much like a snarl. "And why exactly take out a bunch of harmless kids?"

"It is our belief that when you remove the head of the family, you need to extinguish the entire family line so the young don't grow up and exact bloody revenge for the death of a parent. It might seem callous, but it only makes sense."

They heard the clicking of her heels against the stone floor before the beautiful blond appeared in the arched doorway. Benito looked around then; it was clear by the surprise in his eyes that he finally noticed that his guards posted in each archway were missing. He scrambled to his feet reaching for the gun at his belt. Several of his men did the same, some clumsy and some lethally fast depending on their level of confusion and skill. It didn't matter. They were surrounded by men loyal to Casey and Reyes.

"I wouldn't recommend it," Reyes drawled lazily, his own gun pointed directly at Benito's heart before Benito could even draw. Reyes nodded at one of his men who relieved the Mexican boss of his pistol and stepped away from the table.

Casey continued into the room, her four inch heels striking the stone with a lethal finality in each step before she stopped at the edge of the table opposite Benito. She was dressed to impress in silver heels and a snow-white halter dress that flowed around her hips with each step she took. She wore her white-blond hair in long, loose ringlets; old Hollywood style. On her wrists and throat she wore the diamonds Reyes had gifted her on the plane trip over. Held loosely in her right hand against the fold of her skirt was her silver gun. Her eyes, one green and one amber, were glowing with anticipation.

Benito looked from Casey to the woman who had been sitting next to Reyes, the woman introduced as Reyes' wife. "I don't understand," he said.

Reyes swept his hand toward Casey. "No Benito, you do not. This woman is my wife. I trust she is sufficiently stunning?" Reyes asked with a small smirk, as though he was now the one revealing a secret weapon.

"Casey Hernandez," Benito said darkly.

She nodded, her eyes on the man responsible for the murder of her family. "You weren't careful enough, were you Benito? You didn't clean up after yourself; didn't make sure I died with the rest of my family. Shame on you for being so sloppy."

He grunted. "Stupid mistake; allowing Hernandez to keep you when you didn't fall with the rest." He collapsed back into his chair, staring at her with some hostility, but mostly awe, as though he were seeing a beautiful ghost conjured from the pits of his deepest memories. "So much like your mother," he mumbled, then seemed to catch himself and straighten. "Ignacio begged me to allow you to live when you pulled through the initial surgeries. It was a stupid sentimentality, but I was superstitious too, you see? Figured if you survived a bullet to the brain, maybe it was meant to be. Perhaps you were not meant to die with the rest of the Palmieri's. You were always a truly stunning child with those strange eyes; the way you could look right through a person."

She blinked slowly. "I don't remember you," she murmured almost absently.

She placed her hands on the table, listening to his story with rapt attention. Her gun clinked against the heavily polished wood. She'd had weeks to come to terms with the death of her family and indeed with his words, the replay in her head came slower, less like the mad rush of a movie clip that wouldn't stop and more like a slow replay of a black and white film where all the players knew their places. A beautiful ache built in her chest as he spoke because she finally knew how the movie began and how it ended. It started as a horror film, but somehow ended in romance. Her eyes drifted to Reyes where he watched her with rapt possession, his attention unwavering. He'd brought her to this moment and he would carry her through.

Her gaze shifted back to the demon in the shadows, the man that had orchestrated her suffering and brought about the downfall of the Miami Palmieri's. He looked so much smaller in real life than she'd built him up to be in her imagination. He wore a suit, like most of the men at the table. His was light-coloured, she thought, open at the neck and collar with a pocket kerchief. He was likely in his sixties or seventies; his build was slim and he was balding. Now her man, her beautiful Reyes, he could easily carry the mantle of monster with his bold, broad and bloodthirsty presence.

"Go on," she encouraged, "tell us what happened after you allowed Ignacio to keep me."

Benito glared at the beautiful blond apparition and then said viciously, "I ordered the death of any in your immediate line. Though Ignacio begged for children, I told him to make sure there were none. That one or both of you be rendered sterile. I didn't care who as long as there were no children."

She nodded. "You ordered the death of my baby, didn't you?"

"Of course, I did," he said, some of his smugness returning. "I couldn't have a Palmieri spawn rise up and come after me one day. In fact, a few months ago, I'd decided you were too much of a risk. One of my Miami contacts brought me the news that you were beginning to fight against your chains, refuse your medications and talk back to your bodyguards. I couldn't have that."

Casey had begun to suspect the truth of what had happened to baby Jack. His confirmation, though a knife twist to the heart, didn't cause her to so much as flinch in surprise. She wouldn't give him the satisfaction. She took her hands off the table and began walking around the seated men, who were watching the proceedings apprehensively, helpless to do anything but sit and witness the drama unfold, Reyes' surrounding men ensuring compliance. Before she could reach Benito the lovely blond at Reyes side stood gracefully from the table to intercept Casey. No one moved to stop her.

Casey's face softened and she smiled holding her arms out. "Gina."

Gina side-stepped the gun held carelessly in Casey's hand and went easily into her embrace. Though they'd had barely a few days to get to know each other, Sotza had gifted the two women with each other's existence. Ten years earlier when the mafia world had been rocked by the brutal deaths of the Palmieri family, a single living relative, a teenaged cousin, had been whisked off the continent and into safe-keeping, essentially forgotten since she had no other family and had never been considered a direct threat. Except for Sotza, few even knew of her existence. She had been living an uneventful and lonely life in central America and was overjoyed to reconnect with a cousin she thought dead.

"If you don't mind, cousin, I'd prefer to leave for this part," Gina murmured, pulling away from Casey with a grimace. "Much as I'd like to see this little worm squirm, I'm afraid I've never really developed the stomach for this sort of thing."

"Of course, I'll wait until you're safely away," Casey said kindly and, indeed waited for the other woman to make her way out of the dining room before she continued along the table. She stopped next to Reyes and placed her free hand on his shoulder.

Reyes wrapped his arm around her waist and pulled her in tight against his side, breathing her scent. It had been a long few days without her, trusting Alejandro to keep her safe while they gathered reinforcements among cartels loyal to Reyes, ones that were willing to make a move against Benito. Now it was hell watching her stand tall against the man that had destroyed her family and not take the gun from her and kill every disloyal man in the room. But this was her moment, her time to reign.

She was staring down at the jewel encrusted skull with a sort of fascinated horror, before lifting her gaze to Benito's. "The eyes, Reyes... what colour are they?"

"Green, *nena*," he told her.

"Like my mother's."

She lifted the gun and pointed it at Benito's head. Reyes knew she was a damn good shot. He'd made sure of it before they'd come into Mexico.

"Say her name," she demanded.

Benito glared and for a moment and it looked as though he would refuse, but finally he mumbled. "Sandra."

Tears glittered in Casey's eyes and she sniffled and said, "Sandra Palmieri." Then she turned the gun on the skull and pulled the trigger sending shards of skull and jewels flying across the table. Her bullet went right through the skull and struck the man sitting on the opposite side of the table right through the heart. He slumped in his chair without making a sound.

CHAPTER THIRTY-THREE

Casey gaped at the dead man, stunned.

"Holy crap, I didn't mean to do that!" she squeaked and turned horrified eyes on Reyes. "Was he one of ours?"

Reyes chuckled darkly and gave her hip a reassuring pat. "No, *nena*, my guys are all standing in position." His eyes cut to Benito and lingered in disgust. "Real professionals expect an ambush at any moment, especially when hosting an unknown. All these motherfuckers belong to the head of the table. This party belongs to you; shoot at will."

A slow grin spread across her face and she flung her arms around Reyes. He swung her into his lap and kissed her hard on the mouth, slipping his tongue across her lips, demanding access to the treasure within. She opened eagerly and pressed herself against him, heedless of their audience.

Reyes pulled back slightly, his hand tangled in her hair, gripping her hard. "I missed you, Casey. Was the longest three days of my fucking life. Don't you ever fucking leave me again, understand?"

She smiled against him and nodded, ignoring the painful tug in her scalp. "Yes, Reyes. Never again." She was about to kiss him again when a loud bang startled her and she jumped in Reyes' lap and craned her head around to look at Benito who'd brought this fist angrily down on the table.

"Get on with it, whatever this is," Benito sneered. "I don't intend to watch the last Palmieri bitch whore herself at my table. I'd rather go to hell."

Casey felt Reyes stiffen beneath her and reach for the gun he'd placed on the table within easy reach. She ran her fingers lightly down his arm soothing the rage that surfaced so easily on her behalf. Though she loved his protectiveness, this was her party.

"You're absolutely right!" she looked back at Reyes. "Let's not be rude, *mi rey*. Let's get this party started." She gave him her best, most cock-hardening grin and leapt from his lap.

She sauntered around the table, white dress swishing around her long legs, blond hair moving with perfect movie star precision as though she were walking a red carpet. The only thing out of place was the silver gun, which fitted perfectly in the palm of her hand. Reyes had a skull etched into the handle with a rose in place of one of the eyes. Her bloodthirsty Bolivian had true romance in his heart.

Every pair of male eyes in the room watched her with rapt attention as she walked behind Benito. She wrapped her arms around his shoulders and bent to speak in his ear while he tensed under her touch.

Before she could speak, Reyes sent her a warning look and growled from across the table, "No touching, *nena*. We talked about how this would go down."

She rolled her eyes and straightened with a sigh backing away from the Mexican she'd marked for death, hands in the air. "No fun," she mumbled.

"Casey," Reyes warned, standing. "Roll your eyes at me again and your fun is over entirely."

She smiled big and turned back to her prey, wandering

around to where Benito could still see her, but sticking to the rules Reyes had discussed with her and staying out of arm's reach. Reyes had come to stand behind her, arms crossed, to enforce his rule if need be. "Let's make this quick, Benito, since I sense my man is getting impatient. He prefers cartel justice, long drawn out torture sessions as opposed to my American style of shoot em' up and spit em' out." She glanced at the guy slumped in his chair opposite the shattered skull. "I jumped the gun on him a little, if you'll excuse the pun."

"What the fuck do you want with me, *puta*," Benito snarled turning to look at her. "Just get it the fuck over with."

"Oh!" she laughed, her high airy laugh sounding somewhat off-balanced but still beautiful as it echoed through the room. "It won't be that easy! You destroyed my world, took everything I love because of your disgusting tradition of killing the entire family. Now I take the things you love, Benito." She tapped her gun against her cheek and pretended to think about it, then she started listing the names of his family, all the illegitimate children he'd fathered. "Let me see now... there're the children tucked safely in their beds: Santiago, Matias, Rosario, Renata, Juan Paul, Juanita. That's a lot of fun I'm going to be having avenging my *familia* Benito," she finished with a giggle.

Then her eyes turned glacial and all humour fled her face. "Of course, I'm forgetting a few, aren't I, Benny? The ones that are old enough to sit at papa's table and do business." He stiffened in his chair, horror bleeding into his expression as she leaned in as close as she dared, and whispered, "Benito Jr."

She straightened her arm and pointed it down the table, two spots to the right of Benito, straight at a man in his early thirties. Her arm shook a little; not in fear or doubt, but with emotion. Her time for vengeance had finally come and she was utterly and completely elated. Reyes stepped up behind her, his warmth filling her with strength. He wrapped a strong arm around her waist and simply held her as she turned her head, pinned the man to his chair, promised him death with a single look and then escorted him into hell with a single shot to the head.

The men on either side of the now dead man flinched but didn't move otherwise, knowing they would be dead before they leapt from their chairs. Reyes' men surrounded the entire macabre party and though they kept their distance, ensured the politeness of all guests.

Benito howled in rage and fury as grief erupted from him and he slammed his fists down on the table. He jumped to his feet, toppling his chair over. Spittle flew from his lips as he turned toward Casey and lunged, snarling, "You fucking whore, do you know what you've done!"

Reyes dragged her back at the same time as Casey shot Benito in the stomach, sending the older man flying backwards off his feet. He landed on his back and then curled onto his side clutching his stomach with a groan of pain. Casey dropped to her knees beside him, indifferent to the blood that was soaking into the hem of her white skirt. She gripped his arm and spoke almost manically, "You see, Benito? You see, now! It hurts to lose family like this, doesn't it?" She tapped her gun against the side of her head and flinched a little when the heated metal brushed her temple. "Bullets hurt, Benny!"

"You fucking lunatic cunt, get the fuck away from me!" Benito shoved her back, his bloody hands leaving prints on her pale skin.

Casey jumped to her feet, rocking back on her sky-high heels and glared down at him. "I don't think you get it at all!" she snapped. "But you will, you have two more sons here. Renaldo and Santiago sit at this table too."

"No, no! Please!" Benito screamed and tried to grab her, clutching at her skirt.

Casey kicked him away and turned back to the table. A struggle was taking place as Renaldo desperately tried to leave the table while two of Reyes' men held him down. Santiago sat stoically drinking wine next to his brother. Casey knew he was her age. She'd done her homework. She might have admired his bravery, might have even allowed him to live for his simple audacity, except he'd known of the hits on her family and she'd traced countless others to his name. Children. He was a child killer.

She lifted her gun and shot him in the head. She watched dispassionately as he flew back, his chair toppling over, wine glass smashing as it hit the stone floor. Then she nodded at the men holding Renaldo down and turned away as they completed his execution. She smiled and looked down at Benito's expression as the bullet thudded into the table as it exited his son's skull. Benito screamed his anguish at the loss of his sons.

She dropped to her knees and before Reyes could stop her she dragged the suddenly frail looking man into her arms as he lay dying in a pool of his own blood. "Now do you get it, Benito?" she crooned. "It fucking hurts."

"F-fuck you, *p-puta*," he managed to say through a face full of blood, snot and tears.

Then he lunged up at her and reached for her gun just as Reyes gripped her arm and dragged her away from the Mexican arms dealer. "Back the fuck up, Casey!" Reyes snapped sharply. "Don't touch him again, he's like a feral dog that needs to be put down."

Casey stood, blood dripping from her white dress. "I'm not done hurting," she murmured and turned back to the table. "You have one secret here you thought no outsider could find out. The reason you've gone without a wife all these years. No woman to legitimize your children."

Her eyes glowed with vengeful fire, amber and green, as she stared at the man that had sat to the left of Benito without fail for the past thirty-five years. He stared coldly back, ice clashing with fire. He knew what was coming.

"Please!" Benito screamed, blood and spit flying from his lips, when he realized who she was after. "I'll do anything, give you anything! Do not take my Mano, I'm begging you! Jewels, money, all of my trade routes, they're all yours... take them! Please, god, just don't kill him. Please..." he sobbed, finally a broken man. "I'm so sorry."

"Tell that to Sandra Palmieri when you see her," Casey told him and then shot Benito's lover through the heart.

Casey dropped to her knees on the hard stone floor next to Benito and growled, "Hurts, doesn't it, *puta?*"

"Have you no mercy?" he appealed, holding his bloody hand out to her. "You have the face of an angel... but so little mercy."

She laughed bitterly. "Where was your mercy when you gave me to Ignacio Hernandez? Where was your mercy when you ordered the death of my infant son? You should have gone back to that hospital and finished me off, Benito. That would have been mercy."

Real fear flashed through his eyes an instant before Casey filled his head and torso with holes, emptying her gun. Reyes dropped to his knees behind her and wrapped his arms around her, ignoring the spray of blood across her dress, face and hair. He kissed the back of her head and whispered, "What about the children? Do we take the entire line as he tried to do to yours?"

She shook her head. "No, Reyes. We don't kill children."

He grunted and she knew he had his own opinions, probably ones they wouldn't agree on, but this was her party and he'd already agreed to let her make the rules.

"Are you done yet, *nena*, or do you want to kill more of them?" he asked, gripping her hair and tilting her head to the side so he could kiss her neck. She knew it turned him on to watch her shoot. He was a merciless, sadistic son-of-a-bitch. And she loved him.

She tilted her head further to the side, giving him better access, which he immediately took advantage of, heedless of their rapt audience; half of which were pissing themselves in terror and the other half wondering where the insane, ethereal blond came from and where they could get one.

"Maybe one more," she finally said. "For good measure!"

"Okay, *cariña*," Reyes chuckled and helped her to her feet. "Which one do you want?"

She turned her sharp eyes back to the table and immediately pointed at a man she'd recognized the moment she walked into the room. "I know that mean son of a bitch from my Ignacio days," she smiled coldly as he squirmed in his chair. "And he knows me, he's a disgusting piece of shit that would try to put his hands on me every time he thought my bodyguard wasn't looking. I think I'll play with him a little first..."

Casey trailed her gun along the back of the other men's chairs, *thunking* it satisfyingly against the wood, as she approached the one she wanted. He tried pleading with her. "Mrs. Hernandez, C-Casey, so good to see you and looking so fine," he said in a high-pitched voice. "I never meant nothing by it, you know?"

"But it's not nice to terrorize women, Stephan," Casey scolded him, pressing the muzzle of her gun hard against his wrist where it rested on the arm of his chair. She pulled the trigger but nothing happened.

She looked surprised and then giggled and shrugged her shoulders. "Used them all on Benny."

Alejandro came up behind her, squeezed her shoulder and offered his weapon. She grinned at him and shook her head, her blond hair, now liberally streaked with blood, swaying with the movement. "No thank you," she whispered loudly, "just make sure he suffers. Not just for me, but for every woman that didn't have a bodyguard to protect her from this disgusting piece of work."

She turned to Reyes who was at her back, always at her back. "I think I'm done. Can we go home?"

Reyes grinned and wrapped an arm around her waist. "Anything you want, *mi reina*."

CHAPTER THIRTY-FOUR

R eyes turned to Alejandro, his voice full of death. "You
know what to do." Then he escorted Casey from the
dining room.

They walked side by side through Benito's hacienda.
Despite the bloody evening Casey had both instigated and
endured she felt a sense of peace wash over her. She walked
tall next to a man that wanted her height and her power to
equal his. She knew she would never match his level of
brutality and blood lust, but she was a match for him in every
other way. She was his queen and now she'd proved it. She'd
avenged her family in spectacular fashion.

The clip of her heels against the stone pavement was the
only sound that followed them as they made their way
through hall after hall toward the garden where their vehicles
waited to take them back to the airplane. The bottom floor
of the hacienda was glowing beautifully in the rising moon-
light. Casey glanced down at her dress, now covered in blood,
completely ruined. It looked beautiful to her.

"I'm all... red," she whispered, flaring the skirt out away
from her thighs as they walked.

Reyes looked at her, his face filled with dark hunger. "You can see it, *nena*? You can see this colour?"

She smiled over at him and let the fabric flutter between her fingertips. "I can see it if you ask me to, see the things you do. I see them through your eyes, Reyes." She stopped walking, turned and tugged him against her. He stepped easily into her, wrapping his broad hands around her slim hips.

Casey shoved her fingers into his hair and abruptly brought her lips to his, stopping just short of touching them. "You want me, you take me," she whispered, her breath rushing over him. His fingers clenched hard against her, biting into her flesh through the thin fabric of her dress. It felt so fucking good with the fresh rush of vengeance coursing through her veins. "Take everything for you."

With a growl Reyes lifted her slightly and shoved her backwards into the shadows, slamming her against something hard, but he softened the blow with a hand at her back. He wrapped that hand around her neck and forced her head into the perfect angle for the harsh, brutal kiss he took. He ground his hips into hers lifting her body slightly until she was riding his erection. Casey moaned into his mouth as he fucked her with his tongue, stealing her breath until she began to feel faint. She could only clutch his shoulders and take quick breaths when he allowed her to surface.

The moment he released her lips, he attacked her neck with sharp stinging bites. He didn't even pretend he was kissing her flesh, he marked as much of her as he could, fisting her blood-soaked hair in one hand and wrenching it to the side so he could have better access.

"Love you so fucking much, Casey, *mi amor*, *mi reina*. So fucking much more than I ever thought possible," he snarled against her throat. "I will take everything for myself and I will give you the world in return. I am *el rey*."

Casey cried out, her entire body quaking with the fierce emotion ricocheting through both of them. Reyes wrenched her skirt up her body and tore her panties away in one swift move. She screamed at the sting left behind across her thigh and then moaned into his mouth as he shoved his fingers deep into her pussy. She widened her legs, giving him better access. She had no idea how long she'd been wet for, but she was betting it was the moment she walked in on that cozy little dinner scene and set eyes on her man sprawled in his chair like the king he was, owning the dangerous men that sat all around him.

She screamed into his mouth as he pumped his fingers in and out of her, driving her higher and higher, brushing his thumb across her clit with each stroke. Before she could peak he pulled his fingers out and pushed them into her mouth, forcing her to taste herself. He enjoyed doing that, showing her how much he turned her on. She sucked his fingers deep into her mouth, wrapping her tongue around each one, licking the taste of her pussy off his strong fingers while he unzipped his pants and freed his cock.

He shoved her skirt back up around her waist, lifted her right up off the ground and growled, "Legs around my waist, *nena*."

Casey clung to his shoulders and did as he ordered, lifting and wrapping her legs around his waist with his help, then he brought her down on his thick cock, filling her inch by inch. She flung her head back, pressing it against the wall behind her and opened her mouth in a silent scream of joy and pain. Fuck, it was the best thing she ever felt in her life and she wanted it to go on forever.

He wanted her hard and he wanted it rough. He wrapped his arm around her waist, snaked one hand up her back, took a fistful of her hair, forced her head back so he could bite down on her neck and began fucking her hard. He slammed her back against the wall repeatedly, forcing his cock in and out of her. It was like being repeatedly impaled with thick, warm steel. Reyes took her to the edge of her endurance and then pushed her over.

Casey screamed, her voice echoing through the veranda beyond. Her body had no choice but to tighten around his as the friction against her clit and the hard fucking drove her higher and higher toward a ferocious orgasm. Her pussy began to ripple, tighten in anticipation, as he slammed harder against her.

She gripped his hair and held him hard, a scream of pure ecstasy ripping through her as she was flung over the edge into oblivion. She went limp against him as he continued his hard thrusts, holding her up against the wall. Reyes shouted her name against the skin of her throat as he came and slammed his hand into the wall next to her head. She smiled happily as she felt the hot rush of him inside her and squeezed him tight against her body.

They both lay against the wall, Reyes leaning against Casey while protecting her back from the hard stone with his hands. He whispered words of love and praise to her while she snuggled against him. She smiled and held in a giggle. His words were mostly approval of her deadly accuracy with her gun and the way she played with her prey before disposing of it.

She sighed and squeezed him tight. She would have to teach him how to speak of nicer, less blood-thirsty things before their child was born. Which reminded her, she should probably tell him soon, give him a chance to get over being pissed that she'd gone into Mexico pregnant before the baby came.

CHAPTER THIRTY-FIVE

C asey chewed her lip nervously and touched a finger to her still flat belly, soothingly caressing her unborn child as she leaned against Ignacio's old desk and stared unseeing into what used to be her back yard. It still looked the same, perhaps a little less manicured. Ignacio had always been about appearances while Diego was more about security and the bottom line. He would prefer fewer maintenance workers and gardeners on his estate.

She barely listened to the men as they conducted business, which probably surprised Reyes since she'd taken part in almost every facet of his business since Venezuela. And though she'd convinced him to bring her to Miami to reconnect with her former associates and establish herself as his partner, she hadn't been telling him the entire truth.

There had been some blow back to her taking their unborn child into Mexico and putting both of their lives at risk. He'd raged for days, locking her in their bedroom and alternating between terrible fury and attempting to make her see reason. Oh, she'd seen reason. She'd always seen the truth, just not the truth Reyes wanted her to see. Reyes was beyond terrified of losing the only family he now had. He seemed to understand the importance of allowing her to rise up, become the powerful force that would ignite his heart and entrench his cartel in the underworlds of many regions, but he couldn't allow her to do it while pregnant. Something about pregnancy and the added vulnerability to her health seemed to push him over the edge. She'd known he would be that way. These mafia guys were funny about *familia*.

Only after she'd promised to treat herself more like the queen of England than the queen of murder and mayhem did he let her out of the bedroom; though she'd enjoyed some perks in having her favourite man to herself for days on end. They'd outlined the terms of her pregnancy. She was still allowed to stand at his side and negotiate if he deemed the partner safe. And for some reason, he believed Miami was safe. She was about to disabuse him of that notion and likely send herself back into bedroom lockup for the next six months.

She side-eyed Diego, the snake. Worth it.

"Mexico will not be available to you until further notice," Reyes was telling Diego. "You will have to make do with your other connections. I can put you in touch with Sotza in Venezuela; he'll be reluctant to work with an Ignacio associate but he may be willing with a word from me."

Casey snorted lightly, tuned them out and continued to stroke her belly. She wondered if her little jellybean would have black hair or powdery white blond hair. She ignored the look that Reyes shot her. She didn't care if he thought she was being immature. Diego was a piece of shit and there was no chance the regal, deadly Sotza was going to work with him. In fact, she was entirely certain that it would take Reyes a matter of days, if not hours, to learn the truth about Diego.

Reyes was only using the man because he was easy and convenient. She knew, realistically, that most of these guys were their own level of disgusting, the majority without integrity. If Reyes refused to work with all of them, then he wouldn't have anyone left to work with.

Still, Casey wasn't quite done avenging herself and her family. She was biding her time, like any good black widow. Waiting for her chance to lure the fly into her trap. She glanced sideways, wondering if they were going to wrap things up soon so she could murder the crap out of her nemesis, when her gaze drifted to Ignacio's statue, the one she'd always hated so much. Her eyes lit up and she wandered toward it.

She stood studying the naked cherub with new eyes. It had always caused her to wonder if Ignacio wasn't so much impotent as into children. He did seem to prefer her looks when she was younger, more child-like. She shuddered.

She was so absorbed in the horrible statue she didn't hear the men's conversation wrap up or Diego approach her from behind. He slid an arm around her waist, digging his fingers brutally into her hip, causing her to jump in shock. He brought her body back into his, slamming her ass into his cock. She gasped and cried out, but he covered her mouth with his hand. She glanced back over his shoulder and saw Reyes outside the patio doors with his back to her, standing with Alejandro deep in discussion.

"Can't wait to get you alone, Casey. Just you and me, baby," Diego breathed in her ear. "Ah, the things I'm gonna finally get to do to this body. Fuck, it makes me so fucking hard."

Diego, the motherfucker, had done exactly as she'd hoped by biding his time, waiting to catch her alone. Only she hadn't been paying attention. But she had a secret weapon, one he would never guess she could possibly have developed in the past few months. She'd become strong, risen up. Despite the strength in his arms, the black, ugly thoughts in his head and the sadism in his heart, he was no match for Casey. She had her own strength. She was a queen.

She knew he was expecting her to allow his grope, allow him to touch her so he might release her faster. She wasn't sure what his plan was after that though. Did he truly think she wouldn't tell Reyes? Did he think Reyes would believe Diego over the woman Reyes had flown all the way to Miami just to stand at his side. She rolled her eyes. *Please son, take a number, this bitch is his everything.* This is why she needed to show Reyes that Diego should be replaced, the man was just stupid. He probably couldn't negotiate his way out of a paper bag.

She grabbed one of the fingers that Diego had placed conveniently at her waist and snapped it back so hard it broke instantly. He howled in pain, let her go and bent over double clutching his finger. Casey whirled around, intent on kneeing him in the face, but then the statue caught her eye again. Oh, even better! She grabbed it with both hands and hauled the heavy piece of gaudy art work off the pedestal. She lifted it as high as she could and viciously brought it down on the back of Diego's head just as Reyes and Alejandro came rushing in the back door.

Casey let the statue fall from her hands, wincing a little as it smashed Diego's hand where he lay dazed on the floor, whimpering and bleeding. Well that was a happy accident. She'd been having a lot of those lately.

She turned to the desk and reached for her purse where she'd left it earlier, dragged it toward her and began rummaging through it. Reyes took the scene in at a glance and seemed to assess what had gone down. He apparently came to the conclusion that his woman had things well under control, crossed his arms over his broad chest and merely raised an eyebrow.

"What are you looking for, *cariña?*" Reyes asked negligently, eyeing her as she searched through her bag.

"My gun," she huffed, lips pursed in annoyance.

"Well maybe if you carried a reasonable size purse for once, *nena*," Reyes pointed out, amusement clear in his voice despite his words.

Diego let out a pitiful groan from the floor and tried to rock himself into a sitting position while blood gushed from the head wound she'd given him.

She turned on Reyes, fury snapping in her dual-coloured eyes. He smirked, clearly enjoying the sight of her when she was fuming. "Really, Reyes? *Really?*" she snarled one hand still buried in her oversized bag. "You brought me back to the home where you murdered my first husband... and yes, before you say anything, he absolutely deserved it, but you brought me back into this horror show of a mausoleum to be insulted by this creepy little cockroach." When Diego made a sound of protest she kicked him viciously in the knee with the pointy toe of her shoe.

Reyes grabbed her arm and pulled her out of Diego's way before Diego could grab her and drag her to the floor as he clearly intended to do when he swiped for her ankle. "What did he say to cause *this*, Casey? My god, woman, you threw a fucking statue at him," he said incredulously. "You shouldn't be lifting heavy shit while you're pregnant, *nena*. You know better." Alejandro attempted unsuccessfully to cover his laughter with a cough. Reyes pointed at Diego who was trying to pick himself up off the floor and snarled, "Stay down, cockroach."

Alejandro let loose and guffawed. Everyone in the room ignored him.

Casey dropped her purse on the desk with an aggrieved sigh and placed a hand on her hip. "He implied that the moment he got me alone he'd unleash his sadistic tendencies on me. And this time he wouldn't hold back." She eyed Diego with disgust. "Well, this time I didn't hold back, did I, Diego?" she taunted, loathing clear in her voice.

"*Puta*," he spat at her from the floor. "Mob trash! That's all you ever were and all you'll ever be."

Stupid move really, considering Reyes had gone deadly still, his glittering eyes on Casey as she watched Ignacio's number one henchman. The same man who had spent years stalking and torturing her at every opportunity. "Explain your words, Casey," Reyes said, his voice so low and dangerous she barely caught the words. "In detail."

She swallowed and moved her gaze to meet Reyes', knowing instinctively he would want her eyes when she told him the intimate details of what this man had done to her. "He never touched me unless Ignacio ordered it. Ignacio didn't often have the stomach for real punishments and torture unless he had to prove himself in front of his men, but this one," she nodded toward Diego, "just loves fucking people up, and he's had a thing for me for years. He loved getting his hands on me every chance he could. Whenever Ignacio let him off his leash, he would do his best to make my life a misery. Tying me down, locking me up... punching, slapping, pinching, sometimes cutting. He was under orders never to go too far with Ignacio's property... I had to stay attractive, an asset. But I knew, I just fucking knew, he was waiting for the day he could get his hands on me and completely unleash. This disgusting little slug thought today might be the day. Thought maybe you'd turn your back long enough he could finally snatch me up and play with me the way he's always wanted to." She felt Alejandro approach her back as she spoke, his silent warmth supporting her almost as much as Reyes unwavering love.

"And," she whispered, "he was there when my family died. He was only a few years older than me and didn't take part in the shootings, but he was there. I remember he watched as Ignacio pulled the trigger on me." She looked coldly down at Diego who finally had the good sense to cower.

Reyes reached under his jacket to pull his gun from its holster. "What do you plan to do, *nena*?"

"What do you think, *nino*?" she said with a huff, sticking her hand out. "I plan on having a tea party with him."

"Fuck, woman," he growled slapping the gun into her palm. "Told you what would happen next time you called me that. You're damn lucky there are witnesses or I'd have you over my knee."

Without barely looking toward Diego, she shot him in the shoulder and then shouted at Reyes over Diego's cries of pain, "Stop calling me *nena* and I'll stop calling you *nino*!"

Reyes stalked her around the desk and then bent her backwards over the surface with her arms braced behind her, the gun still clutched in one hand. He wrapped one arm around her waist and yanked her into the heat of his body. They both ignored Diego's groans and Alejandro's chuckled amusement.

"I'll call you whatever the fuck I want, Casey, *mi amor*," he growled and reached down to hike her tight skirt up enough that he could wrap her long leg around him.

"And what'll you call me now, Reyes?" she whispered against him.

"*Mi reina*," he whispered back. "Always, *mi reina*."

He pressed his lips to hers. It wasn't a passionate kiss, though the heat that burned so brightly between them flamed to life in her breast, it was a kiss of promise. A seal of their partnership. He had stolen her, he had helped raise her up and now he was declaring her his equal.

Diego took that moment of distraction to lunge for the door in a desperate attempt to escape his fate. Casey gave her head a tiny shake and rolled her eyes, because really, how far did he think he was going to get? He had a vicious head wound, a bullet in his shoulder and three very dangerous individuals stalking his back. She didn't think Reyes would mind a good eye roll just this once since it was directed at the bleeding idiot bee-lining for the door. She broke their lovely little moment, glanced over Reyes shoulder, lifted the gun and shot Diego in the back, right through his black, sadistic little heart.

"Damn, I was really hoping he would get tortured a little more than that," she sighed heartbrokenly, leaning her head against Reyes neck.

Reyes and Alejandro laughed and Reyes leaned down to kiss her pouting lips. "Dammit woman, you're hell on my Miami connections," he grumbled.

She gave him a light shove and stood up to straighten her skirt when he finally gave her enough space. She grinned at him and patted his chest, swinging her bag off the desk. "No worries, darling, I have a contact. She'll be golden once we get rid of her husband and help her clean up. She knows this business like nobodies business. Trust me."

Reyes gave her a sharp look. "A mafia wife?" he said.

Casey gave him a wicked smile. "You think I'm the only one that knows how to shut up and pay attention?"

He laughed and held out his hand for her. "Casey, I don't think you stopped talking since the moment we landed in Bolivia." His warm eyes caressed her. "And *cariña*, I wouldn't want it any other way."

And in a single moment of clarity, the past ten years rushed at her. He was right. She'd kept it all in, barely said anything to anyone because she'd learned to keep Casey in a cage. To never let her out lest she get crushed and destroyed. Then Reyes came along, peeked between the bars and seen the woman within. He smashed the lock, reached in and coaxed her out. He encouraged her to find the will to rise up and become Casey again.

She placed her hand in his and said, "Let's go home,"

CHAPTER THIRTY-SIX

"You take the pain away or I take everything you love!" Reyes snarled from the end of the bed, pointing his finger in the obstetrician's face.

"Reyes!" Casey shrieked, gripping a fistful of blankets in her long, slim fingers and giving him a glare that rivalled even his best death glare. "Either shut the fuck up or leave! Let the man do his job," she snarled from between clenched teeth as another labour pain hit her.

"Not fucking likely, Casey," he growled back and turned to the baby doctor, two nurses and Miguel who were hovering next to his wife. He'd had the birthing team specially flown in two weeks earlier and paid them all exorbitantly to follow Casey's every move, much to her annoyance. "What the fuck are you waiting for?" he shouted at them. "Fix her!"

All three medical professionals stood gaping at him, too terrified of the volatile cartel boss to dare touch his woman while he was in the room. Miguel just rolled his eyes, used to Reyes' temper when it came to Casey. Casey let loose another shriek of frustration, struggled to push herself into a sitting position and reached under her pillow. She yanked her special gun out and, with shaking fingers, maneuvered the safety into the off positon. She shoved a fistful of hair off her face and pointed the weapon at her lover, who watched with dawning realization, a combination of anger and amusement warring for supremacy in his expression. She would pay for this clearly premediated stunt once she was recovered. She never slept with a weapon on her person, which meant she was anticipating his over-the-top concern for her safety and decided to take it upon herself to cut him off.

She took a deep breath and said in the calmest voice she could manage, "You will stop harassing my doctors, Reyes, if you would like to remain for the birth of your child. Otherwise you can leave the room and find out what happened later." Then she broke his heart and ended his tirade with her next shakily spoken words. "I'm scared enough as it is. What if... what if..." Her voice drifted off and she stared at him, her dual-coloured eyes awash in tears as she stared at him helplessly.

He shoved the doctor out of his way and fell to the floor next to her, taking her free hand in both of his and holding it against his lips. "Won't happen, *cariña*," he whispered fervently, pressing the scarred back of her hand against his cheek. "You've got this, my gorgeous *esposa*. You are the strongest woman I know. You will bring our screaming child into the world, *mi reina*."

She reached for him with her other hand, accidentally smashing him in the side of the head with her gun. He didn't flinch as she cupped his face in both hands. Miguel hastily removed the weapon from her loose fingers so she didn't accidentally shoot the baby's father. Casey leaned over her extended belly and urged Reyes further up the bed so she could kiss him.

"Promise our baby will be okay?" she whispered against him, her eyes bright on his.

"You have my word, Casey," he breathed against her mouth. "*Siempre*." Always.

She nodded and squeezed him, pressing her forehead against him. He could tell another labour pain was hitting her, but she barely flinched. Instead she stayed in that moment with him. He could feel her lashes fluttering against the skin of his cheek as she shifted her face and bore the pain on her own. He could feel the savage fury rising up within him, painting his guts black with an inferno of raw emotion. When it came to this woman, nothing mattered except keeping her safe. As much as he wanted the little life within her, he wanted her to be healthy and happy more. Her pain was breaking him.

A tear, the first to have escaped him since the loss of his mother and sisters, slid from his eye and touched his scarred cheek. Casey captured it on her thumb before anyone else could witness his brief moment of weakness. She opened her eyes and stared into his. "Protect us with your life, Reyes," she whispered, "and I will be *tu reina. Siempre*."

He nodded and stood from the bed. He gave her scarred hand one last squeeze before stepping away from the bed. He nodded at the medical team. "You may proceed." When they didn't move, he barked, "What the fuck are you waiting for? She's having a baby, right? Are you just going to watch?"

Casey laughed weakly as they rushed to do his bidding. She looked at Miguel with a smile and patted the bed next to her asking wordlessly for her good friend to join her. He brushed past her husband, having had almost a year now to get over his fear of torture and death, and sat next to her. He held her hand and they chatted in between her contractions.

Periodically, he made sure she updated him on all of her symptoms, particularly anything going on in her head. While her migraines had gotten much better over the past year with the right balance of medications to help and constant progress being made in the field, she was still at risk for possible stroke if her blood pressure rose too high. It had taken months of arguing and both her and Miguel's combined voices to convince Reyes that she shouldn't just be drugged and the baby removed at the right time. The only argument that had worked was that it wouldn't be good for the baby and Casey couldn't possibly handle another child's death.

But as her contractions grew closer together and her blood pressure slowly rose, along with a rising pain in the base of her skull alerting them to a potential migraine, Reyes became more and more agitated. He paced the room like a caged lion, snapping at everyone, ready to pounce at the first sign that something was wrong with his woman or his baby. The obstetrician looked as though he might throw up every time Reyes neared him, but he couldn't bring himself to care.

"Casey," Miguel said calmly from beside her as she gritted her teeth and tried not to push, as per the doctor's orders. She side-eyed Miguel in what looked like a murderous squint. "You need to calm down a touch. Your blood pressure is getting too high and I'm a little concerned."

Reyes' head snapped up and he stopped pacing, staring, waiting to see if she would comply with her personal neurologist. He gritted his teeth and squeezed his hands into fists, trying to ignore the need to tear the world apart, to commit unspeakable acts of rage so that his soul might rest in peace for a few minutes.

Casey squeezed her eyes shut and nodded, trying to breathe through the pain in her head and the terror welling up inside her. He saw the thoughts written on her face the moment she opened her eyes and met his. What if her baby didn't survive because she couldn't manage the pain of birth?

Because she wasn't strong enough to bring the baby into the world without having a stroke.

"Reyes!" she cried reaching for him. "I need you."

Miguel backed away from the bed and gave Reyes room. He immediately climbed in behind her and carefully manoeuvered her until she was resting against his chest with her head on his shoulder. He could feel her heart pounding like thunder through her back where she rested heavily against him. He sat with his legs bent underneath her arms, his warmth surrounding her entire body. She turned her face into his neck, closed her eyes and breathed his scent deep into her lungs, savouring him as tears dripped gently down her cheeks. He smoothed the sweat-soaked hair back off her face and tucked the strands behind her ear before gently kissing her.

"I'm scared," she whispered.

"I know, *nena*," he whispered back. He tilted her face up until she was forced to look at him. "Do you think I would ever let anything happen to you?"

"No," she said instantly. "Never."

"*Nunca*," he agreed solemnly. "You belong to me forever."

She nodded. "Okay," she whispered. "I think I need to push now."

Their daughter was born thirty-seven minutes later. It took another hour for Miguel and Casey to get the severe migraine she experienced during the birthing process under control. Reyes paced the room with their daughter held in his arms, terror clawing at his heart until he thought he would fall to his knees and beg for God to take him if He would just spare Casey this pain. She tried weakly to reassure him, whispering from the bed where the nurses had changed the sheets and dimmed the lights, but she was in too much pain.

When the IV fluids and medication finally took effect, she was able to hold her child for the first time. Miguel and the rest of her birth team left the room. Reyes lay next to her on the bed watching the two most important people in his life with fierce possessiveness. He could already see the future mapped out for them. A whole lot of mother and daughter attempting to negotiate for freedoms he would never allow. And he would love every moment of it.

"What will we name her?" Reyes asked, emotion shining clear in his eyes as he watched the woman he loved cradle their daughter against her chest and hold her as though she would never let go.

"Sally," Casey said instantly, without a single moment of hesitation.

Reyes straightened from behind her, disgust warring to replace his peace. "Absolutely not!"

Casey didn't even bat an eyelash. She traced the tip of her finger down the powdery soft cheek and across the perfect, tiny lips. "Sally is Jack Skellington's counterpart, his other half. Nothing else will do."

Reyes felt something expand and then explode in his chest. Like a bubble he'd been holding onto for all the pain his woman had gone through. She was finally safe and whole. Maybe he would never truly be able to let go of her past, the way she seemed to be doing. Maybe he would continue to search out and torture anyone associated with anyone who had ever harmed a hair on her head... or even looked at her funny. But he was ready to admit that she had moved on. That Casey's inner core of steel had not only strengthened her, but healed her as well.

"Alright, *mi reina*," he said after a moment, caressing first the fine blond of her hair and then reaching past to run a finger over the fine blond that promised to sprout from their daughter's head. "Sally it is."

"Thank you, *mi rey*," Casey whispered, tilting her head back, finally taking her eyes off the child to kiss his jaw.

"But just in case she needs a back-up name one day, how do you like Mariana?" Reyes asked. "It was my mother's."

"It's perfect," Casey said with a smile, then shifted Sally Mariana in her arms and reached for the buttons on her nightgown. "Now do you remember what the nurse said about breast feeding? Can you go get her? And I swear to god Reyes, if you threaten her life, I'll shoot you in the foot or somewhere else painful but useless."

CHAPTER THIRTY-SEVEN

"This was your idea, *nena*," Reyes reminded her while attempting to disguise the impatience in his voice.

She eyed him as though he were about to pounce on her and slowly backed away from him, glancing sideways for escape routes. Sure, it had been her idea, and it had seemed super badass and smart at the time, but now seeing and *smelling* his burnt flesh was making her seriously rethink the brilliancy of this plan. As soon as she'd pressed the burning hot iron to the skin of his neck, pushing hard to imprint the mark of a male crown into his skin she'd started to have her doubts. He'd stood strong and stoic, never once flinching. Only the tiny ripple of his pectoral muscles, bared for the ceremony, gave away his pain. As soon as enough time had passed she'd dropped the small, intricate iron and stepped away, staring in awe at the mark she'd created.

"Wh-what about a tattoo for me instead?" she asked, hoping he might go for a compromise, though she really didn't want a tattoo either and as soon as she was away from the branding ceremony she was bailing on that idea too.

Reyes grunted and approached her. Casey jumped back,

holding her hand out to him, warding him off, her gorgeous white dress fluttering in the evening breeze. The few people attending their wedding and branding had wandered several feet away and were pretending not to hear the exchange. Except for Alejandro, who was laughing his ass off.

Reyes took her hand and brought it to his lips, caressing the scar lightly. Then he pulled her into his arms and held her against his chest. In her bare feet, she was shorter than him and able to lay her head against his uninjured shoulder. "It's won't hurt, *nena*, I promise. I will be with you through every step, it won't be like last time. Our love will carry you through and your strength will ensure you stand tall. Understand, *mi amor*?"

She nodded and murmured, "I understand." And she did. Reyes would never let anything happen to her. The only person that was ever allowed to hurt her was her husband and he made it hurt good. Pain at his hands was pleasure.

They'd exchanged their wedding vows on a secluded beach in Peru, secured by their people and surrounded by only their closest friends and family. Casey's cousin stood between Alejandro and Miguel, looking lovely in a flowing dress that buttoned down her front with Sally Mariana held in her arms, wrapped snuggly in a warm blanket. It had taken very little to convince Gina to come and live with them in Bolivia. Both women had quickly reconnected emotionally, despite the fuzziness of Casey's memories. The more time she spent with her cousin though, the more they came back to her. Gina utterly adored the baby and was happy to share nanny duties when her cousin was exhausted or needed for work. Gina had become such an important part of their household that Casey was beginning to insist she come with them whenever she needed to travel with the baby as she was still breastfeeding and couldn't be away from Sally for longer than a day. Casey noticed that Alejandro had absolutely no problem with this arrangement as he was usually travelling with the group.

"Ready, *nena*?" Reyes asked, pulling her attention back toward him.

Her distracted gaze followed the flexing movement of his hand as he pulled the delicate metal from the heat and lifted it to show her. She tilted her head to the side and gave him a short nod. She took a deep breath and closed her eyes, thinking of everything wonderful he'd brought into her life. Reyes had stolen her from Ignacio and then he'd gifted her with freedom, love, vengeance and a family. She would give him this. A mark that would forever be his.

He fisted her long blond hair in his free hand and tilted her head back, then slowly rotated their bodies so they were turned away from their friends. He leaned in and whispered against her ear, "Open your eyes for me, Casey."

She did. She was facing the sunset. She could see streaks scoring the sky, striking out from the sun and gradually fading across the clouds into the gathering darkness. She wished Reyes could see the beauty in her shades of grey as he wanted her to see the reds, oranges and yellows of his sunset.

"You see the colours?" he asked.

"*Si*, Reyes, I see them through your eyes," she told him.

He used her hair to tilt her head to the side and pressed the brand into her neck. She breathed deep, taking the pain into her soul, knowing Reyes had her. *Siempre*. Forever; the king and his scarred queen.

THE END

ACKNOWLEDGMENTS

Dear readers,

From the bottom of my I heart thank you for reading Scarred Queen. This book was an incredible journey for me. During the writing of this novel I experienced some major changes in my life and Scarred Queen allowed me a sanctuary to turn to when I needed a place to lose myself in fantasy. I've spent my entire life drifting and losing myself in books, either in reading them or writing them. Now I feel so happy and privileged to be able to share my world of fantasies and love of mafia romance with my amazing readers. I hope you enjoyed reading it as much as I loved writing it!

In particular I want to thank Jasmin Quinn for her unfailing and unflinching support whenever I demanded it. She rocks some serious editing skills and didn't even blink when I threatened to fly out to where she lives and throw down with her Game of Thrones style when she dared to suggest one of my characters might have an immature and unnecessary personality quirk (Slurpees are awesome, end of story!). Jasmin's second mafia romance novel, Secrets Inside Her, is due to hit shelves in early March! Thank you to Drew from iDrewthis.com for the absolutely stunning cover, teasers and not-so-patient technical assistance he provides.

A big thank you to Sansa for her gorgeous teasers and amazing administrative assistance with my Facebook group, Nikita's Underworld. To Mia Knight, author of The Crime Lord Series, for making me laugh with her wicked sense of humour and who recognizes a fellow dark comedian. And finally, thank you to the big, wonderful online family of authors, readers and bloggers I've discovered over the past several months! So many of you have provided assistance, valuable advice and encouragement when I needed it most.

Yours sincerely,
   Nikita

ALSO BY NIKITA SLATER

If you enjoyed this book, check out some other works by #1
International Bestselling Author, Nikita Slater. More titles are
always in progress, so check back often to see what's new!

SINNER'S EMPIRE

Book 1 - Sin of Silence - Preorder

Book 2 - A Silent Reckoning - Coming Soon!

Book 3 - Goodnight, Sinners - Coming Soon!

THE QUEENS SERIES

Book One – Scarred Queen

Book Two - Queen's Move

Book Three - Born a Queen

Book Four - The Red Queen (Coming 2021)

Alejandro's Prey (a novella)

The Queens 4 Book Box Set

FIRE & VICE SERIES

Book One – Prisoner of Fortune

Book Two – Fight or Flight

Book Three – King's Command

Book Four – Savage Vendetta

Savage Boss (a novella)

Book Five – Fear in Her Eyes

Book Six – Bound by Blood

Book Seven – In His Sights

Book Eight - Burning Beauty

Book Nine - Chasing Ecstasy (Coming soon!)

Fire & Vice 6 Book Box Set

THE DRIVEN HEARTS SERIES

Book One - Driven by Desire

Book Two - Thieving Hearts

Book Three - Capturing Victory

Novella - The Princess and Her Mercenary

Driven Hearts 4 Book Box Set

THE SANCTUARY SERIES

Book One - Sanctuary's Warlord

Book Two - Sanctuary on Fire

Book Three - The Last Sanctuary

Book Four - The Road to Wolfe

Book Five - Skye's Sanctuary (Coming soon!)

The Sanctuary Series 3 Book Box Set

LOVING THE BAD BOY SERIES

Loving Vincent

Loving Jared

Loving Rico (Coming Soon!)

STANDALONE BOOKS

The Assassin's Wife

Because You're Mine

Mine to Keep (a novella)

Luna & Andres

Kiss of the Cartel

Stalked

AFTER DARK

In collaboration with Jasmin Quinn

Collared: A Dark Captive Romance

Safeword: A Dark Romance

Chained: A Mafia Marriage Romance

Good Girl: A Captive BDSM Romance

Hostile Takeover: An Enemies to Lovers Romance

The After Dark Box Set

Visit **nikitaslater.com** for more information

and the latest updates!

ABOUT THE AUTHOR

Nikita Slater is the International Bestselling dark romance author of the Fire & Vice series, Angels & Assassins series, The Queens series and several standalone novels. Her favourite genre is mafia romance, the bloodier the better, though she loves to write about every subject under the sun. She lives on the beautiful Canadian prairies with her son and crazy awesome dog. She has an unholy affinity for books (especially erotic romance), wine, pets and anything choco-late. Despite some of the darker themes in her books (which are pure fun and fantasy), Nikita is a staunch feminist and advocate of equal rights for all races, genders and non-gender specific persons. When she isn't writing, dreaming about writing or talking about writing, she helps others discover a love of reading and writing through literacy and social work.

Printed in the USA
CPSIA information can be obtained
at www.ICGtesting.com
LVHW051932071023
760218LV00073B/1513

9 781990 355066